BURY THE HATCHET

A BUCK TRAMMEL WESTERN

BURY THE HATCHET

WILLIAM W. JOHNSTONE
AND J. A. JOHNSTONE

THORNDIKE PRESS
A part of Gale, a Cengage Company

GALE
A Cengage Company

Thorndike Press® Large Print Western.
The text of this Large Print edition is unabridged.
Other aspects of the book may vary from the original edition.
Set in 16 pt. Plantin.

LIBRARY OF CONGRESS CIP DATA ON FILE.
CATALOGUING IN PUBLICATION FOR THIS BOOK
IS AVAILABLE FROM THE LIBRARY OF CONGRESS.

ISBN-13: 978-1-4328-8618-9 (hardcover alk. paper)

Published in 2021 by arrangement with Pinnacle Books, an imprint of Kensington Publishing Corp.

Printed in Mexico
Print Number: 01   Print Year: 2021

BURY THE HATCHET

CHAPTER 1

"Guess you heard the good news, Sheriff." Deputy Jimmy "Hawkeye" Hauk hitched up his belt as they began their morning foot patrol along Main Street. The sunrise in Blackstone, Wyoming Territory, always revealed a few drunks who'd passed out in the alleys between the many saloons along Main Street. Some just needed help going home. A few were actually dead from time to time, which required much more attention on the part of Sheriff Trammel and his deputy. "Word is they're hanging Madam Peachtree down in Laramie some time in the next month or so."

"Pinochet," Sheriff Buck Trammel corrected him. "Her name is Pinochet, and yeah, I read about it in the *Bugle,* same as you."

"Pinochet," repeated Hawkeye, as if he was trying it on for size. "Anyway, you got any plans to head down there and see her swing? After all, you're the one who brought her in."

"And the reason why she's swinging." The big man shook his head. "Never was much for witnessing hangings myself, though. Too much of a spectacle for all the wrong reasons."

"After what she done to you?" Hawkeye said. "All them times she tried to have you killed? Hell, she almost had the entire town destroyed while gunning for you."

Trammel had no desire to relive the complexities of the Madam Pinochet matter with his talkative deputy. He genuinely liked Hawkeye and had come to rely on him. He admired the way the young man handled a gun. He wasn't trigger-happy, but he wasn't afraid to shoot when the time came. He was brave and even-tempered, and Trammel was glad to have him at his side.

But if the boy had one failing, it was that he couldn't keep his mouth shut. He'd been born in Blackstone and had never lived anywhere else. He knew everyone and they knew him, but Trammel couldn't call him a gossip. Hawkeye was proud of his new position and the knowledge it gave him. He wasn't old enough yet to know when to talk and when to keep his mouth shut. It was the kind of practical knowledge only years could give him and he didn't have enough behind him yet. Only experience could teach such lessons.

Lessons that Buck Trammel had learned long ago. The hard way.

"They hit us with everything they had." He decided to boost the younger man's ego. "But we fought them off anyway, didn't we? You and me."

The young man stood taller. Even though he was almost six feet tall, Hawkeye barely reached Trammel's shoulder. "Yes, sir. We most certainly did."

Both men looked up when they heard screams coming from farther along Main Street. The town's main thoroughfare was lined with dozens of saloons, gambling dens, and kitchens that all catered to various crowds. Trammel knew the scream could have come from any of them.

When he saw Adam Hagen step out of the Pot of Gold Saloon, he knew the scream must have come from there. Trouble always had a knack for finding Hagen.

The gambler and new proprietor of the saloon lit a cigarette as the lawmen approached him. His red brocade vest and white shirt were as fresh as if he had just put them on, though Trammel imagined his duties at the Pot had probably kept him up all night. "Morning, gentlemen. And what a morning it is! The crispness of the mountain air. The calmness of a town just beginning to shake off the dust of a good night's sleep. The —"

"That scream came from your place, didn't it?" Trammel had no time for the gambler's fancy talk. He knew Adam Hagen to be an elaborate man . . . in his words, in his dress, and in the saloons he had recently acquired. The two men had saved each other's lives several times on the trail from where they'd first met in Wichita to Blackstone. They had once considered each other friends.

That was in the past as far as Trammel was concerned. Their friendship ended the moment Hagen had decided to take Madam Pinochet's place as the territory's chief vice merchant.

Hagen shrugged. "And what if it did? One is apt to hear a scream or two from a house of ill repute from time to time."

Hawkeye spoke out of turn. "The sheriff told you he'd leave you alone so long as you kept things to a dull roar around here. That scream's not part of the bargain."

Hagen smiled at the young man. "Would you look at that? Pin a star on a gadfly and watch him turn into Wild Bill Hickok." He looked up at Trammel. "Has he even begun to shave yet?"

Trammel wouldn't be baited. "You're going to tell me where that scream came from or we're going to kick in every door in the place."

"The change I've witnessed in you since you came to Blackstone is especially fascinating" Hagen frowned. "A few months ago, you were in a lookout chair at the Gilded Lily in Wichita minding drunks and drovers. Now you're the pious lawman of Blackstone." He looked away. "Guess the old saying about beggars and horseback still holds true."

Trammel felt his temper begin to rise. He didn't like Hagen bringing up their former association. He didn't like Hagen at all. Not anymore. "I asked you a question."

Hagen sighed as another scream came from the Pot of Gold, this one louder than the last.

Trammel took a step closer to Hagen, looming over him. "What room?"

"Let it burn itself out, Buck. It's just one of my customers getting rambunctious. I'll handle it myself when he's done."

Trammel pushed past him and stormed into the saloon. Hawkeye was right behind him.

From the boardwalk, Hagen called out, "Room twenty, damn you. But don't kill anyone this time. Death is bad for business."

Trammel ignored the stares he and Hawkeye drew from the men at the gambling tables and standing at the bar. Every working girl in the place ignored their potential customers and looked up in the direction from where the screams had come. They knew that, one day, the screams might be coming from them.

Trammel took the steps two at a time as an unholy shriek came from Room Twenty. He used his bulk to barrel through the door, splintering it from the jamb.

A large man had one of Hagen's girls pinned against the wall by the neck. He held a knife to her eye. Both of them looked at Trammel as the door slammed open and he stepped inside.

The man's knife twitched. "Take one more step, law dog, and I swear I'll —"

Trammel tomahawked the man's knife hand away from the woman as he yanked him away from her. The assailant's grip broke and the woman ran toward Hawkeye as Trammel threw the big man back onto the bed, causing it to collapse beneath his weight.

Hawkeye drew his pistol and held it on

the man as he shielded the young lady from further harm. "Don't move, mister. You're under arrest."

The panicked working girl bolted from the room, knocking Hawkeye out of the way, sending his pistol toward the ceiling.

The attacker bellowed as he clumsily lunged off the collapsed bed at Trammel, his knife held high in his right hand.

Trammel sidestepped the lunge, grabbed the big man's right hand, and pushed the arm farther back. A sickening crack made the man scream as his shoulder broke. The knife dropped to the bed as he spilled onto the floor.

Trammel put his foot on the back of the screaming man's head, pinning him to the ground. "Tell me it's over and I'll let you up."

Hawkeye grabbed the knife off the bed and tucked it into his belt.

Hearing no response, Trammel applied more weight to the back of the man's neck. "Is it over?"

"You broke my arm!"

"I'll do more than that unless you come along peacefully."

"Fine!" the man yelled as best he could. "It's over."

Trammel grabbed a handful of greasy hair

and pulled the man to his feet. The sheriff was about to lead him toward the door when the man's left arm swung around wildly and broke his grip. Trammel staggered back with a handful of the man's hair still in his hands. He launched himself into Trammel, knocking him back against the wall.

The attacker staggered back and threw a left hook that Trammel easily dodged.

By then, Trammel's rage had already boiled over. The sheriff buried a straight right hand into the man's belly, doubling him over. He snatched him by the back of the neck and his britches and threw him through the closed window.

Trammel and Hawkeye looked out the window to see the man had hit the ground and rolled down the small embankment that ran behind all of the establishments along Main Street. His legs were still moving, but barely.

"Looks like he's still movin'," Hawkeye observed. "So he's still alive."

"Yeah." Trammel spat blood out the window in the man's direction. "Let's go get him."

As they turned to leave the room, Adam Hagen was standing in the doorway. "Was that really necessary? Do you know how long it's going to take me to get that window replaced?"

Hawkeye hurried past him, but Trammel took his time. "The girl's fine, by the way."

"I know she's fine," Hagen said. "I just checked on her before I came in here. But you still owe me the cost of a new window, Trammel."

"He pulled a knife on me," the sheriff said as he pushed past him into the hallway. "You remember how much I hate knives, don't you, Adam?"

"And do you know how much a new window will cost me? I'm a businessman now, Buck," Hagen called after him as the sheriff walked down the stairs. "I don't have to be the only one making money here. You could have your share, just like I offered, you know. It's not my fault you're so damned stubborn."

Trammel didn't dignify it with an answer as he went down the stairs to retrieve his prisoner.

Trammel and Hawkeye ignored the injured man's pleas for a doctor as they practically dragged the man all the way back to the jail.

He screamed when they dumped him onto a cot in one of the cells and slammed the door shut. "I need a doctor, damn you!"

"Seems like everyone we dump in here needs a doctor." Hawkeye grinned. "Maybe we're gettin' what you might call a reputation for being rough?"

"That's a reputation I can live with." To the prisoner, Trammel said, "We'll see about getting you a doctor as soon as we've finished our patrol. You interrupted us while we were in the middle of making it, so you'll have to wait."

The man slumped on the cot, his ruined right arm lying limp on the cell floor. "You'd better get me a doctor damned fast, boy. You don't know who you're dealing with."

Hawkeye laughed as he turned the key in the cell door. "Where have we heard that one before?"

"Don't know how many times you heard it," the prisoner said, "but this time, it holds water." He glared up at the sheriff. "I know who you are, Trammel. So do a lot of people."

Trammel knew his name had appeared in the papers a few times as a result of the Madam Pinochet incident. He hadn't been happy about all of the attention, but gunfights and shoot-outs on main streets were big news back east and elsewhere, so he had

16

no choice but to go along with it and wait for it to die down.

"The longer you keep talking, the longer it'll take for you to get a doctor to look you over." He elbowed his deputy. "Come to think of it, we haven't had our coffee yet, have we, Hawkeye?"

Hawkeye played along. "Can't remember that we have."

"I don't know about you, but I'm no damned good until I've had that first cup to start the day. We'd best get ourselves some before we resume our patrol."

"Sounds good to me, boss."

They ignored the man's threats as they left the cells and shut the door leading to the office behind them.

Hawkeye sheepishly laid the keys on Trammel's desk. "Boss, we just had some coffee not half an hour ago."

Trammel sometimes forgot how gullible the young man could be. "That was just for his benefit. You stay here and keep an eye on him. I don't think he'll give you any trouble in his condition, but keep an eye on him just the same. I'll go fetch Doctor Downs right away to take a look at him. His arm's broken, and he probably busted a few ribs when he fell out that window. Don't want him dying on us if I can help it. Get started on writing up the report in the meantime."

Hawkeye eagerly pulled up a chair and took the paper from the bottom drawer of his desk. The boy's spelling was horrible and his grammar was even worse, but he enjoyed writing up reports, so Trammel let him.

The sheriff scooped up the keys from the desk as he left. "I'll lock the door on my way out. Best to keep it that way until I get back. That drunk might have friends, and if he does, it'd be best if we faced them down together."

"I'll be too busy with this here report to do anything else," Hawkeye said. "Say, boss. What did Mr. Hagen mean back there? That stuff about beggars and horses."

Trammel knew Hagen had a unique ability of saying something that could stick in your mind all day. He knew he had fallen prey to it from time to time. "It's an old saying. 'Put a beggar on horseback and he'll ride to hell on account of he doesn't know any better.' "

Hawkeye looked more confused than ever. "Well, you ain't no beggar and Blackstone sure ain't no hell."

Sometimes, Trammel admired the way the

boy's mind worked. "I'll be back with the doctor as soon as I can."

boy's mind wandered. "I'll be back with the doctor as soon as I can."

CHAPTER 2

Trammel enjoyed how Emily Downs's kitchen always smelled like baked bread and coffee. The widow's mother-in-law was a dour old woman who had lost her ability to speak after the sudden death of her son more than a year before, but she hadn't lost her ability to cook.

Trammel was enjoying some of that fine coffee while he sat in the kitchen waiting for Emily to come down from dressing. Upon being named sheriff of Blackstone, he'd rented a room in her house rather than in the run-down hovel that came with the job at the Oakwood Arms or at the Hagen-controlled Clifford Hotel.

Trammel's predecessor — Sheriff Bonner — had used a room at the Oakwood, and given how he'd been shot in the back as he fled his debts, Trammel decided to make his lodgings elsewhere. Mayor Welch, who owned the Oakwood, was annoyed at the loss of income, but the town elders applauded the sheriff for finding much cheaper lodgings at Doctor Downs's place.

Trammel looked out the window as he sipped his coffee. He ignored the black-clad widow's vacant stare from her perch in the chair next to the stove. Her expression never changed, whether she was at church or sitting outside enjoying the sunshine at her daughter-in-law's orders.

But he always felt there was something extra in the way she looked at him. It was as though she could see through all of the fame and glory he had received for bringing Madam Pinochet and her allies to justice. It was like she could see into his very soul and all of the many sins he had committed in his thirty years. He didn't know if that was the case, but if it was, he doubted she'd ever get bored, for there was plenty to see.

"Good morning," Emily Downs sang as she entered the kitchen. She gave her mother-in-law a kiss on the forehead, which garnered no response from her.

"And good morning to you, Sheriff Trammel," she said with false propriety. They were on a first-name basis when they were alone, but kept to formal titles when others were around.

"And a good morning to you, Doctor

Downs," he answered.

She had chestnut-brown hair and bright eyes that were even more captivating in the gentle light of the morning. Her simple dress did an adequate job of disguising the curves of her body of which Trammel had become so fond.

"I trust you slept comfortably."

She turned her back to her mother-in-law to hide her blush, as she had spent a good portion of the night in Trammel's bed. "Most comfortably, thank you." She lifted the coffeepot from the stove. "More coffee?"

He smiled. "Thanks."

"I understand you've already had a busy morning."

Even though he had been the sheriff of Blackstone for several months, the speed with which news spread around the small town at all hours of the day and night still fascinated him. "How the h — ?" He remembered the widow was there and caught himself. "I mean, how did you know? You just got up."

"I heard the screams coming from Main Street and imagined it was something that required your attention. Am I right?"

He chose his words carefully for the widow's sake. "Someone got rough with one of the dance hall girls at the Pot of Gold. Hawkeye and I had to take care of it. You might need to check on the girl involved."

Emily filled her own cup and set the pot back on the stove. "And the man who attacked her? I trust he needs attention, too, thanks to you."

"When you get around to it."

"Is he still alive?"

"Fell out a window," Trammel said. "Busted up some. He'll probably keep until you tend to the girl. She's more important."

Emily strategically moved the kitchen chair so her back wasn't to her mother-in-law and she wasn't sitting too close to her boarder, either. "How bad is he?"

Trammel shrugged. "He fell out a second-story window and rolled down the embankment. His right arm is broken, and I'd be surprised if his ribs weren't cracked, if not broken. His lungs work fine, though, and he's not bleeding much."

"Imagine that," she chided. "Only a half-dead patient for once. You're getting benevolent in your old age, Sheriff."

He couldn't really argue with that. In his time in Blackstone, Trammel had developed a reputation for being rougher than he had to be with some characters, which had led to a drop in crime since the Madam

23

Pinochet incident. His size had usually been enough to discourage most men from stepping out of line, but now that he had some notoriety behind him, men tended to do what he said.

He also knew notoriety was a double-edged sword and it would only be a matter of time before someone decided to test it in an effort to gain some notoriety for themselves.

He would worry about that if and when it happened. For now, he was content with the morning's work while enjoying the widow's coffee and Emily's company.

"The Pot of Gold is Adam's new place, isn't it?" she asked.

"Opened last week," Trammel said. He knew what was coming next. It had been a bone of contention between them for months.

"Did you have a chance to speak with him yet? About mending fences?"

Trammel sipped his coffee. "The opportunity to do so didn't present itself, Doctor. Besides, the fence between us is just fine as it is."

She lowered her cup. "I wish you boys would figure out a way past your differences. You were friends once, Buck. Good friends."

"That was then. This is now. He works his side of things and I work mine." He saw no reason to explain himself, especially in front of the widow.

Hagen had decided to hold on to Madam Pinochet's ledger of illegal actions in the territory. He had also expanded her opium trade against Trammel's wishes. While there may not be any laws against opium in Wyoming or in Blackstone, he hated the practice. In his time as a policeman in New York City and later, with the Pinkerton Agency, he had seen what smoking the sticky tar could do. He had seen good men brought low by the desire to hitch a ride on the dragon's back one more time.

Opium may not have been illegal, but that didn't make it right. Hagen's desire to peddle flesh was bad enough in Trammel's eyes, but he knew if Hagen didn't do it, someone else would. Robbing men of their souls was something Buck Trammel would never tolerate.

"Friendships in this life are so hard to come by," Emily went on. "Especially good friendships like the one you had with Adam. Maybe you could be a good influence on him if you were close to him again."

Trammel laughed as he got up to pour himself another cup of coffee from the stove. "The die for Adam Hagen was cast long before he left Blackstone and only hardened in the years since. There's no amount of praying or cajoling that'll make him change unless he wants to. Or has to, if it comes to that." He poured his coffee. "And if it comes to that, it'll probably be thanks to me." He held out the pot to her. "More coffee before we head out to tend to your patients?"

She drained her cup and gently placed it back in the saucer as she stood. It was a delicate motion, but sounded as loud as a judge's gavel in the quiet of the kitchen. "I'll get my shawl and bag. I'd appreciate it if you'd escort me to the jail to see the prisoner, Sheriff. After that, I'd like to look in on that poor girl he assaulted."

Trammel shut his eyes as she left the kitchen. He knew her tone well enough to know she was upset. He felt the widow's constant glare upon him as he set the coffeepot back on the stove. Her eyes were as vacant as they were alive.

He finished his coffee in two swallows and smiled at her as he set his cup aside. Her look never changed.

He held the back door open for Emily as she appeared with her shawl wrapped

26

around her shoulders and her husband's old medicine bag in her hand. "Can I carry that for you?"

She walked past him into the chilly morning. Trammel sighed as he quietly shut the door behind him.

Out on the boardwalk and still out of view of anyone who might see, she swung her bag and hit him in the side.

Trammel stifled a yelp. "What the hell was that for?"

"For being pigheaded," she said without breaking her stride. "I swear, Buck Trammel, you're a tough man to love sometimes."

Trammel smiled as he caught up with her. She had told him she loved him several times since they had become a couple, but he never tired of hearing it. He easily matched her pace with a little swagger to his step. "So you love me, huh?"

He yelped again when she pinched his side. "Don't get too cocky on me, Sheriff. I might not be a real doctor, but I know all the right places that hurt."

He rubbed the spot where she'd pinched him. "Yes, ma'am."

CHAPTER 3

Ambrose Bowman ignored his guest for a time, preferring to quietly rock back and forth in his rocking chair as he watched the morning sunshine cast its gentle light on the family graveyard behind his house in Wichita, Kansas. It was his favorite time of the day, or at least, it had been since he'd laid his oldest son and nephew in their graves six months before.

Old Man Bowman could remember a time when he did not hold that title, when there were only two graves carved out of the harsh Kansas dirt, for his grandfather and grandmother, who had worked themselves to death making something of this godforsaken land. Now, it was filled with other Bowman dead who had gone to glory since: his father, who had lived to the ripe old age of sixty, surpassing his wife, who'd died while giving birth to Ambrose.

His father had always resented Ambrose

for causing the death of his beloved wife and never let the boy forget it. Even now, as he approached his eightieth winter, he carried the scars of that resentment with him. He had used the feelings to make him the man he had become: the man who controlled the most successful cattle ranch in Wichita.

The man who watched the grass grow tall over his eldest son's grave.

Ambrose did not look at his guest as he told him, "I don't like you, sir. I don't like you or your kind."

"Then why did you send for me?" asked the man.

"I may not like you, but I need you." Old Man Bowman leaned forward and spat, proud of the fact he still had the lung power to clear the end of his porch without difficulty. "I can't do what needs doing myself. I'm too damned old. Too old by a long shot. Maybe older than I should be, depending on which member of my family you ask." He pointed out at the graveyard with a crooked finger. "Many out there, molding in their graves right now, would tell you I should be in there instead of them. They might even be right. But here I am and there they are."

The guest shifted uncomfortably in his

chair. "I'm here because you're paying me to be here, Mr. Bowman. Best get to the point so we can go about our business, or cut me loose and I'll be on my way back to Chicago."

"Chicago." The old man said it as though the word itself was poison. "City folk are lazy folk. They're stupid and easily led like the cattle I've got fenced in just over that rise there. People who do as they're told and sit at desks and take money they've never earned because they've never worked a day in their miserable lives. Penned in together like hogs, scrapping for whatever bits their masters see fit to feed them. That's no way for a man to live. Not if he wants to call himself a man, anyway."

"Never been much for sitting behind a desk myself, Mr. Bowman," the guest said. "If I was, you and I wouldn't be out here having this pleasant conversation on such a fine morning."

"Insolence," Bowman added, continuing his thought. "That's what that is. You have the false confidence of a city man through and through. There was a time I would've taken a bullwhip to you for talking to me that way. Would've whipped you from where you're sitting all the way back to town without even breathing hard."

"Then I guess I'm lucky I didn't know you back then." The chair creaked as the guest leaned forward. "You've gone to great expense to bring me and my men out here, Mr. Bowman. If all you want to do is insult me, that's fine. But the more we talk here, the less time I can dedicate to what you say you want to hire me to do. Now, do you want to keep spitting venom or do you want to discuss the matter at hand? I get paid either way."

Old Man Bowman cursed himself for rambling. His bones may have creaked and sleep may have eluded him, but until six months ago, his mind had been as sharp as a tack. He knew every head of cattle in the field and every penny he had in the bank without having to ask anyone.

But something had died in him the moment he learned of his eldest son's death. Matt had been his favorite among his children. He'd been his first and the best. He had been bred since birth to take over this ranch when Ambrose had been called home either to heaven or hell, depending on what the good Lord decided best for him.

But with Matt in the graveyard with the rest of his kin, neither cattle nor money held much interest for Ambrose anymore. Now, he only lived for one purpose.

Revenge.

"I need you to kill a man."

"I already gathered that." The guest sat back in his chair. "Killing's a dirty business."

"But it's your business, isn't it, Mr. Alcott?"

"It can be," Jesse Alcott allowed, "when the time comes for it."

"And here I was thinking the Pinkerton men did the jobs that needed doing," the old man sneered. "Guess I was wrong."

"I didn't say no. I said it depends."

"On what? Money?"

"That's part of it," Alcott allowed. "A big part of it. But so is who you need killed and why."

"I need two men killed. The men responsible for killing my boy Matt." As an afterthought, "for killing my grandson Walt, too, I suppose, not that he ever counted for much. But don't let my sister hear me say that. She idolized that boy, though I'll never understand why."

Alcott shifted uneasily in his chair once more. "Mr. Bowman, I've read the newspaper accounts of what happened to your son and your nephew. They were killed by a bunch of cowpunchers who got themselves killed up in Wyoming a few months back." He let the words hang for a moment before adding, "The men who killed them are already dead."

"And you think that ends it?" Old Man Bowman's eyes narrowed. "The men who killed them may be dead, but the men responsible for their deaths are still very much among the living. I want you to see to it that they meet a similar end. And I want it done well before someone shovels that last spade of dirt upon my grave out there."

Alcott folded his hands across his flat stomach. "And who do you hold truly responsible for their deaths?"

Bowman's lips trembled with hatred as he struggled to bring himself to speak their names. "A no-good gambler by the name of Adam Hagen. And the bastard who saved him, Buck Trammel."

The old man waited for a response, but when none came he turned to face his guest. He found the Pinkerton man smiling. "What's so damned funny?"

Jesse Alcott's smile held. "I happen to know Buck Trammel. Had a run-in with him on a train headed west back in the spring."

"I don't give a damn about your quarrel with him, Alcott. I care about mine. Will you kill him? And Hagen?"

Alcott flexed his gun hand. He imagined he would be needing it before all of this was done. "Oh, I'll be more than happy to kill them for you, Mr. Bowman. But first, let's discuss cost."

CHAPTER 4

The prisoner grinned through the pain of his broken body when he saw Emily standing outside his cell door. "Well look at what we have here. Hell, if I knew you provided these kind of amenities, Trammel, I'd have gotten myself tossed in here a long time ago." He winced as his broken bones throbbed, but still managed to say, "What's your name, darlin'?"

Trammel hit the cage, making the prisoner jump and wince again. "Her name is Doctor Emily Downs. She's here to treat your wounds and set your arm. If you behave yourself, you'll do just fine. But if you so much as twitch her way, I'll break your other arm. Understand?"

The prisoner's grin disappeared.

Trammel unlocked the cell door and let Emily inside. "I'll be right here the whole time if you need me."

Emily set her bag on the cot and shook

her head as she looked at her new patient's injuries. "It's almost impossible to figure out where to start. I have an idea. How about we start with your name?"

"No way, sugar," the prisoner said. "Just tend to my wounds if you're of a mind to, but my name's got nothing to do with what ails me."

She gently lifted his broken right arm, causing the prisoner to cry out.

Trammel stepped into the cell and grabbed hold of the prisoner's left arm. "Just in case the pain makes you decide to try something stupid."

Emily continued her examination. "The shoulder is definitely separated. Maybe even broken. I might be able be able to pop it back into place, but it's going to hurt."

The prisoner spoke through clenched teeth. "Do what you've got to do, you bi —"

Emily quickly twisted the arm and a sickening crunch echoed in the cell.

Even Trammel winced.

The prisoner passed out.

"That'll certainly make things easier." She continued to examine the arm. "The rest of it seems fine, but I won't know for certain until he wakes up." She ran her hands over his ribs. "Two of them are definitely broken and the rest feel cracked." She moved to his legs and feet. "His ankles are swollen and most likely sprained, though not broken."

She stood up and looked at Trammel. "You weren't exactly gentle with him, were you?"

"I threw him out a window for threatening a woman," Trammel said. "He deserved it. Besides, I save my gentle side for you."

She held a finger to her lips. "Hawkeye's outside. He might hear. Now, pull this one up while I wrap his ribs."

While the sheriff guarded the prisoner as Doc Emily tended to his wounds, Hawkeye rubbed his hands across the sheriff's big desk. It was a mighty fine piece of furniture, one befitting a man of Sheriff Trammel's stature. Not just because of his size, but because of the man he was.

He remembered watching the big stranger ride into town that first day of spring all those months ago. Mr. Bookman, the top hand at the Hagen ranch, had led him and Adam Hagen along Main Street, stopping off at the jail to see Sheriff Bonner before taking Adam to the Clifford Hotel, Hawkeye had just been a runner at the Moose Saloon back then. No one important, really. He'd fetched bottles when the bartender needed them. Swabbed down the floors when the drunks got sick and took care of the sheets in the rooms upstairs. The girls were usually nice to him and gave him tips while everyone else just spat at him. He never let it bother him. He saw no reason why it should.

He had grown up on horseback on his father's ranch and knew he was a good hand. His father had taught him how to handle a herd and a gun as soon as his legs were long enough to reach the stirrups. Not yet twenty, he knew he could still be a top hand one day if someone would give him a chance, but no one was eager to hire on the son of a drunk who had lost his ranch to King Charles Hagen. Now, the same house where generations of Hauks been born was a bunkhouse for cowhands.

Buck Trammel was the first man Hawkeye could remember who had ever looked at him for who he was. Trammel hadn't known about his father being a drunkard when he'd hired him as deputy, and when he'd found out about it, didn't care. He had handed Hawkeye the deputy star in a moment of haste, but it was the proudest moment of Jimmy Hauk's life. He'd never forget the many kindnesses the sheriff had shown him in the months since. The way he tolerated his stupid questions and talking out of turn. He knew he still had a lot to learn about being a lawman and about being a man, and he was grateful to Sheriff Trammel for being willing to teach him. He made it a point to never make the same mistake twice and felt himself grow into the position of deputy with each passing day.

He may not have deserved the star when the sheriff had given it to him, but he had spent every day since trying to live up to it.

He stopped his daydreaming and scrambled to his feet when Doc Emily stepped out from the cells, followed by the sheriff. It was times like these when he realized just how big Buck Trammel was. Hawkeye himself was six feet tall, and the sheriff was a good five inches taller than that. He was broad shouldered and Hawkeye judged him to be about two hundred and thirty pounds. He'd seen the way the man moved when the lead started flying and knew very little of that was fat.

For a city man, the sheriff was good with a rifle and even better with a pistol, but preferred to use his hands whenever possible. Hawkeye had seen him knock a man down with one punch without even swinging hard. He still wasn't as comfortable on horseback as he should have been, but

Hawkeye took pride in giving him subtle hints about how he could ride better. And the sheriff never seemed to resent the advice.

"Morning, Miss Emily," Hawkeye said as the sheriff closed the door to the cells.

She smiled. "You already said that when I came in, Hawkeye. No need to keep saying it every time I walk into the room."

"Yes, ma'am. Forgive me." He realized he was rambling again and stopped. "How's the prisoner?"

"He'll live," Trammel said. "It'll be a while until he's well enough to make the ride down to Laramie to stand trial, so it looks like you'll have to tend to him for a bit longer. Think you can manage that?"

Hawkeye had tended to the scrapes and scars of the girls who worked down at the Moose from time to time, but never something like this. He could learn so much. "Of course, boss. Miss Emily, will you tell me what to do?"

She smiled at his enthusiasm. "We'll talk all about it later. I've set his arm and wrapped his ribs as best I could. He sprained both ankles in the fall, so he won't be able to move much. He also has a nasty bump on his head and is quite dizzy. I'm afraid he may toss up whatever food you give him."

"Ain't the first bit of sickness I've ever tended to, ma'am, so I don't mind."

The sheriff hung the ring of keys on the peg next to the rifle rack. "I'll be able to spell you from time to time, but it'll be up to you to keep him alive. I know you can do it."

Hawkeye felt himself beam with pride. An expression of confidence from a man like Sheriff Trammel was a badge of honor itself. "You can count on me, sir."

Doc Emily and the sheriff traded a glance and laughed. He knew they were laughing with him, not at him, not the way the men at the Moose used to do. He'd been laughed at enough in his young life to know the difference, and it didn't bother him a bit.

"Keep an eye on things while we're gone," Trammel said. "We're going to tend to that girl he attacked. She was sleeping when we stopped by before, so we didn't want to disturb her. I'll be back after the doc has a chance to tend to her wounds."

"I'll be right here. Don't you worry."

Hawkeye heard Doc Emily giggle as the sheriff followed her outside. Then he remembered he hadn't cleaned his pistol since the night before. He set the gun on the desk and got to work.

41

■ ■ ■ ■

"That boy idolizes you," Emily said as they began walking toward the Pot of Gold. "I hope you know that."

"He's just a kid. He doesn't know any better." That sounded a bit dismissive of poor Hawkeye, and Trammel immediately regretted saying it. "He just needs someone to believe in him. He's going to grow up to be a fine man someday if I have anything to say about it."

"You'll have plenty to say about it, believe me," Emily said. "I don't think you could get rid of him even if you tried."

"He's a good man to have around."

Trammel acknowledged the townspeople who waved at him and tipped their hats to him from the other side of Main Street. They were shopkeepers and clerks and bank tellers and merchants who never dared to step foot this side of the thoroughfare. He didn't blame them. The saloons along Main Street were rough places, too rough for the respectable citizens of Blackstone to frequent. There were a few dining halls and respectable saloons along Bainbridge Avenue where they chose to go instead.

The Clifford Hotel was the only attraction

for them on this side of Main Street and it had been built a good distance away from the rowdier places where decent people never dared to tread.

Trammel gently eased Emily to the side when they reached the Pot of Gold. "You'd best stay here while I make sure it's safe for you to go inside."

"For heaven's sake," Emily fumed. "I've had my hands inside people's innards. I've treated broken bones and cracked heads for half my life now. There's nothing in a saloon that'll shock me."

Trammel had seen Emily's work. She'd even patched him up from time to time, and he knew she wasn't a delicate flower. But she was still a lady. What's more, he had come to think of her as *his* lady, and that meant something to him. "It's not for your sake. It's for mine. Please?"

She stomped her foot and turned away. "Stubborn. Go ahead."

Trammel pushed through the batwing doors and stood in the doorway. The place was busier than it had been earlier that morning. All of the tables were filled with men playing cards. The piano player banged away at the ivories, playing a tune that resembled "Old Dog Tray" but was a few notes off. He didn't know if that was the fault of the piano or the man playing it, but none of the patrons seemed to mind.

The working girls flitted among the tables like bees in a flower garden, waiting for anyone who might beckon them to stay.

The bar was doing a booming business. Men stood two deep. A thin line of cigar smoke hovered over the entire room like a filthy halo.

From his perch in the lookout chair in the back, Adam Hagen bellowed, "Atten-shun!"

The former cavalry officer's voice brought the entire saloon to a halt, and an awkward silence fell over the place.

"Ladies and gentlemen," Hagen said as he stepped down from his lookout chair, adjusting the Colt he wore to the side as he walked. "It appears we have a celebrity in our midst and attention must be paid. The right and righteous Sheriff Buck Trammel has come to call and has the look of a man with something important to say." He stopped several feet from Trammel and saluted him before bowing at the waist. "The floor is yours, kind sir."

Hagen's theatrics had annoyed Trammel when they were friends. Now, he looked upon them as almost mocking. He spoke loud enough for everyone to hear. "I'm bringing in Doctor Emily Downs to tend to the girl who got hurt here this morning. I want everyone to mind their manners and their language while she's here. Anyone who doesn't will answer to me."

"Well said, Sheriff." Hagen turned to face his customers. "To put a finer point on it, if I hear one catcall or whistle in the good doctor's presence, I will shoot the offender in the face. Is that clear?"

The patrons grumbled their agreement.

"Good. Next round's on the house as a sign of my gratitude for your cooperation."

The patrons cheered, and the gambling and music resumed.

Trammel held open the door for Emily and she stepped into the Pot of Gold.

"Doctor Downs," Hagen said as he took her hand and kissed it. "Never before has this hovel of decadence and depravity been graced by such a remarkable woman."

"Damn it, Adam," Trammel said. "You've barely been open a week."

"The compliment still holds true."

Emily frowned as she took her hand back. "God, Adam. You're absolutely polluted. What have you been drinking?"

"Whiskey," Hagen responded. "Beer, too, I'm afraid. I'm actually on the verge of sobriety, a condition I intend on rectifying as soon as both of you leave the premises. I take it you're here to call on poor Delilah."

"If that's the girl who was hurt earlier today," Emily said, "then yes, I am."

"How good of you to come. She's in room twenty-two at the top of the stairs, but please allow me to go ahead of you to make sure you aren't disturbed by the carnal sounds from the neighboring rooms. Make straight your path and all that, to borrow a phrase from the Good Book."

Trammel motioned to the stairway. "Get on with it."

"Still as charming as ever, eh, Buck?" Hagen said as he ran up the stairs.

Emily looked back at Trammel and mouthed, *Be nice.*

Trammel followed her up the stairs as Hagen began pounding on doors. "Keep it down in there. We've got a lady present."

Delilah was, indeed, in Room Twenty-two and was already being attended to by three of the other girls of the house. They moved aside when Emily came in with her medical bag, but refused to leave their friend alone.

Emily smiled back at Trammel. "Why don't you boys give us some privacy?"

"Like hell," Trammel said. "No way I'm leaving you alone up here."

"I'll be fine," she insisted. "You can come back to check on me in half an hour."

Trammel didn't like it, but he could tell by her tone that she'd made up her mind. He closed the door before she shut it in his face.

Hagen remained in the hallway, grinning. "You picked yourself a spirited one in Doctor Downs, Buck. I think she's too much woman for you."

"No one cares what you think, Hagen. Not anymore."

"Nonsense." Hagen followed him down the narrow hall. "Quite a few people respect my opinion in a whole host of matters. Just none that you seem to care about. But Miss Emily is far too good for you. Why don't you let me do you a favor and pick out one of the more gentle ones from my herd for you? We both know you're ill-suited to choose appropriate mounts, remember?"

Trammel snatched Hagen by the collar and pinned him against the wall before he realized he did it. "What the hell is that supposed to mean?"

Hagen grinned again. "So things with the fair doctor have progressed in that direction after all. Forgive me, old man, for I didn't know and meant no offense. Though, things being how they are, I suggest you let me go and right now, lest poor Emily finds you suddenly wanting this evening." His eyes flicked down.

So did Trammel's. The gambler was holding a dagger less than an inch below the sheriff's groin. Trammel's grip tightened. "You saw what happened to the last man who pulled a knife on me."

"I did, but he was hardly in a position to do much about it," Hagen said. "I am."

Trammel let him go with a shove, and Hagen slipped the knife back up his sleeve. "You're always full of surprises, aren't you, Hagen?"

"It's part of my charm."

Trammel realized they were standing outside of Room Twenty, where Delilah had been attacked earlier that morning. The broken door hung half shut, and Trammel shoved it all the way in. It slammed against the wall and lost one of its hinges.

Hagen sighed. "You really hate that door, don't you, Buck?"

Trammel ignored him and stepped into the room. It looked the same as it had earlier that morning, though the window had since been boarded up. He looked around the room and didn't find anything out of the ordinary. That was the problem. "You have this room cleaned since this morning?"

"Just boarded up the window and straightened up some of the things you knocked over. I'm still mighty sore about that window, Buck. I hope the town will be prepared to make some reparations."

But Trammel had more on his mind than reparations. "Where are the man's things? His clothes, saddlebags. Things like that?

"I haven't the slightest idea where they are." Hagen threw up his hands when Trammel glared at him. "Honest. I know he had been out back for a time and I had no idea he'd come back in here until Delilah started screaming."

Trammel knew *out back* was Hagen's term for the opium den that operated behind the Pot of Gold. It was a series of tents set up for the purpose of people to lounge while they took a pull on the opium pipe. He claimed he only rented space to them and had no idea what they did back there, nor did he benefit from it. Trammel knew it was a lie but couldn't prove it.

"You and your damned Celestials," Trammel cursed. "I warned you about keeping a lid on that nonsense, didn't I?"

"You most certainly did," Hagen agreed, "and I most certainly have. Our Chinese friends have made certain that none of their clients wander the streets after partaking of the pipe. They ensure all of their customers

49

are fit to travel before they let them go. And like it or not, they've been true to their word. The streets of our fair town haven't been littered by mindless hordes, have they?"

"Only in alleys, thanks to the laudanum you give them to keep them flying."

"No law against laudanum, either."

The damnable part of it was that there wasn't. "Then how do you explain what happened to Delilah today?"

"I'm as lost as you are, my friend. Opium usually makes people passive, giddy even. Why, I've seen the toughest cowpunchers and miners wet themselves and giggle like babies after a spell 'neath the dragon's wings. Never known one to get violent after smoking, unless they were aching for a pipe, which this man certainly was not."

Trammel thought about going in and asking Delilah what had happened, but knew Emily wouldn't approve. Besides, the poor woman had been through enough for one day. But there were other ways to find things out. "I want to talk to the Celestial who runs the den. I want whatever my prisoner left down there while he was smoking."

"Impossible." Hagen folded his arms. "They have an ancient distrust of authority and of lawmen most of all. I'm afraid your predecessor treated them rather poorly and their resentment of the late Sheriff Bonner has carried down to you. I'm not saying it's fair. I'm just telling you how it is. Besides, you know how they are. Anything he left down there has probably been split amongst the heathens by now."

Trammel took a step toward him. "You're their landlord, so you're going to talk to them for me. You're going to tell them that I want to see what that man brought in with him. I'm not asking for it back, and I don't care who has it. But I want to see all of it and I want it now, or I take a flame to that canvas and burn it to the ground."

Hagen closed his eyes. "You have to promise me you won't step foot in the place. I mean it. There's a limit to my influence over them. You know that. If you go barging in there, they'll never talk no matter what you do to them."

Trammel didn't like having terms dictated to him by anyone, much less the town vice merchant, even when that vice merchant had once been his friend. "We'll play it your way for now. But if I don't get his belongings, I'm going to lose patience."

"You'd have to have some in order to lose it." Hagen unfolded his arms and walked out of the room. "And close the door behind you, please. We've got standards to uphold, you know?"

Trammel followed Hagen down the stairs. He left the door open.

Trammel didn't like waiting, but it beat being inside the tent where the air was poisoned with opium smoke. He'd been in his share of dens back in Chicago and New York, and the sweet stench had always turned his stomach. He could barely tolerate the smell of tobacco, but the pipe was something altogether different. Whiskey could bring a man to ruin just as much as opium, but it was different somehow. There was a more social aspect to drinking in a saloon as opposed to lying on pillows and being robbed blind while you drifted off toward oblivion. He imagined his objection didn't make much sense in the grand scheme of things, but he had already made up his mind on the subject and had no intention of changing it any time soon.

Trammel waved away some of the smoke as the tent flap opened and Hagen stepped outside. If he was suffering any ill effects from the fumes, he did not show it.

Hagen stood between the sheriff and the tent. "You're not going to be happy, but I need you to listen to everything I say before you get angry."

"I'm already angry about what happened to that girl," Trammel said. "Might as well tell me the rest of it."

"His clothes are already gone." Hagen quickly added, "He insisted on taking them off before he smoked. After his time was up, he caught Delilah coming in to partake of the pipe herself. He recognized her from the saloon and offered her a good sum to go upstairs. That explains why he was in his britches. You know the rest."

"The hell I do. What about his clothes?"

"As I feared, they've already been scattered among the workers. But the boss said nothing was in them. Your prisoner had already paid them before he smoked and gave the rest of his money to Delilah before they went upstairs. His pockets were empty, and there's nothing to identify him on any of his clothes."

Hagen was right. Trammel wasn't happy in the slightest. "What about his horse? Is that still around or do they already have it on a spit out back?"

The former cavalry officer winced. "What a loathsome thought. They said he hitched his horse outside before he came in the back way, but they haven't touched it. One can never be sure when talking to our inscrutable cousins from the East, but they seem to be telling the truth. There's an excellent chance the animal may still be there, though they didn't see him ride in and have no idea if it's still there."

Trammel knew Hagen was telling the truth. There was nothing more to be learned about the prisoner from the opium den, but maybe the man's horse could tell him something.

"I take it my cooperation has put me back in your good graces," Hagen said.

"Hardly. Because of what happened to that girl this morning, your laudanum privileges are cut off for a week. One word of complaint and I make it a month. I see one drunk in your alley with a bottle in his pocket or at his feet, I blame you and take an ax to every stick of brand-new furniture you've got in your saloon. Do you understand?"

Hagen's eyes narrowed and his jaw set on edge. This, Trammel knew, was the real Adam Hagen. Not the fancy-talking dandy who ran the classiest hellhole in Blackstone, but the same man he had ridden with from Wichita to Wyoming. The man who knew how to handle himself in a fight better than most. The man who could only be pushed so far before he pushed back.

54

Hagen slowly shook his head. "You've really grown to hate me that much, haven't you? Why? Because of this?" He thumbed over his shoulder at the opium tents. "It's not illegal, Buck. It's even encouraged in some parts of the country. Hell, you can get it almost anywhere in San Francisco. Why should I lose out on a buck? Because of your high moral standards? Don't let all that ink they spilled about you in the *Bugle* go to your head, my friend. I know who you really are. And *what* you are, too."

Trammel resisted the urge to grab him again. He remembered the knife and remembered Hagen knew how to use it. "It's not just about the opium. It's about the deal you made with Clay down in Laramie. It's about keeping Madam Pinochet's ledger. It's about you stepping into the same sewer she created when you could be better than that. When you could use that information to make these people do what's right. I know you, too, Adam. And I know what you could become."

Hagen laughed. "So I should just follow the edicts of King Charles and become a humble hotelier until he changes his opinion of me? Not a chance, friend. I stayed away from this place for almost twenty years because it pleased him. But thanks to that ledger and the alliance I've made with Lucien Clay in Laramie, I don't have to do what he wants anymore. I make my own rules now." He looked at Trammel. "Even if that means going against you."

Trammel knew there was more than a hint of truth in everything Hagen had said. He also knew he was not smart enough to stand there and debate him all day. Fortunately, the star on his chest meant he didn't have to. He began heading around the back of the tent to see if he could find the prisoner's horse. "One week, no laudanum, Hagen. I mean it."

He expected Hagen to throw another verbal barb his way, but he didn't.

Maybe Trammel's luck was changing after all.

CHAPTER 5

There was only one horse tied up behind the Pot of Gold, a paint with splotches of black and white all over its body. Trammel was not enough of a horseman to know if the animal was in good condition. Hagen could probably tell just by looking at it, but he would be damned before he asked him for help after the run-in they'd just had. Hawkeye could tell him, if it came to that.

The horse was too busy nosing the crabgrass that sprouted up behind the saloon to care much about Trammel's approach. It seemed like a gentle animal and, from what he could see, well fed.

The saddle was plain and oddly familiar to him, though he could not understand why. There was a saddle scabbard for a rifle, but no rifle. That did not tell him much. One of the Celestials or any number of the other town drunks had probably stolen it. That being the case, he doubted there'd be much of anything of value left in the saddle-bags, but he had to search them anyway.

He opened the left saddlebag first and was surprised to find a thick sheaf of papers inside. He pulled them out and realized they were documents. Letters, mostly, still in envelopes and tied together by an old string. A few thin slips of paper that appeared to be telegrams were in the bundle, too. Since the prisoner was refusing to speak, maybe something in the bundle would speak for him.

Trammel searched the other saddlebag and found only some rags, which had probably been used to dry sweat or wipe down the horse. Given that he already had documents to read, Trammel doubted he would learn much from a bunch of rags.

He had less experience with horses than most men in this part of the world, but he knew men valued their saddle as much as their horses, sometimes even more. They often made some kind of mark on the underside of their saddles to prove owner-ship. He wondered if he might catch a break and find the prisoner's name carved some-where on the saddle.

He pulled up the right stirrup and took a look. What he saw made him take a knee before he fell over.

Something had been branded into the leather of the saddle. Something he had seen before. Something that explained why the prisoner had refused to talk.

Something that made Trammel realize he was in far more trouble than he had previously thought.

CHAPTER 6

Trammel ignored his deputy as he stormed into the jail and unlocked the door to the cells.

The prisoner was awake, sprawled on the cot too small for him. His right arm was wrapped in a splint and propped up on a chair next to him. His ankles were also wrapped in white bandages.

"Aw, hell," the prisoner said. "I don't want to see you, Trammel. How about you send that pretty lady back in here for a spell? She's much better company than you, even for a man in my condition."

The ring of keys trembled in Trammel's hand. It took every ounce of restraint he had to keep from opening the door and pummeling the man to death. He realized Hawkeye was standing in the doorway and threw the key ring to him. "Close the door and step outside."

Puzzled, his deputy did as he was told.

Trammel held up the sheaf of letters he had retrieved from the saddlebags. "You're a Pinkerton."

The prisoner's expression didn't change. "What makes you think so?"

"I found your horse out back behind the opium tents. There's the Pinkerton eye branded into the leather." He pulled out a letter from the pile he was holding. "Then there's about a dozen letters and telegrams between you and Allan in Chicago, telling you to scout out where I was."

"Allan?" the prisoner said. "Didn't know you were on a first-name basis with the grand man himself."

Trammel held up a telegram sheet from the bundle. "Your name is John Somerset. Now at least I have a name to attach to the long list of charges I'll be making against you in Laramie as soon as you're fit to travel."

Somerset laughed. "By the time I'm fit to travel, you won't be fit to do much of anything. You'll be the one facing charges, not me. And not in any court of law, either."

Trammel crinkled up the telegram and threw it at him. "Don't be so sure."

His secrets finally revealed, Somerset got himself as comfortable as he could, given his condition. "Son, all I did was rough up a whore after taking too much pipe. You, on the other hand, killed the son of a very powerful man. Frankly, I like my chances of survival a hell of a lot better than I like yours." He readjusted himself on the cot. "No, sir. I wouldn't trade places with you for all the opium in China."

Trammel had hoped Old Man Bowman would let the death of his family go, but was not surprised that he hadn't. If he had gone as far as hiring the Pinkerton Agency, he was serious. "Who are they sending after me?"

"I haven't the slightest idea," the prisoner admitted. "I don't know who or when or how many and that's the truth. You can kick the hell out of me if you want to, but I can't tell you something I don't know. You know that's how they operate. No one man knows the whole plan except the man in charge, and I'm not him."

Trammel had been lied to enough times to know the truth when he heard it. He also knew how the Pinkerton Agency operated. "They send you here to kill me?"

"You know better than that, Buck. All I was supposed to do was confirm you were here. Sent a telegram saying exactly that when I was in Laramie three days ago. They replied, ordering me to come here and keep an eye on you until the others arrived. What happens after that is anyone's guess. But given your reputation as a hard man to bring down, I'd say they'll be bringing a whole passel of boys with them." Somerset looked him up and down. "Boys like you used to be once upon a time. I hear you were a hell of an operative in your day, big man."

"Operative." Trammel repeated. "Is that what you boys are calling yourselves now? That's a ten-dollar word for a no-good thug."

"Operative. Gunman. Hired killer. Assassin." Somerset shrugged with his good shoulder. "Call it whatever you want. It doesn't change the fact there's work that needs doing and people willing to pay good money to see it gets done. No shortage of people willing to do it, either."

Trammel decided there wasn't much more to be gained by continuing to talk to Somerset. He'd gotten all the answers from the prisoner he was liable to get.

As he turned to leave, Somerset called after him, "I don't know if you're a prayerful man, Trammel, but I'd get myself right with Jesus while you can. There won't be much time once they get here and the lead starts flying."

63

Trammel shut the door behind him and locked it.

The man they called King Charles Hagen sat behind his large oak desk and read through the letters Trammel had given him.

Trammel looked around the room while Mr. Hagen read through Somerset's correspondence. The dark wood and brass furnishings were like everything else in the main house — meant to intimidate the hell out of anyone who happened to be summoned to this place.

The house itself was a sprawling affair built on top of a hill between the two pastures that comprised a good part of the Hagen fortune. Thousands of heads of cattle grazed on the north pasture while some of the finest horses this side of the Mississippi roamed the pasture to the south. As he looked through the windows, Trammel couldn't see the fence line that hemmed in the great man's property, but knew it was out there somewhere. Everything had a limit, even Hagen's empire.

Trammel was sure the setting had intimidated most people, but he had never been one of them. In his time as a policeman and a Pinkerton, he had seen the foundations upon which such empires had been built.

He knew they were built on the backs of people who had been foolish enough to stand in the way of men like Hagen. Their foundations were soaked in the blood of the fools who had tried to stop them. The fine furnishings and woodwork of this house didn't convince Trammel that Mr. Hagen was of a higher class. Trammel knew he and Mr. Hagen were exactly the same, only the latter had found a way to get rich from giving in to his true nature.

Mr. Hagen grunted as he finished reading the last letter and handed the pile to his right-hand man, John Bookman, who had been sitting next to Trammel.

Charles Hagen looked at Trammel from beneath his heavy gray eyebrows. His large nose and deep-set dark eyes reminded the sheriff of a night train speeding past a deserted station. "Have you told my son any of this? I would imagine the same Pinkerton men coming to kill you will be tasked with killing him, too."

"No," Trammel said. "Adam is in the same boat as I am, so there's not much he could do about it."

One of Mr. Hagen's eyebrows arched. "And you think there's something I can do about it?"

"I know there is. The only question is if

you're willing to do it."

Bookman looked up from the sheaf of letters. "Remember who you're talking to, Trammel."

"I know exactly who I'm talking to, which is why I'm here instead of in town." Trammel looked at Mr. Hagen. "What'll it be, Mr. Hagen? You can put a stop to this with one telegram to Allan Pinkerton himself."

The king's eyes narrowed. "You're a forward man, aren't you, Sheriff Trammel?"

"That's why you hired me. Or so you said at the time."

"Which is why, I'm sure, we find ourselves in this current predicament." He gestured at the letters Bookman was reading. "This matter before us is about much more than some old man's vendetta against the men he believed caused the death of his son and nephew."

"We were cleared of those charges as soon as they were made in Nebraska," Trammel said. "Those men were killed by Lefty Hanover and his men, who are molding in a potter's field in Laramie as we speak. Old Man Bowman is looking for revenge in the wrong place. He's blaming me and your son for the deaths of his family members, and he's hired the Pinkerton Agency to get him justice he already has. You can end this if

66

you want to."

"How?" King Charles asked. "By riding to Wichita to speak with the man personally? To talk to a man whose fly-speckled spread is barely larger than my sheep pasture? Preposterous. I wouldn't lower myself to even consider it. Why, it would be cheaper for me to buy the damned place out from under him and turn him into a pauper."

"I wasn't thinking of that," Trammel said. "I was thinking you could send a telegram to the Pinkerton Agency and match whatever Bowman is paying them to come for me and Adam."

"What makes you think I haven't already done that?"

Trammel moved to the edge of his chair. For the first time since finding Somerset's letters, he had a sense of hope. "You have?"

Mr. Hagen and Bookman exchanged glances before Hagen said, "There isn't much that happens in this part of the world that passes without my notice, particularly when some doddering old rancher hires men to kill my son. It just so happens that I have employed the Pinkerton Agency to protect my varying interests from time to time. Mr. Pinkerton himself notified me of Mr. Bowman's quest as soon as he received it."

67

"You already knew?" Trammel had never been a hopeful man, but he allowed himself to become hopeful. "And you've called them off?"

"No."

It was a simple word. Two letters. One syllable. It was a word used by people all over the world every day for a variety of reasons. But when a man like Charles Hagen said it, the word bore the finality of a cell door slamming shut.

Trammel heard himself say, "What do you mean *no*?"

"It's a simple enough word," Mr. Hagen said. "Certainly even a man of your limited education must be able to grasp its meaning. I learned of Mr. Bowman's efforts last week. I have decided to not interfere."

Trammel slowly stood and sensed Bookman had stood with him. "What do you mean it's none of your affair? That crazy old bastard has hired men to come here to kill your son. How can you just sit by and let that happen?"

"I can do it quite easily, young man." Hagen held out his hands to show the expanse of his desk and office. "I do it every single day, for dozens of reasons, and I will do so in this case. Would you like to know why?"

Trammel felt his right hand ball into a fist

and was conscious that Bookman was within arm's reach of him. He also noticed that Bookman's hand had moved to the Colt he had holstered on his hip.

Mr. Hagen went on. "I have no intention of interfering on either your behalf or my son's because it has nothing to do with me. You see, I accepted my son here at Blackstone under the impression that he would be content with the position I gave him as proprietor of the Clifford Hotel and that he would make something of that place."

"Which he's done," Trammel said.

"Yes, he has," Mr. Hagen agreed. "He has succeeded in turning that run-down old castle into a thriving enterprise. But at the same time, he has gone against my wishes and given into the worst aspects of his nature. He has acquired a controlling interest of every saloon on Main Street and cornered the opium market in town. What's more, he has also entered into a lurid, if not lucrative, partnership with that criminal Lucien Clay down in Laramie. He's no better than Madam Pinochet and, in many aspects, is a damned sight worse than that old crone ever was. At least she knew her place and was wise enough to stay out of my affairs. My son, on the other hand, has ambitions that involve destroying the very empire I have spent decades building."

Trammel had hoped Adam had been able to keep his underworld dealings hidden from his father's notice. But as Mr. Hagen had said earlier, little happened in the territory without his knowledge, much less in the town that sat at the base of his hilltop empire.

"I don't bear the boy any malice," Mr. Hagen went on. "He is a Hagen, after all, and Hagen men always hit what they aim for. He'll probably succeed in destroying me if he really puts his mind to it, which he seems to have done." He looked at Trammel. "But I can certainly blame you, Sheriff Trammel. Yes, I blame you very much for his rise as something of a criminal element."

"Me?" Both of Trammel's hands balled into fists. "I haven't gotten a single dime from any of his places."

"But you know they exist," Mr. Hagen said. "And you've done little, if anything, to stop them. Yes, I know the community tends to turn a blind eye to these things, but you didn't come to me when you saw Adam's criminal plans coming to fruition. In fact, you never paid me a visit at all, nor even showed the slightest deference until you thought I might be able to throw money at the problem that faces you now."

"You hired me to protect the town," Trammel said.

"Come now, Trammel." Mr. Hagen laughed. "Surely a man of the world such as yourself should have realized there is no Blackstone without me and that I am your true benefactor. You seemed to have forgotten that since the late Sheriff Bonner pinned that tin star on your chest. Perhaps it's a lesson you'll learn before the last of the Pinkerton men ride over your corpse on Main Street."

Trammel was about to reach across the desk and pull the man out of his chair. He was surprised by Mr. Hagen's quickness as he got to his feet.

He was even more surprised by the double-barreled coach gun Hagen brought up and aimed at the sheriff's head. He was not surprised to feel the cold steel barrel of Bookman's Colt pressed against the side of his head.

"Careful, Trammel," Bookman whispered. "Be real careful."

Trammel didn't move. Despite the disadvantage, he had no doubt he could take both of them. Mr. Hagen and Bookman were holding their guns too close to his hands. He knew he could push Hagen's shotgun toward Bookman, likely killing him and leaving the rich man with an empty gun.

But likely didn't make it certain. And neither of their deaths would serve a purpose. Neither man was any good to him dead. He decided to keep his hands away from his sides as he slowly backed away from the desk and toward the office door. Hagen's shotgun and Bookman's Colt were trained on him the entire way.

"We'll forget about your momentary lapse in judgment just now," Mr. Hagen said, "and allow you to remain as sheriff of Blackstone. However, you're not to step foot on this property again without permission. Any attempt to do so will be met with deadly force. Isn't that right, Bookman?"

Bookman kept the Colt trained on Trammel with one hand. "That's just about as right as anything you've ever said, boss."

Trammel kept slowly backing up, hands away from his sides as he eased out the door. "You boys have made one hell of a mistake here today."

Mr. Hagen spoke to him from behind the shotgun. "I'd say we prevented you from making a mistake, Sheriff Trammel."

"My mistake wasn't as bad as yours," Trammel said. "You pulled a gun on a man with nothing left to lose." He backed into the hallway, then opened the front door and showed himself out.

He didn't bother closing it behind him.

CHAPTER 7

Adam Hagen almost spilled his drink. "Father did *what?*"

"Pulled a shotgun and stuck it in my face." Trammel ignored the glass and the whiskey bottle on the table. He'd need a clear head from now on with all of the enemies closing in on him. "Both barrels. Hammers pulled back, too."

Hagen let out a silent whistle. "I assume Bookman didn't sit idly by while all of this was happening."

"Held a Colt at the back of my head. I had no choice but to back out of there with as much dignity as I could muster, which wasn't much." Trammel looked at the whiskey bottle on the table. The memory of his embarrassment made him want to take a drink. Maybe numb some of the embarrassment and anger simmering inside him. But he knew it wasn't the time for anger. It was the time for cunning. "I feel like a damned fool letting them get the drop on me like that, but I'll admit I didn't expect it."

"Don't be embarrassed," Hagen picked up his glass. "I doubt you're the first man they've run out of their office." He winced and not from the whiskey. "Probably have it down to something of a science. They probably had it all worked out the moment they saw you riding up to the house. But Father rarely lays his hands on a weapon anymore. Feels gunplay is beneath him. You should feel honored that he felt threatened enough by you to go heeled."

Trammel didn't feel anything but frustration. "I'd be a hell of a lot more honored if he'd agreed to buy off the Pinkerton men for us."

"I wish you had come to me with this before going up there," Hagen said. "He won't do that because there's no profit in it for him."

Trammel looked at his former friend. "But you're his son."

"I'm his disappointment." Hagen poured himself a healthy dose of whiskey. "He's already got two adoring sons to carry on the family name and a daughter who dotes on him, so any role I might play in his life is irrelevant. I've also gone that extra step by defying his wishes for me to be a hotelier and instead, have chosen to become the master of vice in this part of the territory."

Trammel sat up straight. He had known what Adam had been up to since they had come to Blackstone, but his former friend had never actually admitted it.

Hagen was amused by his reaction. "Yes, Sheriff Trammel. I'm confessing all of my sins now that the hour of judgment is at hand. As a good Catholic boy, I would've thought you'd appreciate the gesture. Only I have no desire for absolution and I have every intention of making my father atone for his treachery. Not just to me. I've been asking for it for years as far as he's concerned, but for you. He pulled you into this mess by hiring you to replace Bonner, and now he's leaving you to the wolves. That's not right."

Trammel turned his empty shot glass on the table. "It's not right for a father to abandon his son." Hagen's whiskey bottle looked more tempting than ever, but he couldn't risk being drunk and he couldn't abide the epic hangover that was sure to follow tomorrow. "We've got trouble heading our way, Adam, and I'd be lying if I told you the odds are in our favor."

"We've taken on big odds before," Hagen reminded him. "Why, you took out half a dozen men all on your own if the *Blackstone Bugle* is to be believed, which it should be, as I witnessed your wrath firsthand."

Trammel cursed quietly to himself. "I'd wager those damned newspaper reports are half the reason why we're in this mess. If the *Blackstone Bugle* hadn't run stories about me that were picked up by half the newspapers in the country, Old Man Bowman wouldn't have known how to find us. Hell, the Pinkerton men might've found us eventually, I guess, but it would've been harder."

Hagen moved his whiskey glass across the tablecloth as he thought. "How many you think they'll send? The Pinkerton men, I mean. You worked for them for years. You must have some idea how they operate."

Trammel had already done the calculations in his head. "Depends on who's running the group and how many they bring, but you can count on no fewer than six. Closer to twelve would be my guess. They don't like gunplay when honest citizens are around."

"How considerate." Hagen laughed.

"Blood's bad for business. When too many innocents get killed, the same newspapers that idolize them start calling them butchers. If they send twelve after us, they figure it's likely to keep us from fighting back. It's also enough to keep us contained while they go to work."

Hagen did the calculations in his head. "Twelve against two makes it six-to-one odds. Difficult, but manageable, especially with some planning. Throw your rube deputy in the mix and it's three to one. He'll at least absorb a couple of bullets. Might even take one of them with him before he dies."

Trammel brought a thick hand crashing down on the table, causing the whiskey bottle to tip over and begin rolling. Hagen grabbed it by the neck before it hit the floor.

"I don't want that boy run down by you or anyone else, understand? And he's not going to be any part of this. This is our mess, not his. Blackstone's still going to need law when this is all over and he's the one."

Hagen set the whiskey bottle back on the table. "Don't you think you're going a little overboard with your dread of these people, Buck? I mean, I've read all the accounts of the mighty Pinkerton Agency, but how good could they be? You and I aren't exactly going to make it easy on them. We'd been in our share of scrapes before we met each other and quite a few since."

Trammel rubbed his sore hand. "The men they send aren't like the bunch Lucien Clay threw at us in the spring. These are capable men who don't lose their heads when the music starts. They won't be union-busters like I used to be, either. They're not bully boys with clubs and bats smacking around a few starving factory workers. They'll be well-armed, well-trained and well-mounted, most likely ex-army like yourself. Maybe even cavalry. They'll come looking for a fight and know how to handle themselves when one starts. We might get a few of them when it comes to it, but we won't get all of them. Hell, we'll be lucky to take down half before we take on some serious damage ourselves."

Hagen seemed to think about it. "And I assume running is out of the question."

"Will you be serious for once?"

"I'm quite serious," Hagen said. "I consider the matter of my own survival to be the most serious matter I know. I say cutting our losses and making a run for it is a viable option. We've done it before, you know."

Trammel knew. In fact, he had thought about running, though he damned himself for it.

Although he may have gotten his star by

default, it was his now, and he'd grown to like Blackstone. He had a responsibility to the people who looked to him for law and order, and he was proud of what he had accomplished in the six months he'd had the job. He was proud of how he'd changed Hawkeye's life, too. Changed him from being a laughingstock to a young man who was beginning to come into his own. Running out on him would break his heart almost as much as causing them harm by staying.

Even with all of that in mind, Trammel still might consider running if it wasn't for Emily. He couldn't leave her behind and he couldn't take her with him. There's no way she'd leave her mother-in-law in Blackstone. He couldn't ask her to do it.

Besides, the town rumor mill had been churning about the pretty young widowed doctor and her boarder, the heroic Sheriff Trammel. It wouldn't take long for the Pinkerton men to learn about it, and when they did, they'd lean on her to tell them where he might be. She wouldn't know, of course, but they'd hurt her a long time before they believed her.

He'd rather die before he allowed that. And he had no intention of dying.

He had no intention of trying to explain

any of this to Hagen, either. He'd only sneer at the sentiment. Trammel had already absorbed enough scorn from the Hagen family for one day.

"Running would be pointless," he explained. "They'd run us down and kill us. At least in town we've got something of a fighting chance."

"Then the matter is settled. We're staying." Hagen considered that over the rim of his whiskey glass. "We're not without friends, you know."

"You mean the shopkeepers and bankers? Or the drunks and drovers you serve in your saloons? Other than stopping bullets for us, I wouldn't count on them for being much good."

"Forgive me for using the wrong word. I meant we have *partners* whose interests would be ill served if something were to happen to us. Well, at least me. You could benefit by proxy."

"You mean your Celestials?" Trammel laughed. "Sure, if those heathens blew some of that dragon smoke at them, it could give us a chance, assuming they were that stupid, which they're not."

"I'm not talking about the Celestials, either, though they may play their part in all of this before the first shot is fired."

Trammel watched a strange look appear on his former friend's face. A look he couldn't quite read. "I've never been a big fan of puzzles, Adam, and now's not the time to start. Speak plain or not at all."

Hagen held his glass aloft and slowly turned it, watching the way the lamplight of his sitting room danced on the brown liquid. "When I was at West Point all those years ago, they taught us that when modern answers fail us, a wise man must turn to antiquity for guidance."

Trammel was growing anxious. "I'm getting annoyed."

But Adam Hagen would not be hurried. "I find myself pondering a quote from one of the greatest generals of all time, who said, 'Without knowledge, skill cannot be focused. Without skill, strength cannot be brought to bear. And without strength, knowledge cannot be applied.' "

Trammel shut his eyes. "You and your drunken riddles."

"It's not a riddle. It's a quote from Alexander the Great. Ever heard of him?"

Trammel was beginning to wonder if Hagen wasn't already drunk, and therefore useless to him. "Can't say as I have."

"He once held the entire known world in the palm of his hand much the same way

I'm holding this glass of whiskey right now. He didn't build his empire simply by having a bigger army or being more willing to kill than his contemporaries."

Hagen drank the whiskey and gently laid the glass on the table. "No, he won an empire because he was smarter than his enemies. He knew their strengths and weaknesses better than they knew themselves. He knew the decisions they would make and where they would go before they knew it themselves because he studied them before he fought them. He beat his enemies at their own game, and if you and I are to survive this coming calamity, my friend, then we must learn to do the same."

Trammel was relieved Hagen was finally starting to make sense. "How?"

Hagen slowly refilled his glass and set the whiskey bottle aside. He kept looking at the glass as he quoted, " 'Heaven will not brook two suns, nor the earth two masters.' " He winked at the sheriff. "The battle cannot start on Main Street in Blackstone. It must start well before that. In other words, we are going to have to make our own luck."

Trammel flinched when Hagen's hand shot out across the table. "I know we've had our differences these many months past, Buck. I know you are disappointed in me, but now you know why I have had to defy my father in the only way I knew how. You may disapprove of my methods, but you cannot fault my reasoning. I apologize for the damage it has done to our friendship, but we must repair that damage if we are to survive our enemies. We must do it together. I need your friendship and you need mine."

Trammel had met many sorts of men in his travels, but he had never known one who could be as annoyingly charming as Adam Hagen.

He shook the man's hand and not only because the Pinkerton men were coming. "Emily always said we'd patch things up."

"A wiser woman has never dwelled in these parts." Hagen took the cork and tapped it back in the bottle. "Come. We must begin putting our plan into action. We haven't a moment to lose."

CHAPTER 8

"You sure all of this is necessary, Mr. Alcott? I mean, this is a hell of a lot of effort for a sheriff and a drunken gambler."

Alcott checked off an item in his notebook and motioned for Potter to pry open the other box of Winchester rifles. He wanted to have a full accounting of their armaments before they were loaded onto the train for the next day's journey. "Are you in charge of this expedition, Mr. Potter, or am I?"

"Why, you are, sir," said the Missourian. "It's just that the boys are wondering why we need all of this firepower for just two men."

Alcott kept reviewing his notes as though Potter was a mere annoyance. "You're paid to do what you're told, not to ask questions."

Potter set the crowbar aside. "We're paid to know what we're walking into. And bringing this much firepower against a couple of killers is giving the men pause. Now, you might not be paying us to ask questions, but that doesn't mean we ain't entitled to some answers."

Alcott had encountered resistance from men like Potter since the day he joined the agency five years before. They took his New Orleans drawl to mean he was slow-witted. They took his fancy attire as a sign he was a dandy who enjoyed playing at violence more than actually committing it. They did not know that "Diamond Jim" Alcott, as he had been known despite his first name being Jesse, had once been the most feared enforcer on the Mississippi riverboats before Allan Pinkerton himself had decided to hire him.

Riverboat captains who sought to keep order on their gambling vessels had paid a handsome price for his services for years. He kept the working girls honest and dealt cheaters with a harshness that was still remembered up and down the river. Mr. Pinkerton hadn't hired him for his fancy clothes or Cajun drawl. He had hired him because he could be relied upon to know when to kill and when not to.

When in pursuit of men like Buck Trammel and Adam Hagen, killing would be required.

But Potter was right. The men were entitled to some answers, and as Potter was someone they looked up to, Alcott decided to indulge his insubordination just this once. "How long have you been with the agency, Mr. Potter?"

The big man stroked his full moustache as he thought it over. "Goin' on two years, near as I can reckon."

"Then you weren't under Mr. Pinkerton's employ when Buck Trammel was one of us."

"Trammel was a Pinky, too?"

Alcott bristled at the term used for his agency. He held the term *Pinks* in similar contempt, but saw nothing could be gained by debating the point with Potter.

"Once upon a time, Buck Trammel was one of Mr. Pinkerton's best operatives," Alcott explained. "He was a fearsome strikebreaker, but also the man assigned to bring in the worst of the worst. Not on the open plain, mind you, but in cities like Chicago and New York and St. Louis. He's the man who brought in Donald Morgan single-handedly."

Potter's mouth opened. "Trammel did that?"

Alcott returned to his notebook. "Stopped three bullets in the process, but brought the man in alive. He was half-dead when they reached Fort Hancock, but he fulfilled his mission. They say he killed ten men in the process, resorting to his bare hands when his guns went dry. He and Morgan were the only two who made it out of there alive. I'm sure you've heard the stories."

The look on Potter's face told Alcott he had.

Alcott went on. "Adam Hagen is a former officer in the United States Cavalry. Graduated near the bottom of his class at West Point, but led several campaigns against the savages in the Southwest. The years since have served to make him more dangerous and cunning. Blackstone is his home, and it stands to reason that he has many friends there. We may face stiff opposition in our efforts to take him into custody, especially now that Trammel enjoys something of a heroic status after his recent defense of the town this past spring."

Potter blinked as the information sank in.

Alcott had no patience to indulge the dullard any longer. "Now, do you still think all of these rifles and ammunition are too much to go after a small-town sheriff and a drunken gambler?"

Potter picked up the crowbar and pulled open another crate of rifles.

■ ■ ■ ■

Lucien Clay tipped his hat to all of the ladies he passed as he and Adam Hagen strolled through the streets of Laramie. None of them acknowledged his gesture of kindness. He hadn't expected them to. After all, as the owner of most of the saloons and brothels in town limits, he was the reason why their husbands didn't come home some nights.

"You do not seem to be held in high esteem by the fair ladies of town," Hagen observed.

Clay pulled up the fur collar of his buffalo coat a bit higher. "It's always chilly in town, more so when the womenfolk are around. Can't say as I blame them, seeing the services my ladies provide for their husbands. Their husbands treat me even worse. They ignore me on the street, only to act like my long-lost brother when they come to get their itches scratched by my girls and their thirst quenched by my booze."

Hagen laughed. "The pious justification of a vice peddler is a ponderous philosophy indeed."

Clay laughed, too. Despite the fact that Hagen's possession of Madam Pinochet's ledger meant he ultimately held the high ground in the partnership, he had to admit that Adam Hagen was a tough man to hate.

Lucien Clay had been the most prosperous and most feared saloon keeper in the territory for years; second only to Madam Pinochet when it came to influence. Whereas Clay catered to the basest of needs of the territory leaders, Madam Peachtree, as she had been called, had kept extensive records of it. Through her web of snitches, clerks, and mouthy "girls," the madam had long been rumored to keep a detailed ledger on which territory officials were being paid off and how often. She had a list of who visited opium dens and women of the evening. She knew which judges could be bought and for how much.

She had wisely preferred to rule the territory from the tiny town of Blackstone just north of the territorial seat in Laramie. It was within a day's ride of the capital, but too far enough away for casual strangers to pry into her business.

The rumor of the ledger had been enough to keep her safe and under Lucien Clay's protection. Her modest fees for her silence made it easy for Clay to grant it. Her knowledge of who could be bought and for how much had proven to be an invaluable asset over the years.

But the presence of the ledger wasn't confirmed until Adam Hagen had showed it to him one night six months before when he and Sheriff Trammel brought Madam Pinochet to the county jail under the charge of attempted murder. The day that evil woman swung at the end of a rope brought no end of peace to many of the territory leaders, but their peace was short-lived because Hagen had the ledger.

Hagen's allegiance to Sheriff Trammel had always puzzled Clay. He knew the big man disapproved of his friend's opium dens and saloons.

Clay knew the sheriff was aware of the ledger and of his refusal to take part of the profits as his predecessor had done. His relative purity had caused Clay no shortage of concern. He had wanted to eliminate all doubt by killing Trammel, but Hagen forbade it. And as he held the ledger and continued to make entries in it, Hagen held all the cards.

So Lucien Clay decided he would tolerate Hagen and Trammel for as long as it suited his needs. And since Hagen was even more enterprising than Madam Pinochet had been, the arrangement had served all involved nicely.

"What's on your mind, Adam?" Clay asked his partner. "You didn't ride down here from Blackstone just to watch me get ignored by housewives and phonies. I take it you're here about the bounty that has been placed upon your head."

Hagen almost tripped. "Bounty? What bounty?"

"Guess I finally know something you don't." Lucien Clay enjoyed his moment of superiority. Hagen had a price on his head and didn't even know it. It was a small victory Clay decided to savor for a while. It wasn't often one got the chance to see cocky Adam Hagen squirm.

"Got word about it last night," Clay told him. "Word is the Pinkerton Agency has put out a bounty on you and Trammel. Five hundred Yankee dollars to the man or men who bring either or both of you in. Dead or alive. The money is to be split evenly between all those involved in your capture or death." He smiled as Hagen unbuttoned his coat and pulled the Colt from his holster before tucking it in his coat pocket.

"Thank you for getting word to me as soon as you could, Lucien."

"Don't be sore about it. It's just a rumor. Haven't seen any paper confirming it, and I don't know a man worth his salt who'd try to tangle with either of you on nothing more than saloon talk."

Hagen looked around them. "Amateurs can be dangerous, too, as we both know well."

"Yes, sir. They most certainly can. Still, you're safe in town as long as you're with me. Might want to watch your back trail when you ride for Blackstone, though. Even the hope of five hundred dollars is enough to make some desperate folks do some very stupid things."

"I wish I could get word to Buck."

"That big ox?" Clay laughed. "Don't worry about him. If my boys couldn't put a dent in him, some hired guns from back east won't be able to do it. Not unless the bounty is true. Though I must admit that you coming here to Laramie tells me there might be something to it."

Hagen struggled to button his coat with his left hand while he kept his right curled around the pistol in his pocket. "I hadn't heard about a bounty, but there *is* trouble coming our way. You're right about that being the reason why I'm here."

"You mean the trouble coming *your* way, my friend. There's no paper out on me. At least none with my right name on it."

"That's the wonderful thing about our arrangement, Lucien," Hagen said. "It's a partnership in every sense of the word. My successes are your successes, which we share equally and happily. Likewise, my troubles are your troubles, so the calamity that faces me now faces both of us."

"Depends on the variety of calamity."

"The Pinkerton variety."

Clay stopped walking.

Hagen grinned as he walked back to face him. "I thought that might get your attention."

"The Pinkerton variety is nothing to laugh at, Adam. Those boys mean business and they don't play fair. Putting a bounty on a man's head is one thing. If they come to collect personally, that's bad news."

"All the more reason why we must face them as a united front."

Clay didn't feel as playful as he had only a few moments before. "When are they getting here?"

"I'm still trying to find that out," Hagen admitted. "But fortunately, Sheriff Trammel is familiar with their methods. He said we should expect no fewer than a baker's dozen to arrive, most likely by train. Quite possibly from Chicago, where they're headquartered."

"I know where they're headquartered,

damn it. How do you know they're coming?"

"They sent a man to Blackstone to spy on us in advance of their arrival," Hagen explained. "Unfortunately, the man sought to slake his more carnal appetites and got too rough with one of my girls, which brought him to Sheriff Trammel's attention."

Clay had heard about a dustup in Blackstone a few days before. "That the fella Trammel threw out a window?"

"One and the same. The sheriff found irrefutable proof that he is, indeed, a Pinkerton spy. Unfortunately, he doesn't know any more about their plans, which Trammel said is customary for the Pinkerton Agency. He was supposed to spy on us and meet his fellow operatives here in Laramie. As he's currently in bad condition in Trammel's jail, he won't be able to make it, but that won't deter them from their mission."

Clay looked up at the sky and drew in a deep breath. He had run up against Pinkerton men in Colorado and Michigan. They came in like the wrath of God and didn't stop until everything in their path was dust. They always used the right men for the right job, too, so if they were coming, they'd be ready.

He opened his eyes and felt the warm sun on his face. The cold air made him feel alive. The cloudless blue sky was far too pretty to hear such bad news, but there was no way to avoid it. "This is going to be a problem, Adam."

"Only if we don't try to head it off somehow."

"You don't head off a trainload of Pinkerton men, Adam. They run you down and keep on going."

"You know the wonderful thing about Pinkerton men, Lucien?" Hagen took a step closer and lowered his voice. "They're men. And men have needs that you and I happen to understand all too well. Needs that can be catered to in our advantage."

Clay looked down at the shorter man. "What are you talking about?"

Hagen placed a hand on his back and nudged him forward. "Walk with me and I'll explain everything."

Chapter 9

As they finished their afternoon patrol of the town, Trammel finished telling Hawkeye about the trouble that was coming their way. The young man took the news better than Trammel had expected.

"Thanks for telling me, boss, but I don't see as to how it changes things. I'm here for the duration and so are a lot of other folks. I'll get to talking to some of the others in town who'll help. Why, when those Pinkerton fellas ride up here, they'll find —"

"Nobody," Trammel said. "That's why I want you to ride out of town when they get here. The drunks and the townspeople have nothing to fear from them. This isn't your fight, and there's no reason for you to get caught up in it. The town will need someone to pick up the pieces after it's all over. Someone they can respect. That someone is you."

Hawkeye remained quiet as they walked,

as though he was still absorbing everything Trammel had just told him. The sheriff couldn't blame him. Shooting back at men who were shooting at you was one thing. Knowing they were coming was something different.

Hawkeye surprised him by saying, "You know Miss Emily has been helping me with my reading, don't you?"

"Sure I do. Says you're doing fine with it."

"That's thanks to her. One of the things she's helping me read is the Constitution. Ever read it?"

Trammel didn't like the direction this discussion was headed. "Can't say as I have, but I know what it is."

"Well, I'll tell you that it says it's against the law for people to gun someone down just because someone pays them to do it. You've got a right to a trial and face your accusers in open court before a judge. The way I see it, them Pinkertons ain't much better than Clay's men who tried to kill you all them months back. I didn't run then and I sure as hell won't run now."

The boy's bravery, as foolish as it was, touched Trammel. "Just because a piece of paper says something is illegal doesn't keep it from happening. Clay's men were a rough bunch and we stood up to them. You and me. But what's coming our way isn't a bunch of hotheads with pistols and rifles. They've trained for this kind of thing. They've done it dozens of times before. They're well-paid because they're good at it and know what they're doing. They're the best at what they do."

"Better than you?" Hawkeye asked. "You were one of them, weren't you?"

"I was one of them, yes. But we're talking about twelve or more, and that makes the difference." Trammel pointed out to the open country that surrounded the town. "You grew up in this country. You know there are lots of ways a man could die just by riding from one place to another. Your horse could step in a hole or throw you. You could get bitten by a snake or freeze to death on the prairie. You could run out of water and die. But those are risks you take for living out here. Going up against Pinkerton men when you don't have to is a dumb risk, and it's not one I'm going to allow you to take. I'm the sheriff and you're my deputy, so I'm ordering you to get the hell out of town when those men get here."

A couple of townsmen tipped their hats as they passed by. "Afternoon, Sheriff Trammel. Deputy Hauk."

The lawman acknowledged them as they passed. Trammel thought he saw tears in the young man's eyes.

Hawkeye thumbed back at the men who had just passed. "You hear that, Sheriff? They called me Deputy Hauk. Before you came to town, those men would've sooner spat at me before they acknowledged me at all. I was the boy whose father lost his ranch over a card game and died inside a bottle. Because of you, I've got their respect now. Because of you, I've got respect for myself. I was a joke in Blackstone before you came here. Now, I'm Sheriff Trammel's deputy. I didn't have anything before you gave that to me. And I'm not going to let anyone come into town and take that away from me, not even you, sir."

The young man pawed at his wet eyes with his sleeve. "So you can order me to leave if you want to, but I'll be refusin' that order. And if you fire me for insolence, I guess I'll just have to go back to fetching bottles and cleaning up puke in the Moose. But when those Pinkerton men get here, I'll be standing in front of the jail right next to you with a rifle in my hand whether you want me there or not. So, the way I see it, best to skip all that and let me stay on, because I ain't goin' nowhere."

Trammel's breath caught. He'd never had anyone believe in him as much as this boy did. And he was beginning to think that, with him at his side, he just might have a chance to see this thing through.

"So I guess it's settled then?" Trammel said.

"I reckon so." Hawkeye wiped more tears from his eyes. "Now, aside from telling me to leave, what do you want me to do next?"

Trammel checked the clock at the top of the Blackstone Bank building and saw it was going on four o'clock. "Then it means you're about to become a busy man."

"Just tell me what to do, boss."

"How about you pick up Somerset's supper from the Clifford Arms and clear out the cells while he's eating."

"Clear them out? Why, I just swept them this morning."

"I know you did. But I need you to pull the cots and tables so we have more room in them."

"You think we're going to need more room?"

He clapped the young man on the back. "I know we will. Now, on about your business, Deputy Hauk." He watched the young man stride across Main Street to fetch the prisoner's supper from the hotel. He imagined a Mexican general in full regalia would've been hard pressed to look any prouder.

He was about to cross the street to check on the prisoner himself when he noticed movement out of the corner of his eye on the left. It wasn't so much as a movement, but a sudden lack of motion that drew his attention.

He slowly turned to see two ragged men standing in front of the Old Mill Saloon a few doors up from the jail along Main Street. They were older than him, maybe in their forties or more. They weren't like the normal cowpunchers or farmers that frequented the town's saloons. These men were pale with hollow red eyes, likely from hours spent inside a saloon instead of out working for a living. Their clothes were filthy and their crooked beards speckled with gray.

They had pistol butts sticking out of their filthy pants and they were both looking directly at him.

Even from that distance, Trammel could tell by the way they were standing that they weren't nervous at the sight of a lawman or even at the sight of the man they had read about in the papers, for he doubted either man could read. They had the look of men who were not dangerous by nature, but were working themselves up to do something dangerous. Something that might likely get them killed.

Something like going up against him.

He called out to them. "You boys have something on your mind?"

The taller of the two drew first and got off the first shot. Trammel had already ducked and drawn the Peacemaker from his hip before the second man fired. Both shots were hurried and fell well short in the thoroughfare.

The men ran toward him from the other side of the street, firing as they moved. The shots went high, with one bullet striking the corner of the house beside Trammel.

The sheriff brought up his Peacemaker, aimed at the lead shooter, and fired. The bullet caught the man high in the right shoulder, spinning him like a top and making him fire into the air.

The second man kept running and firing. His third shot bit into the boardwalk to Trammel's left. The sheriff aimed and fired again, striking the man in the center of the chest, knocking him off his feet.

Trammel stood up, keeping his Peacemaker in front of him as he walked toward the men. Hawkeye had come running out of the Clifford Hotel, pistol in hand.

"Stay out of it," Trammel yelled at him. "I've got them." He reached the boardwalk in front of the jail. The second man he'd shot in the chest was splayed like a star in the thoroughfare, his vacant eyes staring up at the gray sky.

But the first man was on his backside, scrambling for his gun with his left hand.

"It's over," Trammel called out to him. "Throw up your hands."

The wounded man lunged for his pistol as best he could and Trammel fired, hitting him just above the belly. The man jerked back and collapsed to the boardwalk.

Trammel kicked the second man's pistol off the boardwalk and kept his Colt trained down on the man he had just shot twice. He stepped on the pistol the first man was still reaching for and slid it out of his reach.

"Why'd you go and do a damned fool thing like that?" Trammel yelled.

The dying man struggled to raise his head. " 'Cause five hunnert is five hunnert, mister." His head sagged and his body went limp as his dying breath escaped him.

Hawkeye descended on the dead man, searching his body for weapons, just as Trammel had trained him to do. "What the hell was that all about, boss?"

"From what he said" — Trammel holstered his Peacemaker — "sounds like there's a bounty on my head."

Hawkeye stood up with a bowie knife he had taken from the corpse. "Hell, there's easier ways of making five hundred dollars."

"Not for them." Trammel eyed the crowd that was spilling onto Main Street from the shops and saloons to see what had happened. He was glad there wasn't a strange face among them. "And more will come to collect."

Hawkeye collected the pistol Trammel had kicked aside. "Or die trying, if we have anything to say about it."

But just then, Trammel didn't have anything to say at all.

Because war had finally come to Blackstone.

CHAPTER 10

"You know I'm right fond of you, Sheriff," Mayor Welch told him in the jailhouse just after supper. "You've got a lot of friends in town. Important friends who support you and how you've made it fit for honest people to walk down the street at all hours of the day and night."

Trammel knew this conversation would be coming from the moment he had found out the Pinkerton men were after him. Word of the bounty on his head had only accelerated the process. "Why do I hear a *but* coming?"

"No *buts*, Sheriff. Just questions about what that dead man meant by five hundred dollars. A couple of the boys down at the Mill heard him say it before he kicked off and rumors about its meaning have been flying around town faster than the flu. Can't blame folks for wanting to know what it means, particularly since it seems to mean something about you."

Mayor Welch had always been something of a conundrum to Trammel. He was the type of man Trammel had often despised. A thin, bald man who'd been henpecked by his wife since they day they'd been married and a politician to boot. He ran the Oakwood Arms when he wasn't tending to his official duties and was well known for cutting every corner he could at his guests' expense to make a buck.

But he had been nothing but generous to Trammel since he had come to Blackstone. He may not have liked missing out on the rent the town paid him for housing the sheriff behind the hotel, but Trammel could hardly blame him for that.

He'd always supported Trammel's actions as sheriff, even when some of the saloon keepers complained that he was too rough with their customers.

Trammel had expected the man to fire him as soon as he learned Pinkerton men were on their way to get him. Welch was only a politician, after all, and Trammel couldn't hold that against him, either. He had a duty to keep the town safe, which was why Trammel had put off telling him about the troubles for as long as possible.

But with two dead men in Miss Emily's

barn awaiting burial the next morning, there was no way for him to avoid the issue any longer. He decided to keep the details to a bare minimum, knowing there'd be plenty of questions to follow.

"The dead man was probably referring to a five-hundred-dollar bounty I think was placed on me by the Pinkerton Agency."

"The Pinkerton Agency?" the mayor repeated with a kind of reverence. "Why would they — or anyone else — have a bounty on you? You were one of them once, weren't you?"

"I don't know if that's helped or hurt things," Trammel admitted. "It's for a charge Adam Hagen and I were cleared of before we ever came to Blackstone. Unfortunately, the fact that we were cleared doesn't hold as much water as is should with some folks. I guess that's why they're sending some men here to either arrest me and Adam or kill us. I don't know which and probably won't know until they get here."

The mayor's mouth hung open as he absorbed the news. Trammel expected him to demand his star on the spot, which would present another host of problems Trammel wasn't prepared to face. But he was past the point of being able to control it and would figure it out when he had to. Until then, it was the mayor's show.

Welch's next question took him off guard. "When are these gunmen supposed to get here?"

"I don't know," Trammel admitted. "That guy in the cell back there is working for them. That's the only reason why I know they're coming at all. As for when they're getting here and how many they'll be bringing with them, that's anyone's guess. If I knew more, I'd tell you. Adam rode down to Laramie this morning to get a better handle on things."

The mayor blinked as he looked away. "Pinkerton men. My God."

Trammel saw the man struggling and decided to make it easier on him. "Obviously, this'll bring a lot of trouble to Blackstone, and I don't want that. So if you want me to move on, just let me know. You won't get any fight from me."

If Welch heard him, he didn't show it. "I'll ride up to Mr. Hagen's place this very night. Surely, he'll know what's to be done to stop this insanity before it happens."

"I already spoke to him this morning," Trammel said. "He has elected not to help in any way. Maybe you'll have better luck than I did, but I doubt it."

"You mean he said no?"

"Yes."

"Are you sure?"

He remembered looking down the barrels of Mr. Hagen's shotgun and the feel of Bookman's Colt against his neck. "Pretty sure."

Welch stood up, absentmindedly turning his worn felt hat in his hands. "I . . . I'm afraid I'll have to talk to the town committee about this immediately. They have a right to know what's going on. Or, at least what may happen."

Trammel knew they did. Just as he knew what they would order the mayor to do after he told them. "You can tell them they won't have any trouble from me if they want me to leave."

Welch looked at him as though he'd forgotten he'd been there. "Trouble? Why would they get any trouble from you, of all people?"

Trammel sighed. Welch wasn't making this any easier. "With people coming to get me, I fully expect them to ask me to leave. And I couldn't blame them for it, either."

The skinny man grew indignant. "Like hell they will. After what you've done for us? You've put us on the map, and for good reasons for once. Before you, Blackstone was just a stopover for cattlemen on their way to Laramie. Now we've got some respectability. Why, the bank is talking about financing two new avenues filled with homes and businesses thanks to the stability you've given us." He held up two gnarled fingers. "Two!"

Trammel appreciated his support, but knew the decision wasn't up to him. It was up to the committee, one of whom was Fred Montague, the head of Blackstone Bank and Hagen's employee. "Might not be much of a town left after the Pinkertons get here."

"And there won't be much of a reason for a town if we tell you to run off in the face of trouble." Welch pointed out toward Main Street. "Don't sell our people short, Sheriff. We might not have your experience, but none of us came here on stagecoaches, either. I rode out here on a wagon from Indiana with my family. Buried a brother and a daughter on the trail. Plenty of other people have similar stories, if not worse. We're not apt to roll over for a herd of gunmen riding in here to tell us how to run things. And we're not going to shirk our responsibility to ourselves or to you. We might not be fighters, but we know how to fight. They've got guns, but so do we."

Trammel hadn't expected the little man

to show so much backbone. But he knew what was coming, and it wasn't pretty. "Please don't get them riled up —"

"Please don't sell us short, sir." The mayor moved to the door and placed his hand on the knob. "You aren't going anywhere, Sheriff Trammel. And that is an order!" He threw open the door and stormed outside, flinching when the door hit the wall, before quietly closing it behind him.

Hawkeye came out from the cells, beaming. "See, boss? What did I tell you? Sounds like you've got more friends than you think."

Trammel wasn't so sure. He knew bravery came easy before things started. But once the bullets flew, people tended to change their minds.

"You get those cells cleared out yet?"

Hawkeye said he did. "Piled up the cots over in Miss Emily's barn like you asked. Nothing but bare floors and iron bars now. You mind telling me why?"

Trammel stood up and pulled down a Winchester from the rack. It was time to begin putting Hagen's plan into place before the committee had a chance to vote.

"I don't have to tell you. I'll show you. Right now." He tossed the rifle to Hawkeye. "Let's go. We've got some work to do."

The crowd in the Pot of Gold was bigger than normal for a Saturday night. The hands of the Blackstone Ranch and a few of the other spreads had just been paid and were anxious to spend their money on whiskey and women.

The piano player was banging out some version of "Yellow Rose of Texas" that would have been an affront to any sober Texan, but as no one in the Pot of Gold was sober, no one seemed to mind.

John Bookman was at a table at the back of the saloon with five of the other top hands from the Blackstone Ranch. His newfound dislike for Bookman aside, Trammel had always admired the way he kept a tight lid on his men. He rarely allowed them to come to town without at least one senior man around to keep them in line.

It made what Trammel was about to do all the more difficult to justify, but no less necessary. "You mind the door," he told Hawkeye, "and follow my lead. We're going to be bringing a bunch of these boys back to the jail, and it might not be easy."

"Jail?" Hawkeye repeated. "But why? They seem like they're having a good time."

Trammel pushed through the batwing doors. "Looks can be deceiving."

John Bookman looked up when Trammel began moving through the crowd of cowboys. His left eye twitched as he slowly rose to his feet when the sheriff approached his table. The five men with him slowly stood up, too.

The music died away as the piano player, sensing danger, ran off. The noise from the bar did not die down as the cowboys enjoyed their first night off in weeks.

Trammel stopped a few feet away from Bookman's table. His hand rested on the Colt on his hip. "John Bookman, you're under arrest."

Bookman's right hand inched toward the gun on his hip before it came to rest on his belt buckle. The men with him kept their hands near their guns, but did not touch them.

"Don't be a fool, Trammel," Bookman laughed. "On what charge?"

"Threatening the life of a peace officer," Trammel said. "Interference with the duties of a peace officer. Drunk and disorderly. Disturbing the peace." The sheriff smiled. "Hope to be able to add resisting arrest to the charges before I'm done."

"Go home, Sheriff. Haven't you been

embarrassed enough for one day?"

The other men at the table laughed.

They knew. Bookman had told them. Probably bragged about running him off the ranch at gunpoint.

Trammel felt his rage spark, but tried to keep in front of it. "Let's go Bookman. You're under arrest, and so is anyone else who gets in my way."

"Your jail isn't big enough for all the people who'll get in your way, Trammel. Your timing's off. This whole place is filled with boys riding for the Blackstone brand. You touch me, they'll tear you and your idiot deputy apart."

"*Two* counts of threatening the life of a peace officer," Trammel said. "And inciting a riot. The more you run your mouth, the longer the charges get, Bookman. Now, either you come along peaceful or you put up a fight. Either way, I go to bed happy tonight."

Hagen appeared at the back of the saloon next to Bookman's table. "Sheriff Trammel! Thank goodness you're here. I'd just sent a boy to fetch you 'round to help me deal with these ruffians. Why, Mr. Bookman here just insulted one of my girls by making a most indecent proposal to her."

"That's a damned lie," Bookman swore.

"I haven't talked to any of his disease-ridden girls all night."

"I have three women who say otherwise." Hagen sucked his teeth. "It's a shame, John. What will Father think when he hears of your indiscretion? He'll be most disappointed indeed. Might send you to bed without supper like the bad boy you are."

Bookman brought up his hand, but Hagen's .32 against his neck made him stop.

"Doesn't feel too good, does it, Johnny Boy? Cold steel against your skin. Kind of makes a man feel powerless, even small." Hagen seemed to remember something. "Johnny Boy. Guess I'm the first one to call you that in years. How we tend to forget what we really are when we sit at the right hand of the king."

"You're nothing like your old man, Hagen," Bookman spat. "You're not even worthy of his name. You've been nothing but a disgrace to him since the day you were born. You ask me, those Pinkerton boys can't get here fast enough to put you out of his misery."

"Too bad you'll be in a jail cell and won't see it." Hagen grabbed him by the sleeve and began pulling him out from behind the table, the pistol pressed hard under his jaw. "Get moving."

A fat man Trammel recognized as one of the Hagen foremen stepped in front of him. "You're crossing the line here, Sheriff."

Trammel kneed the man in the belly, then knocked him over with an uppercut. The man behind him grabbed for a chair, but a left hook from Trammel rendered him unconscious before he hit the floor.

A third boss reached for his pistol. Trammel's Peacemaker was in his face and cocked before he had the chance to clear leather. "Don't."

The man moved his hand away from his gun.

"Now unbuckle your belt," Trammel told him. "And let it drop nice and slow."

The man did as he was told and held up his hands.

Trammel heard movement from the bar before Hawkeye yelled, "Anyone moves, I cut loose with both barrels."

Nobody at the bar moved.

Trammel spoke loud enough for everyone to hear. "You're all under arrest for disturbing the peace, public intoxication, and rioting. Mr. Hagen, would you and your people be kind enough to help my deputy escort these prisoners to jail?"

"Why, Sheriff, it just so happens that a few friends from Laramie have joined me tonight and they would be happy to assist the law in any way they could. Wouldn't you boys?"

Five men with rifles trained on the bar appeared from the back and ordered the cowboys to drop their gun belts before herding them Hawkeye's way. The rest of the patrons looked on in silence as the last of the riflemen shoved the final Blackstone man into the street.

Trammel ordered the man he had disarmed to help his fallen friends to their feet and lead them over to the jail with the others. "Mr. Hagen, would you be kind enough to help me escort Mr. Bookman and these men to the jail?"

"Never let it be said that Adam Hagen was afraid to perform his civic duties." He pulled Bookman out from behind the table. "Let's go, Johnny Boy. You first." He shoved him toward Trammel, who caught him by the shoulder before he fell.

"I told you what would happen the next time I saw you, Bookman. Be grateful you're not dead."

"You'll be dead before long. Mr. Hagen will have your head for this."

Trammel gripped Bookman's shoulder tighter. "But seeing as I have you and most of his men, he'll have to come in personally

118

to get it." He shoved him toward the door. "Now move."

CHAPTER 11

Richard Rhoades, late of the *Ogallala Bugle* and now a reporter for the *Blackstone Bugle,* enjoyed the sight of frontier governance playing out before him in the dimly lit environs of the general store.

Mr. and Mrs. Robertson kept a sharp eye on their merchandise as members of the committee milled about the place as the grave matters facing the town were discussed. Most of the smaller items that could easily be pocketed were behind display counters, but the Robertsons had learned through bitter experience that people rarely passed up an opportunity to steal when they didn't think they'd get caught. Especially politicians.

As Blackstone had never gotten around to building itself a formal town hall — Mr. Hagen thought it an abhorrent waste of money — Rhoades knew official meetings were usually held in the dining room of the

Oakwood Arms, for which Mayor Welch would receive a humble stipend from the town for hosting.

However, as the dining room had suffered water damage from a recent storm, and since the Presbyterian Church wouldn't allow such sinful topics discussed in the Lord's house, the Citizens' Committee of Blackstone had no choice but to hold the meeting in the Blackstone General Store.

Trammel stood next to Mayor Welch behind the counter while the members of the committee discussed the impending arrival of the Pinkerton men and the massive arrest of the men of the Blackstone Ranch.

Rhoades noted the gray-haired men in the room all talking at once, raising their voices to be heard as if volume would give greater weight to their words. He had witnessed similar meetings in Ogallala and again, back home in his native Boston. He imagined similar such meetings were probably the same everywhere, from the houses of parliament in England to a village elder's hut in Siam. Why should it be any different in the tiny frontier town of Blackstone, Wyoming Territory?

Rhoades watched as Mayor Welch, bereft of a gavel, stood as tall as he could and held his hands up as he cried for the meeting to come to order. When the attendees refused to acknowledge him, he stuck two fingers into his mouth and let forth with a piercing whistle that silenced them all.

"Quiet, damn you," he said when the crowd settled down. "I hereby call this emergency meeting of the Citizens Committee of Blackstone to order. I want our secretary to enter it into the record that I have called this meeting under protest as I feel it is an unnecessary waste of time."

Rhoades nodded until he felt the mayor glaring at him and remembered he had been elected secretary at the last meeting. He cleared his throat before saying, "Duly noted, Your Honor."

"Very well," Mayor Welch said. "Now, anyone who wants a say will have their chance to speak. But you're going to take turns and only speak one at a time. If this meeting turns into a shouting match, I'll shut it down and walk out that door." He looked at Rhoades. "I want that on the record, too."

The reporter scribbled away. "It's recorded, Your Honor."

"Good. Now who wants to go first?"

Given the events of the past day or so, Rhoades was not surprised to find Fred Montague was the first to ask to be recognized. He was even less surprised that none of the other committee members fought him for the privilege. It was widely known that Mr. Montague was not only the president of the Blackstone Bank, but had been an employee of Mr. Hagen's for the better part of his adult life. And with the passing of Mr. Hagen's lifelong employee Judge Andrew Burlington this past summer, Montague was the only voice for King Charles on the committee.

The banker stood, reminding Rhoades of what everyone expected a bank president to look like. Tall and gray wavy hair. Deep-set, serious eyes and high cheekbones. His dark suit and crisp white shirt gave Rhoades the impression that he could look just as happy approving a loan as he did in denying one. His entire countenance appeared as impartial as it was impeccable, which everyone in attendance knew was a lie. His penchant for young women he referred to as "nieces" aside, the banker had not granted a single loan or made a decision in the past twenty years without considering how it might affect the holdings of Charles Hagen. In fact, Rhoades noted, all of the men in the general store that night did Mr. Hagen's bidding, save, it now seemed, for Sheriff Trammel.

"Your Honor," Montague began, his voice

clear and true, "our peaceful community has been plunged into chaos overnight by the rash actions and indiscretions of one man. I believe anyone is entitled to the benefit of the doubt and I think all of us are entitled to second, third, and maybe even fourth chances."

A murmur spread through the committeemen, some seeming to quote scripture.

Montague continued. "But when the man of whom I speak is our sheriff, I believe that it is only prudent that we must give pause. First, Sheriff Trammel neglected to tell us that he is the subject of an investigation by the Pinkerton National Detective Agency. That is his first offense.

"As a result of that investigation, a bounty has been placed on his head by said agency, which led to the unfortunate demise of two wretched souls looking to collect on said bounty." He looked at Rhoades. "That was his second offense."

Rhoades had never liked politicians or lawmen, but he held a special contempt for bankers above all. "Thank you, sir. I have noted it as such in the record."

Montague held up three fingers. "Then tonight, as if lying and murder wasn't enough, he made a third error in judgment by provoking an incident in the Pot of Gold

Saloon that resulted in the arrest and mass incarceration of not only the top hands at the largest ranch in the area, but most of its workers as well."

Rhoades was still catching up to what Montague had said when he saw Trammel stand.

"That's a damned lie and you know it."

The reporter looked around the store. Surely, such a declaration should bring about some kind of reaction. He had seen this same committee almost break out into a brawl over far less inflammatory claims. But with the large man with the star on his chest standing at his full height — six and a half feet or more by the reporter's reckoning — the loudest sound in the room just then was Rhoades's pen scratching across the paper.

Mayor Welch looked deflated. "That's a very serious charge, Sheriff."

"And one that I can easily prove." Trammel's eyes never left the banker's. "Yesterday, I went to Mr. Hagen to inform him of the Pinkerton problem and ask his assistance in calling off the Pinkerton men. He not only refused to do so, he and Mr. Bookman drove me from the house at gunpoint."

A murmur went up from the men in the

store as Trammel continued. "Hagen refused to help because he already knew about the Pinkerton plan to arrest or kill me and his son. And if Mr. Hagen knew about it, you must've known about it, Montague. Hell, you're probably the one who told him. Weren't you in Laramie a few days ago?"

Rhoades was surprised to see the boisterous banker sputter like a teapot before ultimately looking away. The reporter considered this news, for although he had only been working for the *Blackstone Bugle* for a few months, Montague's reputation as a formidable man was no secret. He had never seen him back down from a fight so quickly, giving further weight to the sheriff's claims.

Then again, Rhoades doubted Montague had crossed paths with a man of Sheriff Buck Trammel's stature before, at least not without Mr. Hagen's guns to back him.

"You and your employer have known about the Pinkerton threat for some time, Montague," Trammel continued, "and you decided to do nothing. You didn't even have the decency to tell me. I only learned about the bounty on my head after I returned fire on the two men who'd shot at me. Adam Hagen was in Laramie and was able to confirm the reports about the Pinkerton bounty are real."

Another member of the committee called out, "And what about that embarrassing scene in the saloon tonight? Was that revenge for Mr. Hagen's perceived betrayal of you and his son?"

Rhoades watched Trammel look in the direction of the voice. "That was an enforcement of the law. He and his employer had held guns on me when I went to the ranch to inform them of the Pinkerton threat. Pointing a weapon at a peace officer is against the law."

"Man's got a right to defend himself and his property," the same voice called out, which was met by shouts of agreement from other people in the audience.

"To defend it, yes," Trammel said. "But not to force someone off their property at gunpoint and not when that someone is a sworn officer of the law. I went to the Pot of Gold tonight to arrest John Bookman for what he had done. The foremen and the ranch hands in attendance tried to prevent me from executing that arrest and were brought in for interfering with the law, disturbing the peace, and inciting a riot."

From his seat in the middle of the store, Montague said, "That's a pretty broad brush, Sheriff. You can paint anything you want with a brush that big."

"You wanted a sheriff who enforces the law, Montague. And that's what you've got. Count yourself lucky I don't lock you up with them as an accessory after the fact."

Another voice called out. "But how do you expect the Blackstone Ranch to operate with more than half of its men locked up in your jail?"

"I'm a sheriff, not a rancher. The men should've thought about that before they broke the law. Am I supposed to treat Hagen's men different from anyone else in this room?" He began pointing at men around the room. "Different from you, Tom? Or you, Billy? Or your son, Will? None of your last names are Hagen. None of you employ a lot of people or own a lot of property. Does that make you any less equal to them in the eyes of the law?"

Rhoades was glad to hear the committee change from being largely on Montague's side at the beginning to actually favoring Trammel's side. Groups rarely listened to the speakers at such meetings, preferring to cheer when their side spoke and jeer when the opposite side had their say.

But the reporter could tell this was something different, something new. Could it be that "the town Hagen built" was turning on its founder in favor of its sheriff ? As secretary, Rhoades could barely keep up with recording the comments, As a reporter, he was delighted over having a new angle to publish for his column. The only question was whether or not the owner of the *Bugle* would allow him to print it.

It took two earsplitting whistles from Mayor Welch to bring the room to silence. "At the outset, I vowed to end this meeting as soon as it devolved into a free-for-all. Congratulations, gentlemen, you have surpassed my lowest expectations. As we are incapable of debating this matter in a civilized fashion, I adjourn this meeting and require Sheriff Trammel to continue his duties with this committee's thanks and full support."

Another great cry filled the store, but Mayor Welch ignored them. He gathered up his hat and coat, shook hands with the stunned Sheriff Trammel, and stormed out of the back room of the store. The remaining committee members continued to bicker among themselves as Rhoades struggled to close out the formal record of the meeting without having his pen bumped by the jostling crowd.

He looked up in time to see Montague in front of the counter where Trammel was standing. It was only when seeing him in scale with another man could Rhoades fully appreciate the size of the sheriff. Yes, he was taller and broader than most, but this part of the country was filled with big men. Trammel had something about him that made him different from the others. A ferocity? Rhodes wondered. A sense of danger? An air of death about him? The reporter couldn't quite describe it, but knew, whatever it was, it easily outmatched the imposing presence of Fredrick Montague.

He was also glad the remaining committeemen carried their ongoing bickering deep enough into the store for Rhoades to subtly eavesdrop on their conversations.

Montague said, "What's your game here, Trammel? I mean your real game. I know arresting Charles's men wasn't your idea. That damned son of his put you up to this, didn't he?"

"Nobody put me up to anything, Fred," Trammel told him. "Not Adam nor Mr. Hagen, neither. Not even you. I did what I did because it's my job."

"You heard what old Walter asked just now. What happens when Mr. Hagen wakes up tomorrow and finds his best hands haven't come home and half his men are locked up in your jail?"

Trammel shrugged. "You're the one who works for him. You tell me."

"He certainly won't be happy," Montague said. "Knowing him as well as I do, I'd say he'll probably ride to town. If he does, he won't come alone and he won't come unarmed." The banker toed at an unseen line on the planks of the general store's floor. "Yes, sir. You'll be in a hell of a bind then. Hagen men in your jail and Hagen men outside it. You sure that's trouble you want?"

"The only trouble I'll get is the trouble I'll save by not riding out there and arresting Mr. Hagen for holding a gun on me earlier today. He rides into town, he won't be leaving it anytime soon."

Montague looked at the sheriff for a long time. "You trying to start a war here, Mr. Trammel?"

"I'm trying to prevent one, Mr. Montague. A war with Pinkerton men. Your boss can stop that if he wants. My aim is to make him want to."

"But just now, you made this grand speech about enforcing the law."

"There's more than one good to be served at the same time," Trammel said. "Your boss has refused to pay off the Pinkertons and end this before it starts. If he changes his mind, I'll consider going easy on his men.

He doesn't? Well, he'll have to figure a way to run his spread with half the men he usually has."

"What's to keep him from reaching out to the Pinkertons and hiring them to get rid of you?"

"That could be construed as a threat," Trammel said, "depending on who heard it."

The banker smiled. "Then I suppose I'm lucky it's just you and me talking."

"And Mr. Rhoades here from the *Bugle*," Trammel said. "You listening to our conversation, Mr. Rhoades?"

The reporter cleared his throat. "I may have overheard a few words as I finished the report of the meeting, Sheriff."

Fredrick Montague blushed.

Sheriff Trammel didn't. "That's your problem, Montague. Sometimes, you forget who you're talking to."

Montague's blush quickly reddened. "I don't forget anything, damn you, and neither does my bank." He leaned on the counter, his face only a few inches from Trammel. "You think the town supports you now? What happens when Mr. Hagen orders me to call in every loan in town? What happens when everyone, including the mayor, has to scramble to pay the bank what they owe on their businesses, their farms, and their homes? How long do you think they'll support you then?"

The sheriff seemed to genuinely consider it for a moment. "You ever see a run on a bank, Mr. Montague? I'd wager not, since you've been working for Mr. Hagen all your life. I've lived through a couple. When I was working for the Pinkertons, I got called in to guard a bank in Chicago after a bank president did exactly what you just said. They yanked him out of that fancy office of his and burned him right in the street. He was long dead and buried by the time we got there a week later, but we did manage to enforce order. Didn't do the bank president much good, of course, but it's amazing what people will do when their livelihood is threatened." He looked at Montague. "So you call any notes you want. Just don't be surprised when I don't come running to stop the lynching."

"Damn you, Trammel." Montague pounded the counter so hard, Rhoades thought he had cracked the glass. "One word from Mr. Hagen and I'll ride down to Laramie myself tomorrow. I'll get the county sheriff. I'll return with judges and lawyers and a small army to force you to free those men. I'll have you hauled out of here in

133

chains and hanged from the highest tree in Laramie before the Pinkerton boys ever get close."

"You'll never make it. I've got Hawkeye over in the jail right now holding a cocked shotgun on half your boss's ranch. If so much as a sparrow accidentally flies into that building, he'll cut loose with both barrels and you'll lose a lot of men as a result. You show up with an army like that, men will die, starting with those I've got in my jail. Maybe even you."

"You think you can hold off Mr. Hagen's will by yourself and an imbecile deputy?"

"That imbecile is smart enough to have your men covered and willing to kill them on my say-so." Trammel also leaned on the counter, the wood cracking against the weight of both men. "Listen, Fred. I'm not looking to pick a fight with Mr. Hagen because I'm bored. I'm trying to get him to do the decent thing by buying off the Pinkertons and saving me and his son from being killed for something we didn't do. The second he calls them off, I open the cells and everyone goes home, but right now, they're the only leverage I've got. You know it's the right thing to do. I know Adam's not much, but he's still a Hagen."

Rhoades watched the banker stand up

straight and fold his arms across his belly as he thought it over. "I have your word that you'll release them if Mr. Hagen tries to —"

"No tries," Trammel cut him off. "He gets them to go back home or his men rot in my cells for a few weeks."

"But we may not hear back from Pinkerton for days."

"I know Allan," Trammel said. "A man like Hagen sends a wire with the promise of money to follow, he'll pay attention. All that talk of justice and law he spouts on about is just for the customers. He cares about the heft of his wallet more than anything else. If the offer's big enough, he'll respond quickly."

Montague let out a long, heavy breath. "I'll take it up with Mr. Hagen right after sunrise. But until then, in a gesture of good faith, could you release the men into a building where they'd be more comfortable? Like the Presbyterian Church, say."

"Not riding to the ranch right now and arresting him for pulling a gun on me is my gesture of good faith. So, the quicker he makes peace with Pinkerton, the quicker his men get out of those cells. Just remember that there's too many of them for us to take to the outhouse, so it's getting mighty ripe in there as we speak."

Montague stormed back to where he had been sitting and pulled his coat from the back of the chair. Most of the other committeemen had cleared out by then, leaving only Rhoades and Mr. Robertson, the storekeeper, in the place.

Montague couldn't leave without one final parting shot. "I'll deliver your message and, by lunchtime tomorrow, you'll have your peace with the Pinkerton Agency. But you'll have no peace where Mr. Hagen is concerned, of that I promise you. He will bring down the full weight of his empire upon you, and only God will be able to help you when he does. And that's not a threat, Sheriff Trammel. That is gospel."

Trammel didn't move. He didn't even flinch. "I've heard that before, Mr. Montague, but I'm still around. You run off to deliver your message, and when I get confirmation that the Pinkerton men have been called off, your boss will get his men back. Adam will go with you to make sure everything runs smoothly."

"Like to add insult to injury, don't you, Trammel?"

"Think of it a an insurance policy for both our sides."

Montague pulled on his hat and coat and

left without bidding anyone good night. Mr. Robertson could hardly hold on to his cheer until after he'd locked the door behind the banker. "I've been waitin' for someone to tell off that popinjay since the missus and me come to town twenty-odd years ago. Never seen anythin' like it in all my years."

The shopkeeper's glee was infectious. Neither Rhoades nor the sheriff could keep from smiling.

"That wasn't my intention, but I'm glad it made you happy."

Rhoades had begun to pack up his writing material into his satchel when the shopkeeper trotted back behind the counter to join the sheriff. "Before you leave, some of the others and me wanted to give you something as a sign of our appreciation for all you've done for us. We didn't want to do it in front of that damned tattletale Montague."

Trammel looked at Rhoades as if the reporter had some idea of what was happening, which he did not.

The sheriff frowned and said, "You didn't have to get me anything at all. I'm just doing the job I'm paid to do."

Mr. Robertson took a wrapped parcel from the case behind him and laid it on the counter with great ceremony. "You already

137

paid a bit for this, but not for the extras we had done for it. Open it up and try it on for size. We hope you'll like it."

Puzzled, Trammel began to untie the twine holding the package together. When he opened the paper, Rhoades saw a fine leather shoulder holster inside. It was made of a rich brown cowhide and, in the dim light of the store, Rhoades was able to make out an inscription burned into the leather.

TRAMMEL
SHERIFF OF BLACKSTONE

Trammel took the holster in his hands. "I'd gotten so used to the one you gave me, I'd forgotten all about this one."

"You brought it in after that dustup you had at Madam Peachtree's place several months ago. The end was ruined when you shot through it, but I thought I had a man who could replace it. Turns out he couldn't do much with it, so me and a few of the others on the committee chipped in and had him make you up a new one. Brandin' your name into the leather was my idea. My wife thinks it's gaudy, but I thought you'd like it on account of it bein' more personal this way."

Trammel slipped it on, and Rhodes could

see it fit like a glove. The sheriff took his Peacemaker from the holster on his hip and slid the big gun into the holster under his left arm. The reporter had always found the sound of leather against steel to be the most elegantly deadly sound on earth.

"Hope it fits," Mr. Robertson said.

Trammel nodded his head. "It fits fine. Thank you and the others for thinking of me."

The shopkeeper grabbed his arm. "You mentioned how you used to wear a rig like that before you come to Blackstone. We figured now would be a good time to give it to you, seein' as how you might be goin' up against them Pinkerton fellas. But you won't be alone, Sheriff. There's plenty of us who'll stand with you if they come to town. We might not be as young as we used to be, but an old man can be dangerous in the right circumstances."

Trammel smiled as he patted his arm. "Let's hope that talking-to I gave Montague prevents it from coming to that. Say good night to Ethel for me."

"Hell, she's already asleep," the shopkeeper said as he followed Rhoades and Trammel out the door. "God bless you, Sheriff Trammel."

Trammel doubted God would, but

thanked Mr. Robertson for the thought just the same.

The night was chilly, headed for cold, as they walked away from the general store. The cloudless sky showed millions of stars and swirls in the heavens above. Rhoades thought it would've been a beautiful evening had it not been for the gaudy music and drunken laughter spilling out of the saloons along Main Street. He abhorred spirits for that very reason. It was a selfish indulgence that ruined everything it touched, not only those who consumed it, but their families as well. He thought if America was ever to become a great nation, it would need to become a temperate nation by casting off the drunken ways it had inherited from England. But with more rabble coming each day from Europe, he doubted temperance would find a home in this country for some time to come, if ever.

He ignored his annoyance at the saloons and focused on Buck Trammel. The lawman was difficult to talk to, and his editor at the *Blackstone Bugle* would chastise him if he did not attempt to get something quotable from this time they shared. "For whatever it's worth, Sheriff, you have my compliments, sir. You withstood a withering barrage from Mighty Montague, and not many men in Blackstone can say that."

Trammel laughed. "They really call him that? *Mighty Montague?*"

The reporter laughed along with him. "Alliteration aside, the name fits. He's a formidable man." Rhoades immediately regretted saying it, as he wasn't sure the sheriff knew what alliteration meant.

"He's not as formidable as he thinks," Trammel said. "Without Hagen's money backing him, he'd be as timid as a church mouse." Trammel looked Rhoades's way without looking down at him. "You going to print what he said back there about calling in the loans people have with the bank?"

"I'll most certainly include it in my column," Rhoades said. "As for whether or not the owner will allow it printed is another matter. But, the *Bugle* is firmly on the side of law and order. Always has been, even when Sheriff Bonner was in charge. Mr. Montague's threats against the people of this town need to be exposed. King Charles has sat on his throne unchallenged long enough. It's time for his authority to come into question." Rhoades stopped walking when Trammel did.

The sheriff turned to him. "I'd appreciate

it if you didn't do that. Not just yet, anyway."

"Why? He threatened to leverage his financial position against those he perceived to be his enemies, sir. This is not only illegal, but un-American."

"And publishing what he said about the loans could stir up more trouble than we need right now," Trammel told him. "I don't like the man any more than you do, especially after he threatened me tonight. But this town's got enough problems. Even if I was to saddle up and ride out at first light, the Pinkertons could still come here looking for me. The people of this town are going to need to focus on them, not fighting the bank or each other."

Being a reporter, that only led Rhoades to another question. "How exactly do you plan on facing the Pinkertons if they do come?"

"With as little risk to the town as possible," Trammel told him. "And don't waste time asking me any more than that, because I'm not going to tell you. I'm all for freedom of the press, but some things are best left unprinted. Like what Montague said about the loans. I'd appreciate it if you could hold back that part until this Pinkerton mess is over."

The reporter didn't like sitting on such an

explosive story, especially one that could prove so damaging to Montague and Hagen, but the sheriff had made a persuasive argument. For a brutal man, he was also a tactical one as well. "All I can do is suggest it to my editor," Rhoades said, "but he's a reasonable man and you have made a reasonable request."

"Glad to hear it."

The two men resumed walking along Main Street. Rhoades was nervous about walking with the big man along the dimly lit streets of Blackstone. Not only did the sheriff have a bounty on his head, making him a target for every desperate man within a day's ride of town, but it was also night and Rhoades had never been able to see very well at night. It was one of the reasons why he'd been a clerk in the Army of the Potomac in the War Between the States. And it was a reason why he had chosen to become a journalist once he had been discharged from service. Technically, he was considered a veteran, but Rhoades did not consider himself to be one. Veterans mounted charges and marched into cannon fire. His typing skills had helped him secure a desk in Washington writing reports.

There was another reason why he was nervous walking with Sheriff Trammel on such a night, for not only could he not help much if a fight broke out, but he was likely the cause of all the trouble the man was currently experiencing. He may not have been given the opportunity to prove his mettle in battle, but he had mettle in other ways. It was why he chose to unburden himself at such a late hour. "I'm afraid I owe you something of an apology, Sheriff."

"For what? Not standing up to Montague back there? You were taking notes, Rhoades. I don't need anyone to fight my battles for me."

"Not that." The reporter swallowed hard and decided the best way to get this over with was to get it over with quickly. "You see, before I came here, I was the reporter for the *Ogallala Bugle*. I'm the man who wrote that article about those women you and Adam Hagen saved on the plains. If I hadn't written it, Hanover and his men wouldn't have found you and neither would the Pinkertons who are pursuing you now." He expected Trammel to react somehow. To hit him, maybe, or at least yell at him.

But the big man did neither, choosing instead to keep walking along Main Street. "You were just doing your job, same as I am. You didn't even mention Hagen's name in the article on account of him not giving it. They would've found us eventually. Hanover and his bunch. The Pinkertons, too."

Rhoades felt he had to come completely clean in order to unburden himself. "I'm not talking about the article, Sheriff. I'm talking about Hanover and his men coming to Ogallala and beating me until I told them that you and Adam had taken a train here. And where it was going. Without that information, they would've had a harder time finding you. That's why I fear all of this is my fault. Had I been tougher, perhaps all of this could've been avoided."

Trammel stopped walking and faced the reporter. "And you blame yourself for what's happening now?"

Rhoades hadn't felt so small since he was a boy. "In no small measure," he admitted.

"Then stop," Trammel told him. "What's done is done, and you didn't have much to do with it, anyway. You didn't cost Lefty his eye, and you didn't kill those Bowman boys. You didn't lie about us or gin up anyone to come after us. You're not responsible for any of it, so quit living like you are. You seem like a good man looking to do good things. As long as you keep doing that, you'll never have to apologize to me for a damned thing."

It was only then that he realized they had stopped across the street from the jailhouse. Trammel said, "I'd love to hear more of your confessions, Mr. Rhoades, but I've got a full house of prisoners to attend to, so I'll bid you good night. And thanks in advance for seeing reason about that Montague business. If you need me to talk to your publisher about it, I will."

Rhoades watched him cross the thoroughfare and walk into the jailhouse without even the slightest look back. He had just bared his deepest shame to the man and he hadn't even batted an eye. It was amazing how all of that guilt he had been carrying with him all the way from Nebraska to Wyoming had weighed him down for so long only to be carried away on the Wyoming wind with hardly a thought.

Sheriff Trammel was a strange man indeed. Strange in all of the best possible ways for the future of Blackstone.

CHAPTER 12

Trammel coughed as he closed the door behind him. The jailhouse had taken on the rank odor of a pigsty and cattle pen all rolled up into one. Even Hawkeye had taken to wearing a kerchief over his face in a pointless effort to help dampen the stench.

"Sorry about being out here," Hawkeye said as he stood up from behind the desk, "but the smell back there is awful."

Trammel couldn't blame him. "You emptying the buckets regularly?"

"As much as possible, and the men are as good about being neat as drunk men can be," Hawkeye said, "but the pit in the outhouse is filling up mighty fast."

Trammel had expected as much. The jail had been built with only four cells. Mayor Welch told him the town balked at the cost at the time, claiming no one would ever remember the jail having more than two prisoners at any given time. Now the four cells held twelve prisoners, one of them a cripple, and it did not take long for the situation to deteriorate into a cesspool.

It was all part of Hagen's plan to turn their misery into an advantage.

Trammel only hoped it worked. "How are the boys taking it?"

"About as poorly as you warned they would," the younger man told him. "The drink is wearing off, and they're crammed in there too tight to sleep or do much of anything. I'd wager things will only get worse as the hangovers set in. I've been called every name in the book as a result, and a few no one's thought to write down yet."

Trammel didn't doubt that, either. "Any of them sober enough for a night ride?"

"All of the bosses are sober. Mr. Bookman and his like."

"Bookman and the bosses aren't going anywhere." Trammel knew holding on to the ramrods that made the Blackstone Ranch work was the only leverage he had over Hagen. "I'm talking about the cowhands from the bar."

Hawkeye thought it over. "Maybe three or so. Why?"

"Because I want you to help me pull those three from the pen, and we'll leave the rest."

148

Hawkeye took the key ring from the peg next to the door to the cells. "Sure, but why? It's already full-on dark out there, Sheriff."

"Because we're sending them back to the ranch with a message," Trammel told him. "Montague's supposed to do that in the morning, but I'd like to give Mr. Hagen a sleepless night if I can. Maybe give us more of an advantage than we already have. They might be in no shape to see in the dark, but their mounts will know the way home. Now, open that door, and let's pick out the best of the litter."

Hawkeye shoved the drunken men along the boardwalk with the barrels of his shotgun. Trammel followed with his Winchester. The Peacemaker tucked in his new shoulder rig felt good. Comfort would be important in the days ahead.

The Blackstone hands endured catcalls and jeers from the patrons of the saloons they passed by. How word of their departure from the jail spread so quickly was beyond Trammel, but he imagined Adam Hagen had something to do with it.

They found Adam Hagen in the middle of Main Street with three mounts waiting for their riders. "These three belong to our guests," the gambler announced. "They all bear the Blackstone brand, anyway, and should see the men home safe enough if road agents don't get them." He seemed to catch wind of the prisoners and frowned. "Or if their stench doesn't kill the horses first. It'll certainly drive the wolves away."

Trammel lowered his rifle to cover the men as they struggled to pull themselves up into their saddles. Hawkeye's prodding with the coach gun gave them added incentive.

"I want our property back," said a cowhand Trammel remembered being called Les. "That means our guns."

"You can hardly walk," Trammel said. "Giving you a gun in your condition wouldn't make much sense for either of us. You can get your things when you come back to town with your boss tomorrow. You sober enough to remember what you're supposed to say to him?"

"Yeah, I got it, damn it," Les slurred. "But he'll likely whip me just for sayin' them words to him."

Hawkeye said, "I can put you back in your cell if you'd like."

Les took the reins and moved his horse away from them. The other two men had already begun riding in the direction of their ranch without so much as a word. Any beating that may face them was obviously better than the conditions of the Blackstone jail.

But Les was in a far more talkative mood as he edged his mount away from the grip of the lawmen. "Damn you, Buck Trammel, and you too, Hawkeye. Mr. Hagen's going to make you pay for what you done to us tonight. Gonna make you pay dearly. And I hope I'll be right beside him when he does."

"Assuming your rump doesn't still sting from Father's lash." Hagen drew his .32 and fired into the night air, causing the cowboy's mount to buck and run off in the same direction the other two Hagen men had taken.

Les's curses of Hagen's soul were swallowed up by the cold Wyoming night and the jeers from the Main Street drunkards.

Hagen sighed as he holstered his pistol. "I suppose I've lost the ranch's business for the foreseeable future."

"You already control all the saloons in town," Trammel pointed out. "And I doubt their hatred of you will kill their love of your opium. Besides, all of this was your idea anyway."

Hagen grinned. "Why do you always have to be so literal? Besides, we wanted to bring Father to heel so he would agree to help us, and this was the best way I could think of to do it. He may not always listen to reason, but he always listens to money. Locking up his cowhands hurts him in the pocketbook. If nothing else, we have certainly secured his attention. I suspect he'll come to town tomorrow to sue for peace. I suggest we all retire early and get a good night's rest, for we are likely to need it. And considering the extensive resources of our enemies, I think it best if we all sleep at the Clifford Hotel tonight. You, too, Hawkeye."

"I've got prisoners to tend to," the deputy said.

"I'll be tending to them on your behalf," Hagen told him. "You've been stuck in there with them all night. You'll get sick if you're exposed to that stench for too long. I'll be happy to spell you until morning. As the good sheriff said, this was my idea anyway. It's the least I can do."

Hawkeye looked questioningly at Trammel, who wasn't exactly sure what Hagen was angling for. "Do as he says, Hawkeye. You've earned it."

"Ask whomever is manning the desk to direct you to the proper room," Hagen said. "And feel free to avail yourself of any women or whiskey you'd like. Courtesy of the house, of course."

"The promise of a clean bed and the absence of that stench'll be enough for me, thank you." He looked at Trammel. "You sure it's okay, Sheriff? I'm fine for staying up all night if you need it. Got plenty of coffee."

"Go to bed," Trammel told him. "And thanks for all your help today."

Reluctantly, the young deputy ambled up to the boardwalk and back toward the Clifford Hotel.

Hagen laughed. "You've got yourself a loyal one there, Buck. I do believe that boy would die for you if it came to it."

"Let's make sure it doesn't come to that." Trammel stepped up to the boardwalk and Hagen followed. "What's this business about you staying overnight in the jail? That wasn't part of the plan."

"The best plans change midstream," Hagen said, "like you sending a message directly to Father without waiting for Montague. That was an inspired tactic, Buck. Beat the lackey to the punch. Frame the message in your own terms. I do believe I'm beginning to rub off on you somehow."

"Don't wish that on me." Trammel wasn't sure he liked the idea of leaving Hagen alone with a jail full of men who worked for his father. "Why should you stay with them and not me? After all, I'm the sheriff. It's my responsibility."

"I'm offering assistance in a time of need," Hagen said. "Besides, why let them rot in a cell when we can put their captivity to a greater benefit? I plan on using the time to remind them of the man they work for. Their varying states of drunkenness will provide fertile ground for seeds of ideas to be planted. Ideas that may flower in the days and weeks and come to our benefit."

The more Hagen spoke, the more convinced Trammel became that leaving him in charge of the jail was not a good idea. "Thanks for the offer, Adam, but I'll stay with the prisoners."

"Do you really think that's wise?" Hagen asked. "I can afford to be bleary-eyed and half asleep when Father comes calling tomorrow, which he most certainly will, as you've given him no choice. But you need to be at your best, for he most certainly will be. And although he's hardly the man he used to be, he's still quite formidable, as will be the men he brings with him to town."

Again, Hagen made perfect sense, which only served to bother Trammel more. It felt like Hagen was always holding something back in order to lead him in the direction he wanted Trammel to go. A direction that ultimately benefited Adam Hagen.

"Why do I always have the feeling that

there's something behind your plans that you're not telling me?" Trammel said.

"Probably because I don't know everything myself," Hagen admitted. "But I promise no harm will come to any of the men. My words will be my only weapon. And I'll be ready to back you up when Father comes to town."

"You think he's really going to show?"

"We've given him no choice," Hagen observed. "It's a point of pride for him now. You've taken his ramrods. You've taken his best men and horses. He'll come to call and, when he does, he won't be happy. Fortunately, you won't have to face him alone."

"I sure hope this breaks the way you think it will, Adam, because if it doesn't, all hell will break loose."

"We're not in a clean business, Sheriff. Neither one of us."

Trammel wanted to say something, but there was no arguing with the obvious.

CHAPTER 13

It was still an hour before sunrise when Trammel watched Emily drive the final nail in the final coffin she was making. "I'm not leaving town, Buck, so you might as well stop asking."

Trammel had been afraid she'd say that. "Be reasonable, Emily."

"I am being reasonable. I'm also the only doctor in town, or at least the closest this place has to a doctor, anyway. It wouldn't be right running out on people at a time like this. It would be worse to run out on you." She eyeballed the coffin she had made and seemed pleased with her work. "And if you ask me again, I'll be mighty insulted."

Trammel began to say something, but thought better of it. He had gone up against unionists, crazed gunmen, violent murderers, and rampaging cowpunchers, but he found himself powerless against a woman half his size.

He sat on the stool by her workbench and slapped his hat against his leg, ignoring the canvas-wrapped corpses of the men he had shot. "Then I guess that settles it, damn it."

"It doesn't settle anything." She set the hammer aside and slid the lid on top of the coffin to measure the fit. He would have offered at help her, but he had found long ago that she took offense at anyone attempting to assist her with her carpentry skills. "It doesn't settle why these men are coming here to kill you and Adam in the first place. And it doesn't tell me anything about why the Pinkertons have a particular hatred of you. I'd imagine it must have something to do with the time you spent with them. Now that's something I'd like to talk about, if you're of a mind to talk about anything."

That was the problem. The last thing he wanted to talk about was his time with the agency. It wasn't exactly the proudest moment of his life.

Trammel had been recruited by Allan Pinkerton himself during one of his many swings through Manhattan about five years before. Trammel had been part of a special group in the Metropolitan Police back then, which was little more than the commissioner's bully boy squad. Pinkerton took a liking to Trammel for reasons the sheriff still couldn't understand and had insisted on hiring him on as one of his operators. His size and temperament had made him a natural fit for strikebreaking in New York and later Chicago. Most of the men he'd faced were loudmouthed greedy politicians who cared less about the workers and more about lining their pockets. They had deserved a good beating and Trammel had no problem giving them one.

But all of that changed one hot Chicago night a little more than a year before. A group of stockyard workers were protesting long hours for little pay. One of their men had gotten trampled to death while unloading cattle after working for over twenty-four hours straight without sleep or food. Trammel had led a group of Pinkerton men to break the line and beat the workers bad enough to make sure they never thought of defying the bosses again.

Trammel had stopped his men from moving in when he saw the condition of the strikers. They weren't the typical stockyard workers who were broad and surly. These men were emaciated and so tired they could barely stand up. They had been working sixteen-hour days for more than a month straight with little time to sleep or rest.

He had attacked scrawny men before, but

usually after they attacked him first. These men just stood there, looking at the Pinkerton men as if they were half hoping to be beaten to death and put out of their misery.

None of Trammel's men would raise a club against them. They took the men, about a dozen in all, to get something to eat and guarded them so they could enjoy their meals in peace.

That's when the trouble came.

The manager of the stockyard found out where they were and demanded the men return to work. Trammel knew the stockyards were good customers for the company and tried his best to keep the man calm.

But the man just wouldn't calm down, not even in the face of overwhelming odds. He took a swing at Trammel and missed. His second and third punches had missed, too.

The manager left with some of his dignity intact, but quickly returned with ten rough-and-ready types armed with clubs and shovels. Trammel and his men defended themselves easily, but the infraction cost Trammel his position with the agency. He turned in his papers before Allan Pinkerton himself could ask for them. He would not give him the satisfaction.

The long trail to forget beckoned and he found himself in Wichita and, ultimately, in

Blackstone, Wyoming, where twelve of his former colleagues were coming to take his life.

Trammel thought of all of this while he sat on the crooked stool in the old barn of Emily Downs. He wondered if he would know any of the men coming to kill him. He doubted he would. All of the men who had been with him that night at the stockyards had not even bothered turning in their papers. Most were from Manhattan and had caught the next train back there.

The agency would be careful not to send anyone he might have worked with out of fear that old allegiances might get in the way of the performance of their duty. Trammel had always been a firm but popular boss. His men often liked him, and he doubted any would raise a hand against him no matter how much Pinkerton might pay them.

No, the men who came for him would be strangers, including the man who led them. He doubted Allan Pinkerton would send one of his top men. After all, Trammel was a sheriff in a small town north of Laramie. Any friends he had would not be of much help, and the Pinkerton reputation would most likely scare off any opposition. Trammel had used that same reputation to his advantage enough times to know its effect. He knew the men who had pledged to stand by him here in Blackstone were sincere enough when they said it. They were probably sincere still. But when twelve men in Pinkerton gray dusters rode in on horseback, even the staunchest resolve had a tendency to waver.

He hadn't wanted to think about any of this, much less discuss it with Emily. He had hoped just asking her to go would be enough, but should have known she wouldn't leave without a few questions first. And even then, she'd follow her own mind. It was one of the many reasons why he admired her. It was why he loved her, if he allowed himself the luxury of such thoughts.

He watched her place her hands on her hips as she admired the perfect fit of the lid on the coffin and couldn't help but smile. He grinned. "You're a pretty good carpenter for a doctor."

"I don't think the customer will complain much." She slid off the lid and placed it against the sawhorses. "Too bad I didn't think to build it deep enough so I could've put both of them in there."

He hadn't known her to be an incredibly religious woman, but she usually had more reverence for the dead. "Why is that?"

161

"On account of the coffin demand in this town is about to rise significantly, if things go the way I fear they will."

Trammel tried a bit of gallows humor to lighten her mood. "You going to build one of those for me?"

"Don't know if we've got enough wood lying around to fit you, Buck. Besides, you won't be needing it for some time to come."

He slid off his stool and took her in his arms. "You sure of that?"

She took his face in her hands. "Surer than anything I've ever known."

When she kissed him, all thoughts of Pinkertons and gray coats and dead men left him.

Jesse Alcott gathered the men in the station warehouse after they had loaded all the munitions and goods onto the train. He stood before them, his notebook in hand, and took attendance, calling each man by his Christian name, or at least the name they had given him when they had hired on. The practice was merely a ceremonial exercise, one to remind them this was an orderly endeavor. In his experience, success came from discipline.

The men needed to be reminded they were now part of a greater enterprise. They had been a motley-looking bunch when he had first hired them back in Chicago and Kansas City. He had intentionally sought out men who were unlike himself. Men comfortable on the range. Men who knew how to fight and weren't afraid to do so. The task before him wasn't one for detectives or operatives, as were many of the cases the Pinkerton Agency took on. This was a hunt, pure and simple, and for that, he would need hunters. He would need killers, and he had them.

As he finished taking attendance, he saw how each man was of varying shape and height and guise. Many were cleaner shaven than they had been when he had found them. Their clothes newer, and their gray hats and dusters showed the world these were Pinkerton men, with all of the deference that name deserved. They were his men, and it was time for them to realize it.

"I want to make sure all of you are clear about our endeavor before we board the train." Alcott closed the notebook and held it clasped in front of him like a preacher holding the Good Book. "All of you know why you're here and the nature of our task, but you may not be aware of its severity. None of you are strangers to violence, and all of you are formidable men in your own right."

The group of gunmen laughed. "Been called a lot of things in my time, Cap," a man named Hodge called out, "but formidable is a first for me."

Alcott allowed the levity to play out until the men fell silent again and he continued. "We will ride the train to Laramie, where we will disembark with our mounts, armaments, and provisions. We will stay in town one night, then proceed shortly after first light the following morning northward to the town of Blackstone, Wyoming. Have any of you ever heard of it?"

The men exchanged glances, and most shook their heads. The man named Maynard said, "Small cow town, ain't it? Think I've been there a few times on drives to Laramie. Not much to it, as I recollect."

"Your recollection is accurate, Mr. Maynard." Alcott preferred to refer to the men this way. He found that when he treated them like gentlemen, they tended to act accordingly and were a bit easier to control without losing the edge for which they had been hired. "Several saloons, a bank, and a few stores. It is home to the Blackstone Ranch, which is owned by Charles Hagen. King Charles, as he's known in that part of the world."

The name seemed more familiar to the men than Blackstone had been.

"I mention this," Alcott continued, "because one of the men we are pursuing is Mr. Hagen's son, Adam Hagen. He's a former cavalry officer and has lived the life of a roustabout. He's a gambler, mostly, and a drunkard." He looked at the men. "Forgive me for repeating myself as both qualities often go together."

The men laughed. None of them were strangers to the vices of the plains.

"He's not to be taken lightly. We believe he has been in Blackstone for the past six months and has succeeded in forming substantial alliances among the territory's less admirable citizens, most notably the criminal Lucien Clay of Laramie."

Alcott had expected the mention of the infamous gunfighter and saloon keeper to rouse his men, and he was not disappointed. "I take it by your reaction that you are all familiar with Mr. Clay and his exploits. We will have no choice but to encounter at least one of the establishments he owns in Laramie, which is why I will have to ask all of you to remain vigilant while in town. He likely has people everywhere who can be counted on to report anything they hear to

Mr. Clay, which would ruin whatever element of surprise we might have in Blackstone."

"Didn't you put out a bounty on this fella?" asked a man named Brown. "I'd say any surprise we had is just about gone."

"That was my attempt to make our path a bit smoother," Alcott said. "I was hoping some amateur might attempt to capture our targets and get lucky. We will know if my gambit was successful as soon as we arrive in Laramie and make contact with our man there."

"Gambler ought to be easy enough to sneak up on while he's playin'," Brown continued.

Alcott hid his annoyance about the interruption. "Mr. Hagen is but one of our concerns, because I believe his accomplice will present us with the most trouble. His name is Buck Trammel, and although I doubt any of you have heard of him, you'll find him most formidable indeed."

"Heard of him?" the one called Licht said. "Hell, I've seen him. Worked at the Gilded Lily in Wichita while I was there for a time. Hit Lefty Hanover so hard, the eye popped right out of his fool head. Saw it happen myself. Never saw a man drop like that before in my life, and let me tell you, Lefty was no man's idea of a bargain."

"He was one of us once, wasn't he?" said a man named Paulson. "A Pinkerton, I mean. I read all about him in them newspaper articles they ran about him after some killing he did a few months back. In Laramie, now that I think of it."

The men grumbled among themselves, agreeing they had either read or had heard something about the Laramie incident. Alcott didn't like that one bit. He wanted them aware of their duties but ignorant of the risks. When men like these got to thinking too much, they became ineffective and, therefore, useless. There were a lot of miles between here and Laramie. He didn't need the men trading tales about Trammel in the hours it would take to reach Wyoming. Trammel was already big enough. He didn't need any tall tales to make him even bigger.

He decided to regain control of the situation. "Buck Trammel is no better than Adam Hagen. He is a murderous thug drummed out of the Pinkerton Agency for cowardice and rank insubordination. Our employer has paid good money to kill or capture these men, preferably kill as it will likely come to that. Remember, dead men don't put up much of a fight, and as many of you have already said, Trammel can put a lot into a punch. He's also known to be more than adequate with a pistol and a rifle."

Until that moment, the tallest member of the group, named Siegel, was whittling away a piece of wood with a bowie knife. He stopped his whittling long enough to say, "The bigger the man, the bigger the target. Big men don't scare me any on account of 'em being tougher to miss."

Alcott liked his way of thinking. "Well said, Mr. Siegel. Now, if there are no further questions, let us board the train and set about doing what we've been paid to do."

CHAPTER 14

Charles Hagen kicked open the door of the bunkhouse and found three of his men passed out in their bunks. The seven other bunks were empty.

"Get up!" he bellowed as his bullwhip cracked through the air and struck one of the snoring men in the hindquarters. "Get up, you worthless lazy louts, and account for yourselves!"

Les, the man who had been struck, sleepily gathered his bed clothes against him as he held up a hand to fend off another blow. "Please don't hit us no more, Mr. Hagen. We were goin' to come tell you what happened at first light, only —"

"Only now it's nearer to eight than it is to dawn and my men continue to rot in a jail cell thanks to you." He cut loose with the bullwhip again, which sliced through Les's left shoulder, causing the man to scream.

King Charles jerked the bullwhip back

across the bunkhouse floor for another blow. The two other men cowered in their beds.

"You should all thank God Almighty that Mr. Montague had the decency to ride up here and tell me what had happened or it would have been closer to noon before I found out."

Les held his right hand over his bleeding left shoulder. "I swear, Mr. Hagen, we meant to tell you, but the sheriff didn't let us go until late last night, and the horses got a mite lost on the way back in the dark and all. You was already asleep, and we figured the sunlight would wake us. I see now we was wrong."

"You were wrong about a lot of things." Hagen tried to keep the quaver of rage out of his voice, lest they think him weak. "Haven't I always warned you boys to watch yourselves when you were in town? To watch your drinking and your whoring and that damnable dragon smoke?"

"And we done like you said, sir." Les flinched for fear of another blow. "But that sheriff took us in anyway. And not just us, but Mr. Bookman and the other bosses, too. Still has 'em locked up, near as I can figure. That Sheriff Trammel said if you wanted them back, you knew what you had to do. He didn't tell me what that was, but said you'd know. Until then?" Les inched further into his bed. "Sir, these ain't my words and I don't want you hittin' me for sayin' them to you."

Hagen kept the bullwhip lax on the bunk-house floor. "Go ahead."

"He said unless you did what he wanted, you'd go broke in a week, in which case it wouldn't much matter what happened to him then." Les flinched when Hagen flicked the bullwhip, only to begin coiling it again.

"Montague," King Charles yelled, "get in here."

The banker pushed past some of the men who had gathered behind their boss at the bunkhouse entrance. "Yes, sir?"

"You sure my son was part of this? You're absolutely certain?"

"He wasn't at the meeting Welch called last night," Montague told him, "but I saw him help the sheriff get these men mounted and out of town. Of that I'm certain. I would have come to you then, had I been confident I wouldn't get lost on the trail as well."

Hagen finished coiling the bullwhip and put it on the hook on the right side of his belt. "Billy, you got my horse ready?"

"She's all saddled and ready to go, sir," replied one of the men at the door.

"Very well. Montague, you ride with us. The rest of you get back to work. We've got horses and cattle that need tending. Double up on the work if you have to. Anson, tend to Les's cut and get him in the saddle. A hangover and a little nick on the arm are sorry excuses for a man to miss putting in a good day's work."

"Yes, sir," Anson said as he stepped forward with a medical bag to tend to Les's wound.

Hagen turned to leave, but Montague moved over to slow his way. "I beg you again to rethink this, Charles. After all, the Pinkerton boys will be here any day now. They'll most likely finish off Trammel for us. And on Old Man Bowman's paycheck. Why not sit back and wait a week for them to do our work for us?"

Hagen kept walking, backing the banker out of the bunkhouse on his way to his horse, a black Morgan one of the men was holding for him.

King Charles took the reins as he climbed into the saddle and brought the horse around to face Montague. "That's the difference between you and me, Fred. You don't mind other men doing your work for you. I do. Those Pinkerton men might be here a day from now or a week or a month or not at all. Hell, they could be perched in front of Trammel's jailhouse right now for all I care, and it wouldn't change a damned thing. I'll have that damn sheriff release my men before I whip him to death before God and the whole damned town, and that's a promise. Because that's what happens to people who cross me."

He looked at the men who were riding into town with him and motioned to five from the bunkhouse. "You boys, follow my lead and don't do anything stupid." He nodded at the man at the far left. "And Billy, keep an eye on Mr. Montague here. He's a careful man and I wouldn't want anything to happen to him."

Hawkeye sat amid the rocky outcropping known as Stone Gate that flanked the road to town from Blackstone Ranch.

He had tied his horse Daisy at the foot of the rocks and hoped to catch sight of any Hagen men before their mounts caught Daisy's scent. His mare was in season and even a gelding might react to her presence. Hawkeye was well aware that he would need every second he could spare to alert the sheriff to Mr. Hagen's approach. He had already followed Mr. Montague to this point when the banker rode out to the Hagen place just after sunup and he judged more than two hours had passed.

The young deputy's stomach tightened as he wondered why Mr. Hagen had not come to town already. What was he waiting for? Certainly he would want his men out of jail as soon as possible. Was he waiting for men from other ranches to ride to town with him? There weren't that many ranches left. Hawkeye's own family ranch was now part of the Hagen empire. The other ranches were half a day's ride away, and none of them were fans of the Hagen family. If he was waiting for them to come to his aid, he would be waiting until hell froze over.

His stomach tightened even worse as he began to worry that Hagen had taken another route to Blackstone. After all, there was no rule that said Hagen's men had to use the main road. They could've gone through the woods, although it would've been a more difficult ride, particularly if there were many of them. But if that was the route they had taken, maybe the sheriff was already in trouble. And where was his deputy? Sitting in the middle of a bunch of rocks instead of doing his duty.

His fears were relieved when he heard the sound of approaching riders coming from the ranch. He removed his hat and raised his head just enough over the rocks to see men cresting the hill. Eight in total, with Charles Hagen himself well in the lead. The group was still too far away for him to identify the others, except to gather they were probably Hagen ranch hands.

Hawkeye scrambled down from the rocks, untied Daisy as he swung into the saddle, and set her to a full-out gallop back to town. She was a good horse and fast, and they made it to Main Street in almost no time at all. In fact, Hawkeye had to pull her up short to avoid hitting a freight wagon as he turned onto Main Street. He found Sheriff Trammel and Adam Hagen standing in front of the jail.

"They're comin'," Hawkeye yelled down from the saddle.

"How many?" Hagen asked.

"Eight riders. Looks like Mr. Hagen's leading them down himself. They look like regular hands, not Pinkerton men, but I didn't have time to hang around Stone Gate to make sure."

"Good work, Hawkeye," Trammel told him. "Now stash your horse around back and keep an eye on the prisoners like I told you."

Hawkeye rode around behind the jail and tied Daisy to the porch rail of the jail. She bucked at the stench from the jail, and it made him feel awful to leave her tied up there, but he did not have a choice. The sheriff was depending on him for this to work, and if that meant poor Daisy had to be uncomfortable for a bit, then that was all there was to it.

He unlocked the back door to the jail and was sure to lock and bar it behind him when he got inside. The men in various stages of hangovers rattled the iron bars as they yelled questions and insults at him. Only Somerset, the crippled Pinkerton man, sat alone in his bunk and kept his silence.

The men quieted down when they saw Hawkeye pick up the coach gun and thumb back the hammers on both barrels. "Simmer down, boys. This'll all be over in a little while. One way or the other."

Adam Hagen fed the last round into his Winchester. "How do you want to handle this, Buck?"

Trammel cradled his Centennial rifle as he thought aloud. "Eight men. One of them being your old man. One other's likely to be Montague. That leaves six hands with your father."

"Cowhands," Hagen pointed out. "Not gunmen. Father always relies on his foremen to do any gun work that needs doing, and you've got all of them locked up inside. The men riding with Father are probably only passable with a gun and not much for fighting. Time spent seeing to livestock has a tendency to soften a man."

But Trammel knew the odds were still three to one, not counting King Charles or Montague. He imagined the old man was probably good with a gun, or at least thought he was. He would have no problem blasting away if his temper got the better of him. Trammel had seen that look in his eyes when he'd aimed that shotgun at him. Sometimes intent was more important than skill, for the sheriff knew it only took a single bullet to end a life. Gun hands or cattle hands, a lucky shot would make a man just as dead.

"You don't need to be part of this," Trammel told Hagen. "This might've been your plan, but it was my decision to go along with it. The responsibility is mine."

"And leave you with all the fun?" Hagen grinned. "How selfish of you. And this is only part of my plan. Wait until you see what I have in store for those Pinkerton men if the time comes." He nodded over toward the Clifford Hotel. "I was thinking of taking up a position over there. I can cover you with the rifle and go to work close in if it comes to that. But it won't. Father has always been fond of sure things, and trading lead with you is a risk he won't be willing to take."

Trammel looked up when he heard the pounding of the earth beneath his feet. "Sounds like they're on their way. Best get in position."

But Hagen was already sprinting back to the hotel.

Trammel hoped like hell Hagen was right about what his father would do. He hoped his plan worked. He hoped he would be enjoying a nice meal this evening with Emily, complete with her mother-in-law's haunting glare.

He yelled at a couple of people who had gathered across the thoroughfare. "Best get off the street. Find a place to hide and stay there until I tell you to come out."

The people heard the approaching thunder, too, and scrambled down Bainbridge Avenue to get back to their homes and businesses.

He saw Mr. Robertson waving at him from in front of his general store, a Springfield rifle in his hand.

"Get back inside before you get shot!" Trammel yelled at him. "What the hell is the matter with you?"

Reluctantly, Robertson went back inside just as Mr. Hagen, atop a black Morgan, rounded the corner to Main Street. Six men trailed behind him, which Trammel figured to mean that Montague was probably hanging back until the situation resolved itself one way or the other.

Hagen brought his mount to a sudden halt about thirty yards away from the jail. His men spread out to flank him on either side.

Buck Trammel and Charles Hagen locked eyes as the sheriff raised his rifle and aimed it at the rancher's chest. "That's far enough, Hagen. One more step and I shoot."

"You shoot, you die," Hagen said.

"What'll you care? You'll already be dead."

Mr. Hagen's dark eyes glowered at the sheriff from beneath the straight brim of his black hat. "You dare talk to me like that in my own town?"

Trammel saw the rancher's hand drop to a bullwhip coiled on his belt. He'd seen what the lash could do to the hide of cattle in Wichita and had no intention of feeling it himself. He racked a round into his Winchester. "That whip so much as flinches, I'll blow you right out of that saddle."

Mr. Hagen's hand wrapped around the whip's handle, but he did not pull it. "You kill me, my boys here will cut you down to size."

But Trammel was not so sure. He might be a newcomer to this part of the world, but he knew bad men when he saw them, and it was clear to him that the men Hagen had brought with him were hardworking men. Good men who would shoot if they had to, but were not fighters. Given how their mounts shied away from the tension, the animals probably were not used to gunfire and would likely buck.

"I don't think so, Mr. Hagen," Trammel called out, "and neither do you. If you did, you would've come in firing."

Mr. Hagen's right hand came away from the bullwhip and formed a fist that he buried in his own leg. "Damn you, Trammel! Damn you to hell."

The sheriff kept the Winchester aimed at Hagen's chest. "You can curse me later. For now, you can tell me what you want or be about your business."

"You know what I want." Hagen cursed again. "I want my men back."

"They were arrested for being drunk and disorderly," Trammel told him. "Inciting a riot. Resisting arrest. Interfering with a peace officer. This town's got laws against that kind of behavior."

Hagen gritted his teeth. "Then I'm here to bail them out."

"You'll have to wait until I finish writing up the paperwork before that can happen. Things have been pretty busy around here the past couple of days, so I haven't had the chance. Nor reason, either."

The rancher's face reddened. "You didn't arrest those men because they were drunk. You arrested them to get back at me for making you look like a fool in my office the other day."

"I arrested them because they were disorderly and were about to obstruct justice." Trammel made a show of thinking about it. "But given your standing in the community, I might be persuaded to release them into your care, providing you promise to keep them out of trouble."

Hagen appeared to take great pride in saying, "John Bookman hasn't caused a lick of trouble since coming to Blackstone twenty years ago."

"I was only talking about your cowhands. Bookman and the other ramrods stay." Trammel swore he saw the rancher twitch.

"On what grounds?"

"On attempted-murder charges for Bookman," Trammel explained. "Aiding and abetting a criminal and obstruction of justice on the others. You can have your cowboys back, Mr. Hagen, but the bosses stay with me."

Despite his earlier warning, a crowd had begun to form on the boardwalks all over town. People were watching the big sheriff keep the most powerful man in the county, if not the territory, at bay.

More important, Hagen saw it, too. He seemed to appreciate the situation and composed himself as he crossed his hands across the pommel of his saddle. Trammel kept the Winchester aimed at his chest.

"Is there any way you might see fit to release Bookman and the others into my custody too, Sheriff? Say if I were to do you a favor? A demonstration of my commitment to law and order, if you will."

Trammel liked where this was headed, but not enough to lower his rifle. "Such as?"

King Charles cleared his throat and spoke to be heard by the gathering crowd. "Such as my directing Mr. Montague to ride to Laramie immediately and send a telegram to Allan Pinkerton himself to see if there was a way to dissuade him from sending his men here after you."

"I'd say that's a generous offer, Mr. Hagen." He shouted over to Adam. "You think that's a generous offer?"

"I would expect no less," Adam said, "as Charles Hagen is regarded as a most gener-ous man. Though it will undoubtedly be quite a sum."

Mr. Hagen leered at his son. "The safety of the town is certainly worth the price."

Trammel lowered the rifle a hair. "I take it Mr. Montague is prepared to leave within the next day or so? I'm afraid I'll have to keep your men until then."

"In that case, he's ready immediately. Fred! Come out here."

Montague rode out onto Main Street on a bay gelding. "Yes, Mr. Hagen?"

Again, Mr. Hagen spoke loud enough for the townsfolk to hear. "I want you to ride to Laramie immediately and telegraph Mr. Al-lan Pinkerton personally. Tell him I am will-ing to surpass whatever price Mr. Bowman paid to send his men after Sheriff Trammel and my son. Do you understand what I want you to do?"

"Most definitely, sir."

"And I shall be glad to accompany you, sir." Adam Hagen, outfitted in a black frock coat and hat, trotted out from behind the Clifford Hotel on a black mare with a wild mane.

Trammel didn't know much about horses, but knew it wasn't a Morgan, though it was still a beautiful animal.

Charles Hagen glared at his son. "That won't be necessary, boy. Mr. Montague has made the trip many times unescorted, least of all by you."

"But I insist, Father," Adam continued. "Why, the road to Laramie is fraught with road agents and other scoundrels seeking to prey upon unsuspecting pilgrims like the good Mr. Montague here. I couldn't live with myself if something happened to such a trusted ally of yours." He grinned at the banker. "Or if he conveniently forgot to send that telegram."

King Charles Hagen closed his eyes, then looked at Trammel. "I take it you'll release my men as soon as they're underway? Including Bookman and the others? With all charges dropped?"

"You'll get your men free and clear," Trammel said, "but charges against Bookman are pending. I'll release him to your care if you'll vouch for him."

Hagen's horse shifted as its rider tensed. "Just get them out of that hellhole."

Adam rode beside Montague's bay. "Well, Fredrick? Shall we?"

Reluctantly, Montague put the heels to his mount and rode off at a gallop. Adam stopped to tip his hat to his father before following the banker on the road to Laramie.

Mr. Hagen turned to the men who had ridden into town with him. "You boys head back to the ranch. No sense lollygagging around here when there's plenty of work to be done back home."

The men seemed all too happy to be on their way and took off for the Blackstone Ranch without a second word from their employer.

Mr. Hagen nudged his horse toward Trammel as the crowd that had gathered along Main Street began to disperse. "I assume I have your permission to watch my men be released."

"You do." Trammel rapped three times on the jailhouse door and called inside. "Let them out, Hawkeye. All of them."

Hagen's horse shied away from the stench emanating from the jail before the rancher brought the animal back under his control.

"Including Somerset?" the deputy yelled back.

Trammel slumped against the building. Sometimes, he forgot how dense the young man could be. "He able to walk yet?"

The momentary silence almost killed Trammel. "No. I don't think so."

"Then best leave him where he is. Let the

185

rest out, including Bookman and his bunch."

Through the closed door, he could hear the rattle of keys and the groan of metal gates opening.

"Now that it's just you and me talking," Charles Hagen smirked down at him, "I've got to hand it to you, Trammel. You're many things, but you're no coward."

The sheriff looked up at the rancher. "Don't push your luck, Hagen. No one's ever pointed a gun at me and lived. No one. You want to keep on being an exception, keep your mouth shut and ride back where you belong."

But Mr. Hagen would not be deterred. "I meant it as a compliment. Not too many men have defied me, especially with only a drunken rambler and a boy backing his play."

It was Trammel's turn to smirk. "You really think that dance back there was seven on one." He shook his head. "No, sir. That was between you and me and no one else. You may have caught me flat in your office, but you're the one backed down this time. And in front of the whole town, too. I guess you'll just have to learn to live with it."

Hagen tightened the reins and the horse moved back a couple of steps.

Trammel rested the stock of his Winchester on his hip, but did not lower it. "Easy, Hagen. No sense in getting killed after getting what you wanted."

The jailhouse door opened and even Mr. Hagen gagged on the stench. His men began to file out of the jail, squinting in the bright sunlight of the morning.

The rancher struggled to keep the Morgan under control as the wretched odor pushed it back. "You men are a disgrace to the brand you ride for, each and every one of you. If I didn't need you to work the place, I'd have been happy enough to let all of you rot in there until hell froze over. Now crawl down to whatever hellhole he pulled you out of, get your horses, and ride back to the ranch. I'll deal with each of you later and in my own time."

One of the ramrods said, "I'm awfully sorry about this, Mr. Hagen."

"Shut your mouth and get going. Now!"

The men walked past Trammel without even a glance in his direction. He was as glad to be rid of them as they were to be breathing clean air. It would take a while to clear the stench out of the jail, but once Montague sent that telegram to Allan Pinkerton, it would all be worth it.

A bad smell was a hell of a lot easier to

clean out than bloodstains.

Bookman was the last to walk out from the jail and tipped his hat to Hagen. "Thank you, boss."

"Thank me by getting them back to work, John." His eyes locked on Trammel. "As for our conversation, Sheriff, I intend on continuing that at a later date."

"Just be ready to finish it when you do."

Bookman turned and looked the sheriff up and down. He saw the Winchester resting on his hip. "I'll be sure to get a word in before it's all said and done. Real soon, too. And when I do, that star on your vest won't count for much."

"Just make sure you take a bath first. You stink, Bookman."

The head ramrod of the Blackstone Ranch walked away, leaving the sheriff and his former patron glaring at each other.

"Boy," Charles Hagen said, "if I was twenty years younger, I'd beat you to within an inch of your life for this."

"No you wouldn't. And you're not twenty years younger. You're just a mean old man used to getting what he wants. You're a bully, Mr. Hagen, and if there's one thing I know how to do, it's how to handle bullies. Now get back to your spread and stay there before you do something you won't live to regret."

Hagen cursed again as he violently jerked the reins, bringing his Morgan about and riding up the road back to the ranch.

Hawkeye appeared in the doorway, the coach gun still in his hand, though Trammel noticed he had at least eased down the hammers. "Damn, Sheriff. I didn't think that would work."

Neither had Trammel, but he saw no point in telling his deputy that. "Well, it did, and that's all that matters."

"Going to be a long time before the jail airs out," Hawkeye said.

Trammel watched the road to Blackstone Ranch until the last Hagen man had ridden out of sight. "It's going to be a long time for a lot of things to air out, Hawkeye."

CHAPTER 15

In the telegraph office in Laramie, Adam Hagen watched Fred Montague write out the telegram addressed to Allan Pinkerton of the Pinkerton National Detective Agency.

When the banker was done, he handed it to the clerk, but Hagen snatched it from him and began reading it.

"I've sent telegrams before," Montague said.

"None this important," Hagen said as he began to read it over.

"I've sent telegrams moving over a million dollars of your father's money from one account to another."

"None as important to me." He finished reading the telegram and handed it to the clerk. "Send this out as soon as possible, my good man. Mr. Montague will be glad to pay the fee."

Montague dug out the money from his vest pocket and paid the clerk the amount due. "We'll be right outside waiting for the reply, so when it comes, you won't have any difficulty finding us." He glanced at Hagen. "At least I'll be close, anyway. I'm sure my friend here will find comfort in the arms of a soiled dove."

"And miss the moment my father delivers me from the clutches of villainy? Perish the thought." Hagen whisked off his hat and gestured toward the door of the telegraph office. "There's a lovely bench just yonder where we can await the news together."

Montague stormed out as Hagen told the clerk, "When the reply comes, you give it to me first or I'll be mighty cross, understand?"

The clerk nodded quickly that he did.

Hagen tugged his hat back and walked outside, where he sat next to Montague on the wooden bench. "So, how shall you and I pass the time, Freddie? Shall we discuss the weather? A brisk afternoon, I'd say, even for this time of year. A bit early in the season for a frost, don't you think? Though I fear we may get one this evening." He made a show of pulling up the collar on his coat. "It's certainly chilly on this bench with you."

"As it should be." Montague refused to look at him. "In all of my years on this earth, I have never met a son who worked so hard at being a disappointment to his own father."

"I disappointed Father the day I was born, Freddie. We both know that."

Montague looked at the men and women moving to and fro in both directions on the street. "That's because you were never different from anyone else. You always resented him for not being the man you wanted him to be rather than the man he is. And your father is a great man, Adam. You might be too blinded by your hatred for him to see that, but that doesn't make it any less true."

"You've always been a loyal employee, Freddie. No one can take that away from you."

The banker turned as best he could on the cramped bench to face him. "Charles Hagen arrived in this territory with nothing and managed to carve something out of the wilderness."

Hagen's bark of laughter drew stares from men and women passing by. Even a shopkeeper across the thoroughfare looked up. Hagen tried to cover it up with a cough.

"Forgive me, Freddie, but I didn't think you were serious. I've heard that old folktale all my life and it's as comical then as it was now. Men like Hauk and the other men Father bought out or forced out may have started with nothing, but we both know

Father had a healthy trust fund from Grand-father with explicit orders to not come back until he had at least doubled it."

"And he quadrupled it," Montague said with a tone of pride. "Why, it may even be worth five times that amount when you consider his mineral and railroad holdings, not to mention the oil wells in Texas."

"A million dollars from one of the oldest families in Boston gives one quite a head start," Hagen countered.

"It's just as easy for a wealthy man to become poor as it is for a poor man to become wealthy." He looked at Hagen for the first time. "But you know all about that, don't you, Adam? You've been doing pre-cisely that for almost twenty years."

Hagen turned on him. "I didn't ask to leave Blackstone, Freddie. Saint Charles pushed me out and gave me no say in the matter whatsoever."

"All these years later and you're still the same resentful little boy you were when he sent you away to be a man."

"I didn't need to be sent away to become a man."

"Sounds like a boy talking to me," Monta-gue said. "And, just like a boy, you still took your father's money all those years you were in exile. I should know. I'm the one who transferred the funds and kept his books."

"As money was the only thing that ever mattered to that old man, I took great delight in defiling myself with his ill-gotten gains."

Montague surprised him by springing to his feet. "How dare you? Your father never acquired a yard of land that wasn't bought and paid for at a fair price."

"If believing that fiction helps you sleep better at night, I won't try to dissuade you from thinking so. But do sit down, Freddie. You're making a scene, and besides, indignation was never your strong suit. You've been taking orders from Father for far too long to act prideful now."

Montague reluctantly took his seat on the bench, though as far away from Hagen as the narrow space would allow. "Pride is what got you in this predicament in the first place, Adam. Did it ever occur to you that your father cast you out of his house as a test to see what kind of man you might become if left to your own devices?"

Hagen stifled another laugh. "Had that been his intention, he wouldn't have tossed me out with only the clothes on my back. No, he knew my weaknesses even then and knew money was important to me. He used it as a weapon to keep me away, just as he's ising it with my brothers."

"Benjamin and Caleb and Daniel are thriving in their respective positions within the various family enterprises," Montague said.

"Nice little lambs, those three," Hagen observed. "Toiling away in far-flung reaches of King Charles's empire like Roman centurions patrolling Britannia. Dependent enough on him to be subservient, but sufficiently dispersed so as not to threaten to unite against him." He looked at the banker. "I have no illusions about my hatred for the man, Freddie. I know I'm unfair and unwilling to give him a break, but not even you can be so gullible that you don't see the nature of things. The true nature of Charles Hagen. At least I hope not. I may never have held you in particularly high regard, but I never took you for a fool."

"I wish I could pay you the same compliment," Montague said. "I sincerely do. But given the decisions you've made since returning to Blackstone, that would be a tall order. Why, you've even managed to corrupt poor Sheriff Trammel, as evidenced by his foolhardy actions against the ranch."

Hagen's laugh was louder than the first. "Oh, Freddie, you're as gullible as I am a fool. No one has ever been able to corrupt a man like Buck Trammel into doing anything, except believing that Father hired him to genuinely enforce the law."

"Of course he did," Montague countered. "Why else would one hire a sheriff in the first place?"

"To enforce the law of King Charles the First of Blackstone," Hagen explained. "And Trammel's perceived treachery is Father's own damned fault. I don't deny trying to turn him against the ranch, but I wasn't able to actually do it until King Charles and Bookman stuck guns in his face. Trammel might not be familiar with the ways of the wilderness, Freddie, but he understands force and violence. Father only *thinks* he does. And today, he learned what happens when you take such a man lightly."

"Trammel better not get used to that star your father pinned on his chest. He's not going to have it for much longer."

"Then Father should get used to the idea of a revolt, because Sheriff Trammel has become much more than his employee. If today's run-in has shown the good people of Blackstone anything, it's that Father is just a man like any of them. And any man can be beaten. He may still have you and the bank and all of the titles your bank holds on various properties, but there are enough people in town who have seen a gap in the impressive Hagen armor." Adam leaned in closer to Montague. "King Charles was never as tough as he let on. Now the rest of the town knows it, too. How long do you think it'll be before someone else tests him? How do you think they'll react when he hits back?"

Montague leaned closer until his nose was only a few inches away from Hagen's nose. "He'll burn the town and everything in it before he allows anyone to take it from him. Not you. Not your gigantic friend. Not the Pinkerton thugs, either. No one. He can always start over, Adam. He'll do it if it's just to show you he can."

"But he can't burn it down." Hagen grinned. "Not if I burn it down first."

The clerk cleared his throat from the doorway of the telegraph office. Hagen noticed he was holding an envelope in his hand. "I've just received word back from" — he looked around and obviously thought better of saying Mr. Pinkerton's name in public — "from *him.* Which one of you am I supposed to give it to?"

"Give it to Mr. Montague here," Hagen said. "We'll share the news together. Head back inside and await our reply."

The clerk did as he was told and went

back inside to the warmth of the telegraph office.

Hagen looked over Montague's shoulder as he read the telegram.

FEES ACCEPTABLE STOP
RECALLING MEN TO
CHICAGO STOP

It was signed Allan Pinkerton.

Hagen cried out and slapped the banker on the back. "Rejoice, Freddie! A crisis has been averted."

Montague folded the telegram and slid it into the inside pocket of his coat. "One crisis, perhaps. But another rises in its place." He looked at Hagen. "Your father won't forget what happened in town today, Adam. And he won't forget your hand in it, either. There will be a full reckoning on his part, one way or another."

"Nonsense." Hagen waved it off. "He's just used to old lackeys like you jumping whenever he snaps his fingers. His ego is bruised. He'll get over it in a couple of days."

"No, I don't think he will. Not this time. I've seen that look in his eyes only a few times before, usually when he changed his mind about something, which doesn't happen too often as you know." Montague stood up. "You're not a son to him anymore, Adam. You're just another obstruction in his way. A rancher who won't sell out. A nuisance to be dealt with. And he will deal with you eventually in his own time and in his own way." He set his hat on the front of his head to brace against the wind. "I'd clear out of Blackstone if I were you, and I'd take Trammel with you. Do it before your father makes you do it."

"Or dies trying." Hagen fixed the banker with a cold stare. "I've wandered this world enough because of him. King Charles can try to uproot me from town if he wants to, but it'll be a hell of a lot harder than he thinks."

The banker looked disappointed, but not surprised. "And Trammel?"

"Buck speaks for himself. If he stays, fine. If not, that's fine, too. He's got his fight with Father, and I've got mine." Hagen concluded with a final thought. "You've served the old man well for a long time, Fred. You'd continue serving him even better if you remind him what happened the last time he went up against us. He lost. And he'll lose again. That's a promise and a fact. If he stays on his ranch, he'll have no trouble from me. But if he stirs trouble in town, I'll bring my displeasure to his door-step."

Montague dipped his hat into the building wind. "I take it I won't have the pleasure of your company on the ride back to Blackstone. I'm sure there's probably a new crop of Laramie 'girls' for you to inspect."

Hagen stood up without putting his hat on. "Those kinds come in all types, Fred. Some wear a bustle and powder themselves with rouge. I can think of a much more appropriate name for those who wear suits and call themselves bankers."

Montague's ego had clearly taken enough abuse for one day and he stormed off toward his horse without bidding Hagen good-bye.

He did not want the banker's empty gestures anyway. As he walked along the boardwalk alone, Adam Hagen could not help but have a spring in his step. He had gotten what he wanted. What he needed. The Pinkerton men had been bought off and he could turn his attention to other matters, such as solidifying his grip on the town of Blackstone once and for all.

First he would take the town, then the ranch, and all of the glory his blessed vengeance would afford him. Vengeance for being forced into exile. For missing the death of his mother. For losing the love of his brothers and barely knowing their sister. For making him what he had become and for all the nasty deeds he had been forced to perform along the way.

It was he who should have had his choice of representing Father's business holdings elsewhere. As the oldest, it was his birthright. Instead, Father had taken that away from him and left him with nothing but an allowance and a name. Adam Hagen would see to it his father paid for that — in one form or another — before one or the other of them was dead.

Anger and vengeance were thirsty business, and the ride back to Blackstone was a long one. He wanted a drink and to share his good news with his partner Lucian Clay before embarking on the vengeance trail.

He found Lucien in his office at the back of Molly Malone, the new saloon he had opened up in the same space that had been an apothecary the last time Hagen had been in town. He had wandered this part of the world for more than half his life and the constant change of one business into a completely different enterprise never ceased to amaze him.

Clay's office was larger and far more ornate than his previous setup. Larger by more than double, Hagen figured. He wondered if this was the reason Clay had decided to open the Molly Malone in the first place. Unlike Hagen, Clay placed great importance on trappings like fancy drapes and fine bedding. Hagen wasn't above such indulgences, but would rather see the money go toward the front of the house or the guest rooms where the suckers could feel like kings while they pushed their money at him for another dance with Lady Luck or a few enchanted moments with a willing lady.

"You're a sight to behold, Lucien," Hagen said as he entered Clay's office. "The very model of efficiency."

Clay looked up from the mass of papers and ledgers scattered across his desk. He had trimmed his beard since their last meeting into something of a Vandyke. "Back so soon, Adam? I figured I wouldn't see you until after winter."

Hagen gestured at his own face. "I approve of the new look, Lucien. It gives you a more severe, yet dignified countenance."

The vice merchant shrugged. "A new girl from New Orleans suggested I give it a try. Gotta say, I'm rather fond of it." He closed one of the ledgers and sat back in his chair. "But I'm pretty sure you didn't ride all the way from Blackstone to compliment me on my looks. You're here about that Pinkerton business, aren't you?"

Hagen threw back his head and laughed. "Good God, Lucien. You're the only man in the territory with as sharp a mind as myself. I suppose that's why we get along so well."

"Or in spite of it. Any new developments on that front, by the way? With those Pinkerton boys, I mean."

Hagan tossed his hat on Clay's desk and took a seat. "Give me a drink and I'll tell you a pleasing tale."

Clay opened the bottom drawer of his roll-top desk and pulled out two glasses and a full bottle of whiskey. He poured four fingers of the amber liquid for both of them and put the cork back into the bottle. "That's not the swill I serve the suckers out there. This is my own reserve stock from my family's place in Kentucky. Brought all the way here by train, too."

Hagen was surprised by the news. "Just when I thought it was impossible for me to be any fonder of you than I already was, you go and tell me your family makes their own bourbon. Why, if this keeps up, I'll put your name forward for pope."

"That'll be the day." Clay clinked Hagen's glass and sipped. "So, what news of the

203

Pinkerton men?"

Hagen sipped his bourbon, too, choosing to savor it as much as the good news he had come to share. "It's over. My plan worked. Trammel and I were able to force Father into buying off the Pinkerton thugs. What's more, I even had Montague send the telegram. Using Father's own right-hand man to spite him was just too poetic a stroke for me to resist."

Clay observed his partner. "So they're not coming to Laramie? The Pinkertons, I mean."

"They may already be on their way." Hagen shrugged. "They could be aboard the next train into town for all I know. It doesn't matter anymore, does it? The fact that they have been bought off and no longer pose any danger to us is the important thing. Now our operations will continue to run flawlessly without interference from the pesky Pinkertons lurking about looking to do us harm." Hagen raised his glass to Clay. "This is a good day, Lucien. A cause for much celebration. Our partnership will continue uninhibited."

Clay forced a smile, an effort that did not go unnoticed by Hagen. "Of course it is, Adam. A day to long be remembered."

■ ■ ■ ■

After they had managed to kill half the bottle of his family's bourbon, Lucien Clay walked Hagen to his horse and watched him ride off back to Blackstone. He marveled at his partner's ability to ride a straight line no matter how much he'd had to drink. Clay had been drinking his family's bourbon since he was old enough to stand on his own and even he felt the effects of the powerful liquor.

He not only envied his partner's sobriety, but resented it. For in some ways, life would be easier for Lucien Clay if Adam Hagen fell off his horse and broke his damned neck.

Clay had spent the last hour or so listening to Adam crow about how he had finally managed to bring his father to heel. But the fool was too blinded by glory to realize that no one ever brought a man like King Charles Hagen off his throne so easily. He had not been able to build an empire in the wilderness by allowing people to get the better of him. And Clay knew he would never allow one of his sons — especially the same son he had driven away from the family home — to be the one to ruin him.

Clay's own father despised him, and for

all the men Lucien had killed in his day, he would not dare go back to Kentucky and face his own father as Adam had done.

The Adam Hagen he had first met back in the spring had impressed him as a shrewd and courageous businessman. Just because one's trade was vice did not mean he had to be unprofessional about it. Hagen had proved to be a practical man, too. Yes, he had Madam Peachtree's ledger, but he hadn't mentioned it since their first meeting except to confirm what new entries should be made in it. He didn't lord its power over Clay or over any of the many men listed in it, either.

He preferred his power to be implied rather than implicit, an arrangement that suited the egos of all involved. The demands he had made of the men in Madam Pinochet's ledger had come in the form of a request, not demands or threats, and were always followed by cordial thanks from Hagen. He made those indebted to him feel like they were doing him a favor and that, Clay noted, was a valuable gift to possess.

But Adam Hagen's conflict with his father had changed him in recent months. His thirst for revenge for being banished had moved his judgment in a different direction. It was clear that he was no longer content o control the flow of women and drugs and whiskey and politicians throughout the territory. He wanted the glory of pulling King Charles off his throne. He wanted to see his father grovel before his feet while he watched the great ranch house burn in flames before him.

No, Adam Hagen was no longer the practical man who had politely forced his way atop the criminal enterprises of the territory. His quest for vengeance had made him a liability Lucien Clay could no longer afford. He had seen this happen to good men before, better men than Hagen. Men who'd let their love of drink or women destroy them. In those cases, the signs were clear and easy to deal with before they got out of hand. Sometimes, they were even able to recuperate and become useful again. Lucien Clay counted himself as an example of this.

But Adam Hagen was a different sort of man. Despite appearances to the contrary, he wasn't given to excess without reason. Clay doubted Hagen's judgment was slipping or that he had even changed. Revenge against King Charles had likely been his reason for working with Clay from the start. His motives had always been clear to himself, but now, Clay saw them clearly, as well.

And just like Charles Hagen, not many

men could say they had pulled the wool over Lucien Clay's eyes and lived to brag about it.

Clay walked along the boardwalk until he reached the telegraph office.

The clerk, whose name he never had a reason to remember, scrambled to his feet. "Yes, Mr. Clay?"

"I understand Mr. Hagen was here earlier. He'd sent a telegram to Mr. Pinkerton in Chicago."

The clerk demurred. "Telegraphs are privileged communication, sir. I can't in all good conscience —"

"Stop your damned sputtering," Clay interrupted, already annoyed by the clerk's attempt to deny it. "I'm asking you to send a telegram to Mr. Pinkerton from me."

The clerk sat back at his desk and eagerly picked up a pad and pencil. "Of course, sir. What would you want it to say?"

"Tell him I'd like some information. Tell him I'd like to know when his men are expected to arrive here in Laramie."

Chapter 16

Trammel was cleaning the Winchester while Adam Hagen told him about his earlier triumph over Montague at the telegraph office in Laramie. Trammel was more interested in the smell of the gun oil masking the stench that still hung heavy in the jailhouse even hours after the prisoners had been set free. It was already past dusk and he hoped the cold wind whistling through the open doors of the jailhouse would air the place out a bit. Somerset's complaints about being cold were mercifully drowned out by the constant flow of air. With Hawkeye taking a much-deserved rest, Trammel was minding the prisoner while Hagen told his heroic tale.

Hagen finished his story and concluded with, "What's the matter? I thought you, above all people, would be pleased by my good news."

"You're pleased enough for both of us,"

Trammel said. "And that telegram you got didn't say anything about calling off the bounties they placed on our heads."

"I would think news of you dispatching the two men who tried to claim it will serve to quell any further attempts on our lives," Hagen said. "At least until word spreads about the change in the Pinkerton men's course."

"Still cause for worry."

"Not you, Buck. You know, for a man who claimed he wasn't good with a gun six months ago, you've developed quite a reputation as a gun hand."

"I've had plenty of practice." He finished wiping down the rifle before reloading it, then started on the Peacemaker. Things being as they were, he felt better always having a loaded weapon within easy reach. "You think your old man will stand by his telegram? It would be just as easy for him to send one of his men back to Laramie to send another telegram calling off the deal and telling Pinkerton to send his men."

"Not a chance." Hagen shook his head. "That's why I wanted Montague to send it. Another telegram countermanding his first would only serve to make Father look foolish in the eyes of Mr. Pinkerton. And if there's one thing my father prizes above all other things, it's his pride."

"That's what worries me," Trammel admitted as he opened the cylinder and dumped the bullets into his hand. "We showed him up pretty good today. He's not liable to let that go unanswered for long."

"Just like the men who died trying to collect on that bounty, he'll learn the cost of crossing us. I plan on seeing to that personally."

Trammel glanced at Hagen before beginning to clean the pistol. "There's no *us* here, Hagen. The split between you and me still stands as long as you're allowing the Chinese to peddle opium out back of your place. And that ban on laudanum out of your places stands for the rest of the week."

"I expected no less." Hagen sighed dramatically as he stood. "Never let it be said that Sheriff Buck Trammel can allow a bit of good news to ruin his day. I, for one, refuse to join you in your misery. I plan on retiring to my room and celebrating my good fortune with the comfort of a fine meal and the company of a beautiful young woman." He pulled his hat on as he left the jail. "And, with that, I bid you a good evening."

Trammel didn't bother responding as Hagen left the jail. Focusing on cleaning the

211

Colt took his mind off his troubles and the ugly scene with King Charles earlier that day. He wished he could have been as relaxed as Adam appeared to be, but he couldn't. He had seen the look in Charles Hagen's eyes before he had ridden out of town. Their war was not over. If anything, it was only beginning.

He also knew there were hundreds of desperate men within a day's ride of Blackstone who would gladly kill both of them or either of them for the bounty that was still out on their heads. The reputation Trammel had found as a gunman — the one that Hagen took great joy in boasting of — would only serve as a greater temptation for someone to try their hand at making a name for themselves. Killing Hagen would make them money. Killing Trammel would give them fame, and to some men, that was more important.

Trammel also knew there was an excellent chance the Pinkerton men may not get word of Mr. Hagen's counteroffer and may come to Blackstone anyway. Life in this part of the world was much different from city life, where consequences were more immediate. Everything took longer to happen on the frontier. Everything, that is, except the speed of a bullet.

The boom of a shotgun echoed outside, causing him to drop the Peacemaker on the desk. Two sharp pistol shots quickly followed.

Trammel grabbed the Winchester from the desk and ran for the door, ducking at the sound of another shotgun blast as the jailhouse window shattered inward.

"I hope that took your damned fool head off, Trammel!" Somerset yelled out from his cell.

Trammel ignored him as he stole a quick look outside. He saw Adam Hagen lying on the boardwalk, flat on his back. The pistol in his left hand was aimed at the darkness across the street. Trammel knew something was wrong, as Hagen was right-handed.

A wagon sat at the edge of the darkness of Bainbridge Avenue. A wagon that had not been there earlier.

"You hit?" Trammel called out to Hagen, thinking the gunmen, whoever they were, must be at the wagon.

"Barely a scratch," Hagen answered. "Got a bead on two cowards across the street, though."

Trammel looked in time to see a man rise up from behind a horse trough to take another shot. Hagen fired once before Trammel could raise his rifle. The gunman's head jerked from the impact of the bullet before he fell backward into the shadows.

"There's still at least one more," Hagen yelled, "hiding next to his friend. I think I winged him before I fell."

Trammel aimed the Winchester in the general direction and called out, "Come out with your hands up before you get hurt."

"I'm already hurt, mister," a man yelled back. "Might as well have the money, too."

Trammel fired at a glint of light from the shadows before another blast of buckshot peppered the jailhouse wall, well to the left of Trammel. The sheriff held his position, waiting for another shot, but none came.

"I think you got him," Hagen called out.

Trammel was not so sure and remained crouched in the doorway. "That all of them?"

"I don't know," Hagen answered. "I think so."

In other circumstances, the sheriff would have been surprised by Hagen's admission of ignorance on any matter at hand, but a gunfight was no time to be awestruck. "You think you can cover me while I come get you?"

"If you get here fast enough."

Trammel broke cover and ran toward Hagen at a crouch. More gunfire erupted, striking the jailhouse wall behind him as he dove and landed on the boardwalk on his elbows. More shots came his way, but none came close to striking him. He held his rifle as he used his elbows and knees to crawl as flat as he could toward Hagen. The gambler returned fire, giving Trammel as much cover as possible.

When he reached his friend's side, Trammel saw why Hagen had switched his gun to his left hand. His right shoulder was a red mess and bleeding heavily.

Trammel rolled onto his left side and aimed his rifle at the wagon, waiting for something to shoot at.

"They're too scared to break cover and fire down at us," Hagen told him. "The damnable cowards!"

One of the men yelled back, "You'll see how cowardly we are when we spend that money for bagging your miserable hides!"

Trammel fired in the direction of the voice, but doubted he hit anything. To Hagen, he said, "Think you can get to your feet?"

More gunfire came from the shadows across Main Street. Rifle and pistol fire, round after round smacking into the dirt of the thoroughfare and the wooden supports all around them. The bullets landed everywhere but where Hagen and Trammel were lying.

Realizing they were firing blind, Trammel pulled himself into a crouch, grabbed Hagen by the collar, and began dragging him backward along the boardwalk that ran between the jailhouse and the Clifford Hotel. Hagen emptied his pistol in the direction of the wagon. One man cried out, but Trammel did not see anyone fall.

When he had pulled Hagen deep into the darkness of the alley, Trammel dropped off the boardwalk and crouched next to Hagen in the muddy thoroughfare. "Sounds like you got one of them with that last shot."

"Liable to be my last shot, too. My shoulder's useless and I'm empty." Hagen let his head fall back against the boardwalk, knocking his hat aside. His breathing grew shallow as he said, "Keep your rifle trained on the direction of those shots. One of them is liable to break cover to try to finish us off. That'll be your chance to even out the odds."

Trammel felt at Hagen's shoulder and found nothing but a pulpy mess. "How many you figure are out there?"

"I counted . . . at least three guns that last time. Lucky for us that none of them seem able to shoot worth a damn. They had us dead to rights just now."

Trammel knew it, but did not want to think about that. "Let's hope their aim doesn't improve." He began patting down Hagen's belt. "Let me reload your pistol before I try to flush them out."

But Hagen weakly pushed his hand away. "Don't be a damned fool. You've got plenty of rounds left in that Winchester and I'm about to pass out anyway. Leave me here and inch over to the side of the Clifford Hotel. They're firing from the left side of the place and it should afford you plenty of cover."

Trammel heard gunshots ring out from the direction of the Clifford Hotel and dragged Hagen even farther away before Hagen said, "They're not firing at us. They're firing up at the Clifford. Someone's shooting at them from the hotel!"

Trammel remembered he had sent Hawkeye to sleep in one of the unused guest rooms while the jail aired out. "That stupid kid will get himself killed."

"That stupid kid's the best chance we've got to stay alive." Hagen pushed Trammel away. "Move! Go now while they're distracted."

Trammel ran atop the jagged mud of the thoroughfare before leaping atop the boardwalk along the Clifford. He moved at a crouch toward the corner, holding the Winchester at his side as the boom from the twin barrels of Hawkeye's coach gun were answered by pistol and rifle fire. He brought up the Winchester when he reached the corner of the hotel.

He saw one of the men across the street stand up in the back of the wagon, probably to get a better shot at Hawkeye. Trammel fired, striking the man in the chest and sending him spinning before he dropped out of sight. Trammel spotted another gunman lying prone beneath the wagon and dove to his right just before the man cut loose.

The bullets went wide as Trammel tumbled into the mud and rolled onto his stomach. Instinct and reflexes caused him to bring about his rifle as he jacked in another round and fired. The bullet struck the man under the wagon in the face.

Trammel was flat on his belly in the middle of the dark street, exposed with at least one more gunman remaining. He kept the Winchester level as he pulled himself up into a crouch to give him better range of fire.

Seeing the top of a man's head in the back of the wagon appear, he levered another shot and fired, but the shot was rushed. His bullet flew wide into the Wyoming night.

The man in the wagon brought up a pistol just as six shots rang out from the Clifford Hotel. Trammel had a clear shot and cut loose with two quick shots. The man's body jerked from the impact of the bullets from two directions. Trammel watched him drop to his knees and sag backward against the wagon wall. Even in the dim light spilling out from the Clifford, Trammel could see the gunman was bleeding from several holes in the chest.

"That you, Hawkeye?" Trammel called out from his position.

"Sure is, boss," Hawkeye called back. "I'm hit, but I'm okay. I think that's all of 'em."

Trammel had made that same mistake, too. He had to be sure. "I'm coming out from the alley. Cover me if you can, but don't shoot."

Trammel got to his feet and slowly walked toward the wagon, keeping the Winchester at his shoulder as he moved. He'd been wrong about the number of gunmen before. Now that he was out in the open, the same mistake could prove deadly.

Seeing no movement from behind the water trough or anywhere else, he crossed the street and came around the corner of the wagon fast, aiming at anyone inside.

One man was slumped over on his side, dead. The one he and Hawkeye had peppered with shots was still alive, but barely. His breath came in shallow, weak gasps as life leaked from the holes in his chest.

Trammel knew by the shabby dress of the men he could see that they were probably not Pinkerton men, but he had to be sure.

He poked the dying man with his rifle as he asked, "Who sent you?"

The man panted as he struggled to shake his head. "Nobody sent us, boy. We came for . . . for —" He never finished his sentence. He slumped over and died next to his friend's corpse.

Trammel checked the area behind the wagon and saw two more corpses in the shadows.

He finally lowered the Winchester.

The dead man had said it all. No one had sent them. They came for the money.

The bounty on their heads was still in force.

And with Hagen and Hawkeye wounded, Buck Trammel was on his own.

Same as always.

CHAPTER 17

In the aftermath of shoot-out, the elegant lobby of the Clifford Hotel had been transformed into something of a field hospital. While Emily worked on Adam Hagen's right shoulder on the great table in the dining room, Mrs. Welch finished wrapping the bandage around Hawkeye's head. His deputy had suffered nasty cuts from the window shattering when the men returned fire. He had also hit his head on a chair as he fell and had been dizzy ever since.

Trammel stood vigil just inside the doorway of the hotel. Both his Winchester and the Peacemaker in his shoulder holster were fully loaded. He had plenty of spare ammunition tucked in his pockets and on his belt, too.

Main Street was uncharacteristically quiet. Not even the tinny pianos and bawdy singing of the drunks from the saloons along Main Street broke the unsteady silence that had settled over the town of Blackstone.

"I'm sorry I wasn't more useful to you and Mr. Hagen," Hawkeye said. "Guess I was in a deeper sleep than I thought."

Trammel kept an eye on the street. "You did fine. Probably saved Adam's life. You definitely saved mine."

"You really think so?"

Mrs. Welch admonished him for fidgeting and ruining her attempt to bandage him. "Sit still or this bandage will come out crooked. And I'll not have any man I tended to walking around town with a sloppy bandage."

"Sorry, Mrs. Welch," Hawkeye said. "Did you mean what you said just now, Sheriff ? You really think I saved your life?"

"I know you did." Trammel went on in an effort to make the boy feel better. "That last shooter had me dead to rights out there and you finished him off. I owe you one, Deputy."

Mrs. Welch said, "You're all lucky to be alive, if you ask me. Why, if this boy had been standing one inch to the right, his head would've stopped that bullet instead of the windowpane."

"I'll pay for the window, Mrs. Welch," Hawkeye said. "I didn't mean to cause anyone any trouble on account of my mistake."

"You won't pay for anything, young man," the mayor's wife said. "Lucky for you I was a nurse in the war, or else you'd have to wait for Mrs. Downs to finish with Mr. Hagen before you could be tended to."

Trammel had seen the gash on the boy's forehead and knew it could've been a hell of a lot worse. That shard from the busted windowpane could've just as easily gone into his eye as crease his head. But he didn't like to dwell on what could have been. He didn't want Hawkeye to dwell on it, either. And lucky for him, he was still young enough to believe he didn't have to. "You think he'll live, Mrs. Welch?"

"He'll live," she assured him. "But he'll likely have a scar to remind him how lucky he is to still be alive."

Hawkeye would've pulled away from her if she hadn't held him still. "A scar? On my forehead where everyone can see it?"

Trammel grinned at the vanity of youth. "It's okay. You'll find women tend to be awfully fond of scars. And the stories that go with them."

That seemed to simmer the boy down a bit. "I guess they are, at that, aren't they?"

Mrs. Welch sighed. "Youth is wasted on

the young."

Trammel went on. "Gives you something to tell the grandkids about years from now while you're sitting in your rocking chair in front of the fire. You can tell them how you got that from a bullet creasing your head way back during the Battle of Blackstone in the winter of eighteen seventy-six, by God, when you gunned down thirty men single-handed right out there on Main Street."

"But it was just a piece of glass," Hawk-eye said.

Mrs. Welch and Trammel laughed.

The mayor's wife said, "Don't worry, honey. The years have a tendency to add grandeur even to the most boring of tales."

Trammel looked up when the door to the dining room opened and Emily came out holding a white towel covering the front of her dress. "Sheriff, may I see you for a moment?"

Trammel's gut clenched. He knew from her tone that it was not good news about Adam Hagen.

Trammel shut the dining room door behind him to keep anyone in the lobby from looking in. Hagen deserved his privacy.

He saw his friend lying unconscious on the main table of the dining room. The sheets beneath him were soaked with blood and the bandage around his right arm was already growing red. Though he already knew the answer to the question, he had to ask. "How is he?"

"Not good," Emily told him. "I know it might not look like it, but I've managed to stop most of the bleeding. I'm afraid he has already lost a lot of blood."

"What brought him down?"

"Buckshot," she said. "A single bullet wouldn't have caused so much damage. Judging by the number of pellets I was able to pull from his shoulder, I'd say he caught half of the blast. He would have been dead otherwise."

"Do you think you got them all?"

"I won't be sure until I re-dress the wound in a couple of hours," she admitted. "These things have a habit of taking time to come to the surface. But by then, it might not matter."

Trammel felt the room tilt around him. "What do you mean?"

"I mean there's an excellent chance that I may have to take his arm, Buck."

"Is it that serious?"

"It could be. I've done what I can to stop the bleeding, but his shoulder still suffered a lot of damage from the blast. Even if he keeps the arm, I would be surprised if he ever regained full use of it again."

Trammel looked down at the once-proud man laid low and bleeding on the same table where he had held many a feast with his friends since returning to Blackstone. The same man who had been on top of the world only seconds before leaving his office and walking into a wall of gunfire. The man who was delighted by the prospect of bringing down his father was now in a battle for his life.

And he had still managed to kill some of the men who had done this to him.

This man who had once been nothing more than another drunk in the Gilded Lily in Wichita had since become Trammel's friend. This man had led him to a place he could finally call home in the godforsaken world.

Despite all of their differences in all of the months since, Trammel still considered Adam Hagen his friend.

"What can I do?"

"There's nothing any of us can do for the moment," Emily confessed. "I'm not enough of a surgeon to do more than I've already done. And I don't know what more I can do. If he loses his arm or dies, I —"

Trammel drew her close to him and held her. She was not crying, but close to it.

"This isn't your fault," he whispered. "You didn't shoot him, and you didn't put the bounty out on his head or mine. You're the only reason he's lived this long, and I bet not even the finest army surgeon could've done a better job of patching him up. You know that and I know that. Adam will know that, too, in time."

Emily wrapped her arms around him, but kept her hands away from him. "I have blood on my hands."

"So do I. More than you."

"It's a miracle you weren't shot, too."

"I don't think I qualify for miracles, but it's nice to think so." He gently eased her away from him. "Mrs. Welch is tending to Hawkeye right now. Why don't you take a break and check on him and let her come in here to keep an eye on Adam for a while?"

"And what will you be doing?" A look of fear came to her eyes. "You're not going out there alone, are you?"

"Not a chance. I've got the mayor and some of the others watching Somerset over in the jail. I'll head over there and send them here so you're protected. I'll just be across the street, I promise."

"But Buck —"

"They built the place like a fortress, remember. No one can get me while I'm in

227

there. As long as you're safe, I'm happy."

She moved away from him and dried her eyes on her sleeve. It was the least graceful, yet most beautiful gesture he had ever seen her make. "Just make sure you don't get yourself shot, Sheriff Trammel. I'm pretty tired right now and can't promise I'll perform to the peak of my abilities."

Trammel smiled. "I'll keep that in mind, Doctor."

His smile faded when he looked at his friend lying atop the bloody sheets on the dining room table. *Don't die on me, Hagen. Don't die.*

CHAPTER 18

Trammel pulled his Peacemaker when he heard a heavy pounding on the jailhouse door. Despite the stench that still hung heavy in the air, he had thought it best to shut all of the doors after that night's attack by bounty hunters.

He ignored the sound and sat quietly, hoping whoever it was would just go away. He hoped it had been thunder. The drizzle that had started a couple of hours ago had turned into a full-blown storm. A visitor at that time of the night could not possibly be good news. He'd already had his full share of bad news for one day.

When the pounding came again, Trammel knew it wasn't thunder.

He cocked his Peacemaker and aimed it at the door. "Who is it?"

"It's Charles Hagen," the voice said. "Let me in."

Trammel didn't lower the pistol. "You alone?"

"Yes, damn you. Now let me in out of this godforsaken weather!"

Trammel went to the door, unbolted it, and quickly stepped aside. He kept the Peacemaker leveled at the door. "It better just be you who comes in, Hagen. Anyone else gets shot."

The rancher strode into the jail like he was sleepwalking. His clothes were soaked and a steady stream of rainwater ran from the brim of his hat. Trammel quickly slammed the door and bolted it without checking to see if anyone else was outside. His Peacemaker trailed the rancher's movements.

Hagen looked at the pistol. "Haven't you had enough blood for one night, Trammel? Put that damned thing away."

Trammel eased the hammer down, but didn't put the pistol away. "You took a hell of a chance barging in here this time of night. Especially after how we left things."

The rancher showed no sign of hearing him. He wore a blank expression and his arms hung limply at his side. "Is he still alive?"

Trammel took him to be asking about Adam. "He's over at the Clifford Hotel.

Why don't you go see him for yourself?"

"Because I'm in here asking you. Is he alive?"

Trammel decided the rancher had not come to cause trouble and tucked the Peacemaker back under his arm. "He was alive when I left him a couple of hours ago."

Hagen nodded slowly. "Will he live?"

"I don't know," Trammel admitted. "He caught a hell of a shotgun blast to the shoulder. It looked pretty bad to me. Doctor Downs did what she could to stop the bleeding, but there's a good chance his right arm will never be the same. He might even lose it."

"*Doctor* Downs, is it? The Widow Downs is more like it. Her husband was the real doctor. She's nothing more but a damned veterinarian's assistant who picked up some doctoring from looking over her late husband's shoulder."

Hagen's obvious grief was the only reason why Trammel didn't beat the rancher to within an inch of his life for talking about her that way. "Emily was enough of a doctor to save your son's life. I'd say you should be grateful."

"I've sent one of my men to Laramie," Hagen told him. "A couple of doctors will be here as soon as the horses can get them here."

"I know Emily sure could use the help."

Mr. Hagen ignored that. "Who did this to him, Trammel? Was it the damned Pinkertons? Who were they?"

"No. Just bounty hunters. Five of them. They're all dead now, so we don't know where they came from. But they weren't Pinkerton men, you can be sure of that."

"How do you know?"

"Because I used to be one," Trammel reminded him. "And we'd both be dead if they were." Trammel didn't know if it would help, but he added, "Adam fought bravely. He took down at least two of them by my count, even with his left hand."

Hagen's head lifted a bit, and he said with a bit of pride in his voice, "That was my doing. Taught the boy how to shoot equally well with both hands as soon as he was old enough to hold a gun. Served him well at West Point, from what I was told. His skills with a horse and a gun were the only reason he graduated."

Trammel had no way to know if that was true and did not care. "Your son is across the street right now on a dining room table clinging to life. I'd go see him now while you still can."

The rancher looked in Trammel's direction. "Too ashamed to see him yourself?"

Trammel sat behind his desk. "And just what the hell is that supposed to mean?"

Hagen pointed at the star on Trammel's chest. "I gave you that thing in the hope that you might bring some law and order to this town, but all you've brought is violence and death. Why, since the day you rode in here, the shootings and killings have gotten worse. It's more of a sewer now than it was when Bonner had that star."

Trammel knew the man was grieving for his injured son the only way a powerful man knew how — by lashing out at the nearest target.

But Trammel had never agreed to be the rancher's whipping boy and he would not start. "Aside from the trouble Adam and I brought with us when we got here, Blackstone's been a peaceful place until now. Old Man Bowman and that damned bounty he put out on us is the reason for this, not me."

Hagen turned on him and roared. "My boy would be alive and well if it wasn't for you and that trouble you caused in Nebraska!"

Trammel remained calm in the face of the rancher's rage. "Your boy would have been dead and buried in a shallow grave in

Wichita for the past six months if it wasn't for me. And I wouldn't be getting shot at now if it wasn't for him." He slowly got to his feet. "But Adam wouldn't have been a drunken rambler in Wichita or anywhere else if you'd treated him well when he was a boy. We can chase that dog for the rest of the night if you want to, Hagen, or you can spend that time with your son. You should be there — like a father should be — in case he wakes up." Trammel couldn't help but add, "Even a father like you."

Hagen glared at him.

Trammel glared back.

And, as had happened before, the rancher looked away first. "He's not my son."

Trammel closed his eyes. "For God's sake, Hagen. He might be dead in the morning. You don't have time for this nonsense."

Hagen's eyes glazed over as he looked deep into something that could only be seen in his own mind. "I mean it, Trammel. Adam was my sister's boy. She died bringing him into this world."

Trammel found himself slowly sitting back down in his chair. "What?"

"Adam's father," Hagen continued, "his real father, if you could call him that, was a sweet-talking no-account who lived in town. He had his fun with my sister and turned her out without a second thought for her or what he had done to her. I took her in before the baby came and promised to raise him as my own before she breathed her last. Saw to it that the man who threw her away was swinging from a tree before her body was even cold." Hagen nodded to himself. "Me and Johnny Bookman did that bit of work together. Saw to it the wolves scattered that no-account's bones clear across Wyoming, by God."

Trammel watched a single tear streak down Hagen's weathered cheek. "My sister was the only person in this entire world who made me human, Trammel. The only one who knew the real me. She kept my damned temper in check. Hell, my own wife couldn't even do that. When my sister died, she took a large piece of me with her."

Trammel had no words. He had heard a lot of stories in his time as a lawman and a detective. Confessions often came with the job, especially when a man was slapped in irons or staring down the barrel of a gun. He'd heard begging and boasting and lying at the worst moments of people's lives. But he had also heard the truth enough times to know when he heard it, which was why he knew he was hearing it from King Charles Hagen.

Adam Hagen was not his son.

And suddenly, the entirety of a haunted man's life made sense.

It explained Adam's exile. It explained why Charles favored the other boys over Adam and why Hagen had sent him away at such a young age. He reminded the rancher too much of the indignity suffered by his dear sister and the loss of her as a result.

The sudden weight of this knowledge almost crushed Trammel. He could not imagine the impact it would have on Adam if he ever learned of it. When he could find the words, the only thing Trammel could ask was, "Does he know?"

The rancher barely shook his head. "I doubt it. He might have an inkling somewhere in the back of his mind, seeing as how he's so much different from me and my other boys. Any family resemblance is passing and comes from my sister, not me. No, he's got the look of his father. His unfortunate temperament, too. Must run in his blood stronger than any Hagen blood in his veins, by God, much to his misfortune."

Hagen looked at Trammel. Whatever fire that may have been in his eyes when he had first walked into the jail that night was gone. "My late wife knew, but the only people who know the truth about Adam are me, John Bookman, and now you, Sheriff. I'd appreciate it if we could keep it that way. No matter what happens to him now or in the coming days."

Trammel sat quietly while he listened to the rain hammer the jailhouse roof and Somerset's snoring in the back. It would have been almost peaceful if it had not been for the dour Charles Hagen standing in the middle of the room without saying a word.

Trammel was not sure there was anything to say, but he came up with something. "Go see your son, Mr. Hagen. He's as much yours as he is anyone else's in this world. And whatever he is, it's because of how you decided to treat him. I'll keep your secret, but not your conscience. If he dies before you see him again, that's your burden. Go to the hotel or go back home, but I won't tolerate your presence in my jail anymore."

King Charles Hagen did not look very much like royalty as he shuffled toward the door, unbolted it, and opened it. Trammel watched him framed in the doorway, standing there waiting, almost as if he hoped someone might take a shot at him, too. He reluctantly stepped out into the night, with only the cold wind and rain to greet him.

Trammel went over and shut and bolted

the door without checking to see if Mr. Hagen was still there. He wasn't sure it mattered one way or the other.

He looked up when he heard laughter coming from the cells.

"The things a man hears when he wakes up in the middle of the night," Somerset said.

Trammel slowly walked back to the cell block. He found Somerset sitting on the edge of his cot, his immobile right arm still lashed to his side, his bare feet on the cold floor of his cell.

"And just what is it that you think you heard, Somerset?"

"Old King Hagen weeping and moaning about his dead sister," the Pinkerton man laughed. "And sticking him with her unholy spawn to raise."

"Adam Hagen is a love child, abandoned by his real father and shunned by his adopted father. Someone's going to pay very well for that bit of news."

"Unless he's lowered his standards since I quit," Trammel said, "I don't think Allan's going to pay very much for idle gossip."

"Maybe he won't," Somerset allowed, "but plenty of others might. Lucien Clay, for instance, or maybe one of them reporters in Laramie. And if you're nice to me, maybe I'll cut you in on a piece of what I get. What do you say?"

Trammel pulled his Peacemaker and slammed the butt of the pistol on Somerset's left hand.

The prisoner cried out as he tumbled back onto his cot. "You broke my damned hand!"

Trammel tucked the pistol back under his arm and walked out into the office. "I'll break more than that if you ever breathe a word of what you heard here tonight to anyone else." He slammed the door to the cells shut and locked it.

He had heard enough bad news for one night.

CHAPTER 19

The next morning, Lucien Clay made sure he was awake in time to meet the 6:23 train down at the station.

Knowing how impressionable these Pinkerton types were to appearances, he pulled his best suit out of the cabinet and had one of his girls give it a good brushing. It was a black affair, which was intentional given the purpose of his impending meeting. He found that serious colors in the territories always threw the city folk off their feed. They were accustomed to reading about how frontier people lived in rags or tan clothes. Clay hoped a dash of dignity would give him something of an advantage on whoever was leading the small army of Pinkerton men.

He needed any advantage he could get, coming in so late in the game.

He found two white gloves in the bottom of his dresser and decided they would add just enough of a dramatic touch to his ensemble. He remembered reading in one of the newspapers from back east that gloves had become fashionable again in Paris, London, and New York.

He had already finished off two mugs of coffee by the time he heard the train whistle sound as it approached the town. He pulled on his hat and coat before he took a stroll down to the station to greet the new arrivals to Laramie, Wyoming.

He nodded in greeting to all who stepped off the train, but was only truly interested in meeting one passenger in particular that rainy morning. Well, one passenger and his companions.

He found the man the telegram had told him to look for. Six feet, dark hair only beginning to be speckled by the gray of advancing years. His suit simple, save for a shiny gold watch chain that spanned his middle and the unmistakable gray duster that showed him to be a Pinkerton.

Clay could play the gentleman when the occasion called for it. He removed his hat as the man stepped down from the train. "You must be Mr. Alcott, I presume?"

Alcott eyed him for a moment before answering, "You presume correctly, sir." The Pinkerton man took him in from head to toe. "I take it you are not the man I was supposed to meet, as I was informed he was a sort different from you."

Clay appreciated the man's vague caution. A cautious man could always be trusted to be corruptible. "I am afraid you are correct, Mr. Alcott. Although I may not be the man you expected to meet, I am a man you will be happy to know. My name is Lucien Clay and I am the proprietor of many fine drinking parlors here in town." He removed his gloved hand before extending it. "Welcome to Laramie."

Alcott regarded the hand for a moment before shaking it. "The pleasure is mine, Mr. Clay, though I'm afraid your reputation precedes you, sir. You're more than just the owner of a few saloons. I have heard you are also a major provider of vice in this part of the territory."

"And you are no mere detective," Clay responded, "but the infamous riverboat enforcer Diamond Jim Alcott, the most feared man on the Mississippi once upon a time."

Alcott did a poor job of hiding his response to the flattery. "Surely, I don't need to remind a saloon keeper of how men like to better themselves by enlarging the stories they've heard in their travels."

"Not in this case," Clay said. "I was on the *Jolly Tinker* the night you sent Pierre Sangre to hell, so my knowledge of your exploits comes firsthand. In fact, it's the reason I'd like to buy you a drink. Several, in fact, if you'll allow me."

It was clear to Alcott that this Clay was no fool, and the mention of his infamous battle with Bloody Pete on the *Jolly Tinker* riverboat told him there was more to Mr. Lucien Clay than he had first believed. "I have a company of men and horses and material to tend to at the moment. Perhaps another time?"

"Perhaps you'll come to visit me over at the Molly Malone just over yonder." He motioned to the building with his hat. "I not only want to have the honor of buying a brave man a drink, but to also discuss the contents of the telegram you received while making your way to our town."

Alcott took a step back as he stood a bit taller. "What do you know of it?"

"I know that Mr. Charles Hagen contacted Mr. Allan Pinkerton and outbid Old Man Barrow's vengeance against Buck Trammel and Adam Hagen. I know that you've good reason to hate Trammel personally as well as professionally. And I know you hate to waste your time and efforts on a fool's errand, even when you're well paid for it."

Alcott's eyes narrowed. "You appear to know quite a bit for a man who claims to be a simple saloon keeper."

"The train often lays over here in Laramie." He turned and gestured to the rows of saloons in town. "Their crews need places to eat and enjoy themselves as a railroader's life is a lonely one. I count many of them as my friends, and friends have a way of telling each other things."

He could tell Alcott was intrigued, which meant it was exactly the best time to break away. "But I am afraid I've monopolized your time enough, Mr. Alcott. As you said, you have several important matters to attend to. Stop by the Molly Malone when you're finished and we'll discuss more over the warmth of a good fire and good whiskey."

As Clay headed back to his saloon, Alcott called out, "It may not be until well into the afternoon hours. Perhaps evening."

Clay smiled but did not turn around immediately. *Alcott hadn't said no.*

Clay turned and said, "I have nothing but time, Mr. Alcott. Stop by when convenient. The door off the alley is the most private if you'd prefer. Through the bar is the same difference."

Clay's smile held all the way through to his office. He may have just bought himself a Pinkerton to add to his already impressive collection of corruptible officials.

Lucien Clay wasn't surprised when his lumbering bouncer Brian rapped his knuckles on his office door some five hours later and told him, "A Mr. Alcott is here to see you. Says he's got an appointment."

Clay pulled two glasses and a fresh bottle of his family's bourbon from his bottom drawer. "Show him in, and make sure we're not disturbed unless I call for you. Not even if the damned building's on fire."

He remained seated, pouring the whiskey as Alcott entered the office. Brian closed the door behind him.

The Pinkerton man took off his hat and smiled. "No flourish or handshake, Mr. Clay? No cultured airs of welcome to your place of business? I must confess I'm a bit disappointed."

Clay glanced at him as he poured the second glass of whiskey. "You mean that display I put on down at the station? That was for the benefit of the locals who think I'm just a swill-pushing thug. In here, I decide who thinks what."

Alcott seemed to be enjoying himself.

"Which is to imply you're not. A gentleman, I mean."

Alcott tossed his hat on the desk before sitting down. "If you really were on the *Jolly Tinker* that night, you know Pierre Sangre deserved his fate."

"Oh, I was there." Clay handed a drink to Alcott, which he eagerly took. "Pete had it coming. He never knew when to quit while he was ahead, but I'm wagering you do." Clay grabbed his own drink and tried to clink Alcott's glass. "Cheers."

But Alcott pulled his glass back. "What are we drinking to?"

Clay thought about it for a moment. "To good alliances old and new."

Alcott clinked glasses and the two men drank.

The men set their glasses on the desk and Clay quickly went about refilling them. "You'll find that's the good stuff, too. From my family's own still back in Kentucky. It's not the rotgut we overcharge for out there."

Alcott frowned. "Some of my men are out there right now drinking your rotgut."

"Which serves them right," Clay said. "After all, you're in here for a reason. The same reason why I'm no longer working behind the bar and own my places. Several of them, in fact, all across the territory. You and me, we've risen above such things. We've achieved a certain station, wouldn't you say?"

"Beyond that of booze-peddlers and river-boat killers?"

"The world's big enough to have a place for the talents of all concerned," Clay said, "especially for men like us."

"Is that why I'm here, Mr. Clay?" Alcott asked. "Because we're so similar in temperament and experience?"

"That and because I know what it's like to be burned unexpectedly." He picked up his drink, but saw no reason to propose a toast. "I know what it's like to have vengeance in your grasp, only to lose it through no fault of your own at the last possible second. I also know it's even better when there's a profit to be made on the enterprise, and legal, too." He leaned forward. "I know Trammel humiliated you on that train last spring by sucker punching you in front of a carload of gamblers. I also know Old Man Bowman was going to pay you to avenge his dead son until Charles Hagen paid Allan Pinkerton money to call you off."

"You seem to know a lot, Mr. Clay."

"I know because the man who was behind it all sat in that same chair as you only a few days ago and told me all about it. Bragging, you might say."

Alcott set his glass aside. "You mean Trammel?"

"I mean Adam Hagen," Clay said. "Trammel's just a thug with a star on his vest. Hagen's the real brains behind all of this. When King Charles refused to buy off Pinkerton, Adam backed his father into a corner to the point where he had to pay. I won't bore you with the details, but you can rest assured it was impressive as hell. Even I thought it was genius."

"So Hagen got what he wanted," Alcott said. "Since I'd imagine you and Hagen have come to some kind of an agreement, anything that benefits him should benefit you as well. Correct?"

"Should but doesn't." Clay knew he would have to choose his next words very carefully. If he didn't tell Alcott enough, he and his men would leave town. If he told Alcott too much, such as the part about Hagen having Mrs. Pinochet's ledger, Alcott might find it and keep it for himself. Clay would just be trading one master for another.

He walked a thin thread as he said, "I've decided that any man crafty enough to back Charles Hagen into a corner is far too dangerous for me to trust in business.

Normally, I'd just have to grin and bear it while hoping for better things. But normally, I don't have an army of Pinkerton boys at my disposal."

Alcott stood up. "We are not mercenaries, sir."

"The hell you're not," Clay said. "And since that door stays shut until I open it, you might as well sit back down and hear me out, because you're not going anywhere."

He watched Alcott slowly retake his seat.

"Now," Clay continued, "I can't pay you more than whatever King Charles paid your boss to have you back off. However, certain things have transpired in the past few days that may make the vengeance you seek a little more attainable."

"What could I attain now that I could not attain with twelve trained gunmen at my side?" Alcott asked. "These men are not city ruffians like Buck Trammel, Mr. Clay. These men are all former cavalry or lawmen or ramrods who have never been east of the Mississippi. They have never known the comforts of city life and have never sought them out, either. They're killers, Mr. Clay, killers through and through. And at my direction, they will take to wiping out any town at hand, be it Blackstone or even Laramie itself."

Clay let Alcott run on without bothering to correct him. He knew Blackstone would be easy enough to take once a torch was put to some buildings at each end of town. But Laramie, on the other hand, would prove a much harder challenge, even for a small army of Pinkerton men.

As Alcott's arrogance served Clay's purpose, he allowed it to go unabated for the moment by taking a different tack. "You have now what you had before you boarded the train, Mr. Alcott. The necessary force and ability to take down a town if necessary. What you don't have is information. Your spy isn't here to give you his report, is he? A Mr. Somerset, I believe."

Alcott's eyes narrowed once more. "You have him?"

Clay shook his head. "No, I don't, but Trammel does. Your man lost his faculties a few days back and took to attacking a soiled dove in the Pot of Gold, one of Adam Hagen's many establishments in Blackstone. Unfortunately for your man, Trammel heard her screams, interceded, and threw Somerset out a window."

Alcott looked at the floor. "So he's dead."

"He's very much alive and in Trammel's cell as we speak. I understand he suffers from a variety of aliments, including a broken shoulder, two broken legs, and a skull that rattles a bit more than it used to."

"Good God," Alcott said.

"I'm afraid the Almighty has little place in this part of the country, Mr. Alcott. But fear not, for I think your strategy against Trammel and Hagen has been far more successful than you currently believe."

Alcott raised his chin to him. "Explain yourself, sir."

Now that he had him hooked, Clay decided it was time to reel him in. "Not until we come to an understanding."

Alcott leaned forward. "This may be your establishment, but it is currently occupied by twelve of my men. That door may stay shut, but I assure you my voice is powerful enough to carry through it. One raised word from me and those men will set to burning it — and everything within it — to the ground."

Clay produced the Colt Navy pistol he kept in a holster under his desk and aimed the long barrel at Alcott's face. "And one shot from in here will set my men a-shooting outside, and they won't stop until all of them are dead." He thumbed back the hammer. "Not that you'll care, of course, because by then, you'll be rapping on the pearly gates yourself, praying for Saint Peter's benevolence with the keys.

Alcott sat back in his chair, but Clay didn't remove the gun.

"What are your terms, sir?" Alcott asked.

Clay eased down the hammer on the Colt, but laid it on his desk, pointing at Alcott to show hostilities between them were paused, but not yet resolved. "I will give you information on how you can accomplish your mission without violating the orders you have received from Mr. Pinkerton."

"And how do you suggest I accomplish an impossible task?"

"By agreeing to my terms, which involves the simple task of killing Mr. Adam Hagen."

Alcott blinked. "The very man I was ordered to not kill."

"One of two, but given the events of the past forty-eight hours, a task easier to fulfill. You ensure his death and I will be in a position to provide you with suitable protection from the wrath of Mr. Pinkerton and even King Charles Hagen."

"Because without Hagen," Alcott concluded, "you're in charge of the territory, aren't you?"

Clay saw no reason why he should explain himself to the hired help. He simply extended his hand across the desk. "Do we have a deal? You'll earn far more from me than you will as one of Allan Pinkerton's errand boys."

Alcott looked at the hand but did not shake it. "Why such a generous offer to a man you don't even know?"

"Because I know the caliber of man you are, and I know you don't allow insults to stand for long. I know you don't like the orders you have received from Pinkerton and your vengeance left unachieved will burn a hole in your belly the whole long ride back to Chicago and for long after. I'm offering you the best of all worlds. Satisfaction, a place to stay, and a steady stream of money in your pocket for the foreseeable future. It's a fine deal a less intelligent man would readily take, which means you should have shaken my hand by now."

Alcott regarded Clay's hand again before shaking it.

"Good," Clay said. "Now that we have an agreement, let me tell you how we can both get what we want. Your enemies have been whittled down from three to only one."

"How?"

"By the bounty you or Mr. Pinkerton placed on their heads. Some men came to collect yesterday, and Adam Hagen was gravely injured. Mr. Hagen himself sent for our town doctor, who rode out in the middle of the night. So I can only assume that Adam is in a bad way. Trammel's deputy, an idiot boy named Hawkeye, has also been injured and is unfit to fight, not that he would've been much of a challenge for you and your men."

"And what of Trammel?"

"Untouched, near as I can figure, but without anyone but a couple of aging store-keepers to back him against you, I'd say there are enough of you to apprehend him. Or kill him, should you choose. Makes little difference to me."

"As long as Hagen's dead," Alcott concluded.

"A deed which should prove to be easy enough for a man of your talents and experience. Surely you and your men should have no problem getting rid of a half-dead cripple and an outgunned sheriff. As impressive as Trammel may be, he's still only one man."

Clay watched Alcott absently massage his jaw. He wondered if that was the spot where Trammel had slugged him.

"Yes," Alcott said. "I believe you're right." He looked at Lucien Clay. "I think we'll work quite well together, Mr. Clay."

CHAPTER 20

Adam Hagen woke, staring at the ceiling of his bedroom. He knew it was his bedroom, because he remembered the jagged crack in the plaster that ran from just over his bed to behind the wallpaper to his left. He knew the crack well, for he had spent countless hours staring at it since returning to Blackstone as he planned his next moves to secure his place in the territory.

As he stared at the crack, his thoughts turned again to worries. *Can Lucien Clay be trusted? Are the Celestials holding back money from their opium trade? Is Judge Stack's latest crooked ruling recorded in the ledger? Where is the ledger? Is it safe?*

He gave a short nod. *Yes, of course it is. Worry about something else.*

Okay. How far can Father be pushed before he bans his men from going to town? What still needs to be done to finally pull King Charles off his throne?

He frowned. *What about Buck? How far can he be pushed before he treats me like every other criminal in Blackstone?*

These thoughts and dozens more flew through his mind several times on any given night before a fitful sleep finally took him. He often woke slowly, groggy, the next day, his head usually sore from too much whiskey and not enough food. Whatever female companionship he had procured the previous evening was usually still with him, for the girl was allowed to sleep later if she had been requested by the boss.

And Adam Hagen was the boss. He most certainly was.

Boss or not, at that particular moment, Hagen could not recall how he had gotten to his room the previous night. He usually kept his wits about him, even when he drank heavily.

Why can't I remember what happened last night? Surely whoever is with me will know.

He patted the left side of the bed and found it cold and empty.

Strange. I never go to bed alone.

He raised his head to look around and the stabbing pain that flashed through his entire body in one blinding moment reminded him of everything that had happened.

The gunfight outside the jailhouse. The

fire in his right arm. The man across the street that he had shot through the head. Trammel dragging him backward along the boardwalk, followed by the deepest blackness he had ever known. The sweet smell of ether and the metallic smell that could only be blood. His blood. Voices, too. Hushed and gentle at first, then harsh and demanding. Fever dreams? Nightmares? There was no way to know for certain.

The only certainty was the cracked plaster ceiling and his intolerable pain.

He felt a heavy pressure on his chest, as if a large hand was pushing him down on the bed. He fought off the pain enough to dare open his eyes and found it was, indeed, a large hand pushing him down.

A hand belonging to Buck Trammel. "Take it easy, Adam. Don't move too much."

Hagen blinked away the tears that had come not from emotion, but from the pain. "If you're here," he whispered, "I must be in hell."

"Nope. You're still in Blackstone." Trammel removed his hand. "And just barely at that."

Hagen turned his head, slowly, and saw his entire left arm wrapped in thick white bandages. "What happened?"

"You caught a healthy dose of buckshot in your right side," Trammel told him. "High enough to take a chunk out of your shoulder."

Hagen had been a soldier and knew the severity of shoulder wounds. Cheap novels made them out to be little more than paper cuts, but he knew better. "How bad is it?"

He heard the hesitation in Trammel's voice. "I'll get Emily to come in and explain it to you."

Hagen grabbed for him with his left arm, but the renewed pain made him immediately regret it. "Damn it, Buck," he said through clenched teeth. "Will I keep the arm?"

"Seems like it for now," Trammel said. "Emily operated on you right after it happened. She stopped the bleeding and saved your life. Your father brought up a couple of doctors from Laramie who took over from there. Even they had to admit she did a hell of a job."

The news made him almost raise his head, but he remembered the pain it might cause and thought better of it. "Father did that?"

"I was surprised, too," Trammel admitted. "They worked on you some more and it looks like you'll keep your arm. They said it might even be back to normal eventually."

Hagen's empty stomach ran cold. He knew what loaded phrases like that meant to a man in his predicament. "What do you mean by *eventually*?"

Trammel didn't answer right away. "Emily or one of the doctors would be better able to answer that than me, Adam."

"Unless you've become a reckless man since I've been unconscious," Hagen snapped, "you always choose your words carefully. If you said *eventually*, you said it for a reason. Why?" He saw Trammel grit his teeth.

That big lantern jaw of his was set on edge as he clearly wrestled with what he should say. He had already said too much.

Hagen lost patience. "Damn it, Buck. Just tell me!"

So Trammel did. "You almost lost your arm, Adam. Hell, you were close to gangrene setting in even after the second doctor got here. But they used an old Indian trick and fought the infection, so you got to keep your arm. But the damage is bad. I heard them tell your father you won't have much use of it for the better part of a year, if ever." Trammel pawed at his mouth. "The doctors could explain it a hell of a lot better than I can, but that's the gist of it. You pushed me to tell you, so there it is."

By instinct, Hagen tried to ball his hands into fists. The left one did. The right one did not move. In fact, he couldn't feel anything in it at all. "You mean I'm paralyzed?"

"They splinted your arm and wrapped it good and tight so you can't move it," Trammel told him. "It's going to have to be that way for a while. And don't ask me how long, because I don't know. They said it has to be that way to make sure you don't tear anything while it heals. I remember they said in a month or so, they'll be able to know for sure."

"But right now, as we sit here in this room, I'm a cripple." The words hit him harder than Trammel's big hand on his chest. "A cripple."

"Knock that off right now. You're laid up, just like you would be if you had a busted leg or a bad case of the flu. Like that *spy*" — Trammel spit out the word — "Somerset we have over in the jail. We won't know if you're a cripple for some time, but if it's any consolation, the doctors said they would've taken the arm if they didn't think you could use it. As for how much you'll be able to use it, there's no way of knowing yet."

Hagen shut his eyes as the words and the

pain mixed together in a terrifying brew. For the time being, he would not be the man he was. The man he had become and still planned on being. And there was an excellent chance he may never be the same again. People had already grown to resent him as a boss in the territory. As a cripple, they would not hesitate to pick him apart piece by piece. Not even the contents of the ledger would be enough to save him.

Besides, how could a one-armed man be expected to make entries, much less protect it? He opened his eyes when he heard Trammel stand.

"I know this is a lot to take in, Adam. I'll send Emily in to look at you. She'll be happy you're awake. A lot of people will be. We've been worried about you."

"How long have I been out?"

"A week, give or take," Trammel said.

Hagen looked at him. "You can't be serious. That long?"

"I'm afraid so. You mumbled a lot of nonsense, but nothing to be embarrassed about. Well, nothing you should be embarrassed about, anyway."

But Hagen was concerned about other things. The fever dreams. The harsh words jumbled with the soothing words. The voices of men, not Emily. "Who was with me? Did

I say anything about the ledger?"

Trammel shook his head. "After all of this, after all you've been through, you're still worried about that damned ledger of yours?"

"Until I can find a way to defend myself," Hagen said, "that damned ledger of mine is the only thing keeping me alive. Now tell me who was here with me. Please!"

"You were by yourself a good bit of the time," Trammel told him. "I checked in on you when I could, and so did Hawkeye. Emily saw you several times a day. Otherwise, your door was locked."

"What about my father?"

Trammel's eyes narrowed. "What about him?"

"Was he here with me? When I was delirious, I mean?" He wasn't sure Trammel knew what *delirious* meant, so he added, "When I was babbling, I mean."

"He was only here the night you got shot and the day after when the doctors came up from Laramie. The room was pretty crowded with the doctors and your father, so I wasn't here then. Why?"

Hagen's clearing mind was too flooded with questions to provide any answers. "Did the Pinkerton men ever come to town?"

"No sign of them," Trammel told him. "I

haven't heard anything about them being in Laramie, either, but that doesn't mean they aren't there. They could already be back in Chicago for all we know." After a pause, he continued, "You're going to need to settle down or you're going to pull out some of Emily's fine stitch work."

"This is not the time for settling down." The fog of the last few days confused him as he tried to find a way to push the right words out. "I need you to do something for me. Something for the both of us, really."

"You're breaking into a sweat. Now you either take it easy or I'm not doing anything for you."

Hagen felt the room begin to spin. Trammel was right. He was no good to anyone if he passed out again. There was too much that needed to be done. "I need you to listen very carefully to what I'm about to say. My father wasn't here out of any paternal concern. He didn't bring those doctors here from Laramie to save my life. He brought them here because he was trying to get me to tell him where I hid the ledger."

Trammel sat in the chair next to the bed. "That's a pretty low thing to accuse him of, Adam. I don't like the man any more than you do, but he came by the jail the night you were shot. I could tell he was genuinely worried about you."

"Worried, perhaps, but not about me. It was about what might happen to the ledger if I died before telling him where it was."

The more he spoke, the more he could feel his mind begin to clear. But with clarity came a growing pain from his shoulder. He spoke through it. "I know you and I haven't been on good terms lately, Buck. I know you disapprove of my opium business and feeding laudanum to my customers, but I never force anyone to do anything they aren't willing to do and pay handsomely to do. I don't have hawkers pulling people in, and the customers have to ask for laudanum. That's why I've been able to keep the reprobates from getting out of hand in town. I would make a lot more money if I actively sought out new customers."

Trammel crossed his arms across his chest. "Yeah, I know. That's why I've allowed you to keep up that side of your business. But what does that have to do with your father or the ledger?"

"The contents of the ledger will give him the power I'm beginning to build. If I died without telling him, he might never find it. Yes, the threat I pose would go away, as it would if I'm just a cripple. But if he has the ledger, he can control the entire territory and what happens to me doesn't matter."

The expression on Trammel's face changed. "Adam, he asked you about where you hid it, didn't he?"

"I think so." Hagen shut his eyes and tried to remember, but all he could hear was an echo of mumbled voices seeming to blend into one. The voice of Charles Hagen. "I think I told him I kept it in my office at the Pot of Gold."

Trammel ran his hand across his broad jaw. "You really think he'd sink that low? To question you about it while you were on your deathbed?"

"Of course." Hagen managed a smile. "The closer we are to death, the closer we are to the truth. What better time to get me to open up than while I'm in a stupor — at my weakest?"

The look on Trammel's face showed that he wasn't so sure.

Hagen could feel the desperation beginning to build in his chest, which only served to feed the pain. "Maybe you're right. Maybe it was just nightmares. But maybe it was real. I can't be sure, and since I'm in no condition to walk over to the saloon and check my office for myself, I need you to do it for me. See if he went there looking for the ledger himself."

Trammel seemed to think it over. "You realize you're asking me to help you find the one thing that's keeping your criminal enterprise going."

"I'm asking you to make sure it's safe. It's the only thing keeping the wolves from devouring both of us. That ledger is the only reason why Clay pulled his men off you last spring in Laramie. It's the reason why I keep him and the rest of the officials in this territory from pulling me down and this town along with it. Your exploits have made as many enemies in Laramie as my opium trade. The entries I've kept making in that ledger are our best insurance policy against our demise."

"That's a pretty big stretch, Adam."

"The people who shot at us were desperate men in over their heads, looking for money. If Clay or my father get their hands on that ledger, they get the power that comes along with it, and they can do with us what they will. And that's not good for either of us."

Trammel stood up and walked over to the window. Hagen was not sure what he was looking at, since the window only looked out on a narrow alley. Maybe he was thinking. Hagen hoped he was thinking the right way.

Trammel turned back to Hagen. "Since you put it that way, I'll walk over to the Pot of Gold and look for it. But say I don't find it. Where else should I look?"

Hagen laughed, and the pain that shot through his body made him immediately regret it. "Nice try, Sheriff. I didn't say I actually kept it there. I said I think I told Father I kept it there. Just look at my office and see if it looks like anyone has rifled through it. You know how neat I am, so you should be able to see if anyone has been careless."

"And if they haven't?"

"Then all of this has been nothing more than the fever dreams of a cripple," Hagen said. "But if I'm right, you and I have to keep a closer eye on Father than ever before."

Trammel stepped away from the window and stood over Hagen's bed. "You don't keep the ledger there, do you?"

Hagen trusted him, but only so far. "Check the office, Buck. For both of our sakes, especially since your Pinkerton friends may still have a role to play in all of this."

Trammel moved to the door. "I'll take a look and let you know if I find anything. Is it open or do I need a key?"

"Check the top drawer of the dresser there," Hagen said. "You'll find a key in there."

Trammel checked in the drawer and, indeed, found a key, which he took. "In the meantime, I'll let Emily know you're awake. She'll probably check in on you in a while."

"But do not tell Father," Hagen warned. "Not under any circumstance. I know he will find out eventually, but let that happen on its own. I don't want him knowing until he has to."

The sheriff opened the door. "You're not a trusting man, Adam."

"Knowing who to trust and who to suspect has kept me alive this long." He smiled. "I trusted you and look at where that got me."

"Rest. I'll be back in a while."

Before heading up the street to Hagen's office at the Pot of Gold, Trammel stopped by the jail to check in on a couple other people in town.

Emily was back in the cells taking care of Somerset's injuries, while poor Hawkeye sat with his head on the desk. He still had not recovered from the head wound he had received during the shoot-out the week before.

Emily had originally thought his only

wounds were from the cuts and the splinters, but as time had shown, he had rattled his brain when he hit the chair. He was still dizzy, and his vision went double every so often. Emily had told him bed rest was the best medicine for him, Trammel had even gone as far as to order him to stay in bed, but the young man was stubborn. Although he was not steady enough on his feet to go on patrol, he insisted on staying in the jail to keep an eye on the prisoner.

Trammel hoped the kid got better soon. He was a tough young man, and the sheriff was confident that he might become a hell of a lawman someday if he lived long enough. He just hoped the boy's brain healed quickly. He had known plenty of men who were never right after a hard knock to the head. He did not peg Hawkeye as the type who could live with that kind of infirmity.

Just like he did not think Hagen could live with being a cripple.

"Morning, Sheriff." Hawkeye tried to stand when Trammel walked into the jailhouse, but quickly sat down again as another bout of dizziness took him.

"What did I tell you about getting up?" Trammel checked the bucket Hawkeye kept by the desk for the moments when the dizziness upset his stomach. For the first time in days, it was empty. "How are you feeling?"

The young deputy put on the bravest face he could. "Haven't gotten sick once today, Sheriff. I'd call that progress."

Trammel knew head injuries could take a long time to clear, if ever, but he took a clean bucket as a sign of progress. "Keep up the good work. Is Miss Emily seeing to the prisoner?"

"She's all done," Emily Downs said as she stepped out from the cells carrying her medical bag. "The prisoner is healing quite nicely, for what it's worth. Seems to have broken the fingers on his left hand somehow. Any idea how it happened?"

Trammel fondly remembered rapping him on the hand with the pistol of his Colt when he threatened to talk about Adam not being a Hagen. "He tell you anything?"

"No," Emily admitted. "Claims he must've rolled over on them in his sleep."

Trammel was glad the Pinkerton man was keeping his silence. "Well, you can forget about Somerset's problems for a bit, because I've got some news that should brighten your spirits for a change. Adam is awake, and it looks like it's for good this time."

Emily clapped, and Hawkeye cheered before getting dizzy again.

"His fever was so high," Emily recalled, "I was worried he might never recover."

"He's recovered just fine. I told him you'd be in to see him in a bit." Trammel walked with her outside, but asked her to slow down as soon as they got clear of the jail.

"What's wrong?" she asked.

Trammel was still bothered by what Hagen had said about his father. "You took care of Adam most of the time he was sick, didn't you?"

"Me and Mrs. Welch split the duties during the day, yes. Why?"

"Do you remember if his father spent a lot of time in his room?"

"He was there when the fever got high," Emily told him. "He insisted on taking care of him, even when we couldn't. It was quite a relief for us at the time. When the doctors went back to Laramie, care for Adam fell entirely on us."

Trammel winced. There may be something to Hagen's concerns about his father and the ledger after all. "Yeah, I'm sure it was."

"Why do you look so sad, Buck?" Emily placed a hand on his arm. "Adam's awake now. That's good news. Why, even if he can't use his arm, it looks like he'll live and that's a cause for happiness, isn't it?" She frowned again. "I certainly hope you're not allowing your petty differences about his other businesses dampen your enthusiasm for his well-being."

"Far from it," he assured her. A part of him wanted to tell her everything Charles Hagen had told him about Adam not being his son. It would have been easier to share the knowledge with someone. But the secret was not his to share, not even with Adam, so it was his burden to bear alone. "He asked me to go to his office and get him some things."

"See?" She pecked Trammel on the cheek and went off on her way to tend to Adam. "He has only been awake for a few minutes and he's already looking to get back to work. I bet he'll be using that arm in no time!"

But the sheriff's smile faded as he watched her hurry to Hagen's bedside. Because he was not just concerned about Adam Hagen's arm. It was his ledger.

And what it might mean if someone had searched the office for it.

CHAPTER 21

At the Pot of Gold, the bartender hovered near Trammel like a hummingbird as the sheriff used Hagen's key to open the office door.

"This is highly irregular," Ben Springfield said. "I know you're the sheriff and all, but I don't like the idea of you going through his things without Mr. Adam Hagen hisself bein' here." It was almost as though he was afraid of what Trammel might find inside.

Trammel felt his patience begin to fail him. "Who do you think gave me the key? Now get back behind the bar where you belong and quit causing trouble." He waited until Springfield reluctantly went back to work before venturing into the office.

Using only the long rectangle of light that filtered into the office from the bar outside, Trammel had no trouble seeing someone had been there since Adam had left it before the shooting.

The chair behind the desk had been carelessly pulled aside. The items on the shelves had been hastily shoved aside during what could only be described as a frantic search for something. Papers Trammel remembered being arranged in a neat pile had been toppled over on the desk and spilled out onto the floor.

It was obvious that someone had done a sloppy job of searching the place, probably because they did not care about getting caught. And they did not care if Hagen or anyone else found the mess. By then, it wouldn't matter. Either Adam would be dead or the ledger would have been found. Either way, the need for secrecy would be over.

But nothing was over as far as Trammel was concerned. Not until he knew if the ledger was safe.

He struck a Lucifer and lit an oil lamp by the door, which cast a better light on Hagen's ruined office.

He shut the door to keep Springfield and the nosy saloon customers from seeing too much and began to move around to the back of Hagen's desk. The more he looked, the worse the scene became. All of the drawers had been pulled out of the desk; their contents dumped onto the floor before the drawers were cast aside in a pile in a corner of the room. The large bottom drawer that looked like a door had been kicked in.

Trammel bent and shined the lamp inside. The space was empty. No sign of the ledger. Even the bottle and glasses he knew Hagen kept there had been taken. It seemed odd to him that someone would steal a bottle of whiskey in the office of a saloon of all places. Maybe the thief or thieves had celebrated finding what they were looking for?

As he imagined the desk would be the first place the thief had looked, he supposed the rest of the wreckage was a result of the frustration of not finding the ledger.

He cast his lamp around the ruined office and saw no other signs of any disturbance. No signs of the whiskey bottle or the broken glasses, either.

Trammel had investigated his share of robberies when he had been with the police in Manhattan and later with the Pinkerton Agency. He could not remember a case where thieves had done all of this damage just for a couple of swigs of whiskey.

He could also not remember a time when the empty glasses and bottles hadn't been found anywhere at the scene, either. Trammel swept his boot through the contents of the desk that had been scattered on the floor and listened for that brittle sound of glass being shifted.

He heard nothing.

He held the lamp beside the ruined bottom drawer to see if the glasses and bottle might've been broken when someone kicked in the drawer. But there was no sign of broken glass or spilled whiskey inside there, either.

Who would set about ransacking an office, but not break the glasses and bottles inside the bottom drawer? Not even by accident?

Trammel had the answer almost as soon as he asked the question. Someone who knew they would be there. Someone who knew enough to be careful not to break them. Someone who had been in the office before, perhaps many times.

That ruled out Charles Hagen, but not someone else.

Trammel locked the office door behind him and blew out the lamp. He would not need it where he was going.

Ben Springfield was back behind the bar leafing through the morning edition of the *Blackstone Bugle*. A few men were seated at the tables, playing cards and sipping beer.

Springfield did not bother to look up from his paper when he heard Trammel stomping his way. "You done with your snoopin', Sheriff?"

Trammel snatched him by the collar and yanked him over the bar. The few patrons still in the saloon either scattered or kept their mouths shut as the big sheriff pinned Springfield against the bar.

"Damn it, Trammel. You've got no cause to treat me like this."

"I'm going to ask you this one time," the sheriff said. "I catch you lying, I take to backhanding you from one end of this bar to the other. Understand?"

Wide-eyed in terror, Springfield nodded his head quickly.

"Why did you tear apart Adam's office?"

"Someone did that? Why —"

Trammel brought his big hand back to strike him, and Springfield began to shout, "Don't hit me, damn it! I admit it! I did it!"

Trammel lowered his hand. "That's good, Ben. Now tell me *why* you did it."

"Because I had no reason not to," Springfield said. "Everyone thought Hagen was going to die. What else was I supposed to do? Just wait until it actually happened before gettin' what I've got comin' to me? That lousy friend of yours drove me out of business. Hell, Sheriff, I used to own this place. Now I just work here with a measly cut of the profits, which don't count them opium tents in the back. No, sir. He keeps what them Chinese fellas give him all to his ownself."

Trammel hadn't been certain Springfield had robbed the office until that moment, but it made sense. He was the only one who probably had a key to the office or had enough time to get one made. He could have searched the office during off-hours when fewer people were around to notice what he was doing. There was no question in his mind that Springfield was behind it.

No, another question was more important. The sheriff's grip on Springfield's collar tightened. "Who put you up to it? And don't tell me you did it on your own. I won't believe that and you know what happens then."

Springfield moaned as the sheriff had finally managed to hit the truth. Trammel's right hand flinched backward and the bartender began to tell all that he knew.

"John Bookman paid me to do it," the bartender said quickly. "He showed up here one night around closin' right after Hagen got shot. Don't go askin' me which night it was, because I don't remember for certain.

He told me he wanted me to let him inside. He figured I had some old keys lying around back from when I owned the place. But Mr. Hagen changed out the lock on the office door when he took over and never saw fit to give me a copy. He wanted to kick in the door, but I wouldn't let him leave me with that mess. He said he'd come back with the key and get in there himself."

Trammel knew the answer to his own question. "But you had a key, didn't you?"

"Sure did," Springfield admitted. "Had two made when Adam only wanted one. I couldn't get in there when he was inside, but I went in there whenever he wasn't around. Seein' as how badly Bookman wanted in there, I knew there had to be something worthwhile in there and I didn't want him finding it first."

Trammel had figured that had been the case. *Bookman. Who works for King Charles.* Adam had been right after all. It was not just a dream. They had been pumping him for information while he was recovering from the gunshot wound. He was fighting for his life and his arm, but all they cared about was that damnable ledger. Adam might not be Charles's son, but he was still blood. He deserved better than that from an uncle and the only father he had ever known.

The sheriff shook Springfield. "You broke into the office alone, didn't you?"

"Damned right I did," he eagerly admitted. "Went in nice and gentlelike, so much so that Adam himself wouldn't have known I was there. Even got the desk drawers open with a couple of hairpins from the girls upstairs so no one would know I was even there."

That explained quite a bit. "And all you found was the whiskey in the bottom drawer."

"Found plenty more than that," Springfield said. "Not that any of it did me any good, on account of me never learnin' how to read."

"That so?" Trammel snatched him hard by the collar. "Then why did I see you reading the newspaper on the bar just now?"

"Leafin' through it and readin' it are two different things," Springfield protested. "Ask anyone. I don't know how to read. Hell, Denny Stack had to keep my books for me when I ran the place."

Too obvious a lie for a man like Springfield to make, Trammel released him with a shove. Keeping his focus on what had happened in the office, the sheriff said, "But you knew Adam kept whiskey in the bottom drawer of his desk."

"Yes, sir," Springfield said, "and I'd be damned before I let John Bookman or anyone else have it. Adam raved how good t was, and as he was near death anyway, I took it for my ownself. Finest whiskey I ever tasted."

Trammel didn't much care about the quality of Hagen's taste in whiskey just then. He cared about the state of the office. "So that mess in there was created by Bookman when he searched it after you?"

"Yes, sir. I begged him not to make a mess, but he told me that was my problem. He was awful forceful about it, but I don't think he found what he was looking for, on account of him bein' angry and trashin' the place."

Trammel could imagine Bookman losing his temper like that. "Did he tell you what he was looking for?"

"Kept sayin' somethin' about a ledger," Springfield told him. "Said he needed to find it. I told him where they were but old Mr. Bookman still wasn't satisfied. He was just kept getting' angrier and angrier until he turned that room into a whirlwind of paper. Never saw a man get so angry without someone gettin' dead right after."

"And why didn't you clean it up?"

"On account of Mr. Bookman telling me it wasn't necessary to go through the fuss. He said Adam was nearer to death's door than he was to living and that all of his possessions would belong to King Charles soon. We could worry about cleaning it up later. Until then, I was to keep the bar running and not tell anyone about what happened here."

That didn't make any sense to Trammel. Adam had no love of his father and he doubted he would leave any of his properties to him in his will. "You're absolutely sure you don't know when this happened?"

Springfield thought on it further. "About four days ago. Right after Adam went and got himself shot."

"And when did Bookman tell you he was going to be taking over Adam's businesses?"

"Said it would be about a week at the most before Adam died and things changed over to King Charles. I don't know how he figured out that number, but he was so damned angry when he up and stormed out of here that he wasn't of a mind to tell me more."

Trammel took a step back as the facts fell into place for him. Adam had been shot more than four days ago. A week could mean five days or seven, depending on the way a man wanted to look at it.

Either way, the deadline Bookman had mentioned to Springfield was coming up soon if not already passed. Whatever he was planning to do must be close at hand.

Adam Hagen was in more danger than he thought, especially now that he was alive.

Trammel ignored the looks he drew from the patrons as he bolted from the Pot of Gold Saloon and along Main Street, back toward the Clifford Hotel.

CHAPTER 22

Trammel knew Adam was in trouble when he reached the hall to Hagen's room and found the door half open. He pushed it all the way open and found John Bookman struggling to keep a pillow over Adam Hagen's face. The wounded man was putting up the best fight he could, given that he was fighting off his attacker with one arm wrapped in bandages as Bookman put all of his weight on the pillow.

From behind, Trammel fired a left hook around Bookman's shoulder that connected with his jaw. He pulled him off Hagen and followed it up with a right cross that sent the ramrod stumbling backward until he crashed into the dresser.

Bookman regained his balance and threw a quick roundhouse right that mostly hit Trammel's shoulder and didn't slow the big lawman down. He grabbed Bookman by the shirt and tossed him into the hallway.

Bookman hit the wall hard enough to lose his balance and fall to the floor. Trammel closed the distance before Bookman could get to his feet. The ranch boss got to his knees and buried furious lefts and rights in Trammel's chest and belly, but the sheriff used his elbows to block most of them.

When Trammel did throw a punch, it was an uppercut that connected with Bookman's jaw and snapped his head back. He landed hard on his backside and cried out from the pain. He reached for the gun on his hip, but Trammel stepped on his arm and pinned it to the floor. "That's enough, Bookman."

The foreman roared as he tried to move Trammel's leg, but found he did not have the strength to budge it.

Trammel put more weight on the arm. "I said it's over, damn it. Quit reaching for the gun and tell me who sent you and why."

"Why do you think, you idiot?" Bookman said through clenched teeth. "Not even you can be that dumb."

Trammel had an idea, but he needed Bookman to tell him first. He needed Adam to hear it, too, assuming he was still alive. "Tell me and I'll let you get up. If not, you wake up in jail with a broken arm. Your choice."

Bookman laughed despite the pain. "I

made my choice a long time ago. I chose Charles Hagen to be King Charles of the Wyoming Territory and I haven't had a complaint since. Not you or his illegitimate nephew in there can ever make me regret that choice. Not one damned bit."

Trammel leaned hard on Bookman's arm. "Shut up, damn you."

Bookman shouted through the pain. "You hear that, Adam? I was there the night you were pulled kicking and screaming into this world. I'm the one who tied the rope around your father's neck — your real father — and gave him to the wolves after it was all over."

Bookman pointed with his free hand toward Hagen's room and lowered his voice. "I should've done the same thing to him. That monster in there has been nothing but a disgrace to the family since the day he was born. I was ready to smother it back then if Mr. Hagen had let me, but he'd promised his sister he'd watch out for it. And all it has done is brought pain and misery to everyone who has tried to love it ever since. All you caught me doing tonight, Sheriff, was something I should've done thirty years ago.

Trammel brought his boot across Bookman's face, knocking the man out. The sheriff bent and took the gun from Bookman's holster and the knife he kept in his boot. He patted him down, but failed to find any other weapons. He stood up when he heard what could only be described as whimpering coming from Hagen's room and wondered if his stitches had come undone in his struggle with Bookman.

He rushed into the room and dumped Bookman's weapons in a chair by the bed before tending to his friend. He tucked the pillow back behind Adam's head and a quick check of the bandages showed no new spots of blood.

But the tears on his friend's face told him the wounds he suffered now were not the kind that could be bandaged or sewn together. At least not by any surgeon Trammel could name.

The sheriff sat on the edge of the bed. "I guess you heard all that."

"Every single word of it," Hagen said through the tears. "I suppose I always knew the truth in the back of my mind, but lacked the courage to ask the questions myself. All of those years. All of that anger. All of the lies. If I had known he was my uncle all along, at least I would have understood the hatred and resentment. I caused the death of his sister, for God's sake. I would have at least been able to see why he treated me like that. But to wander around wondering what I'd done to anger him so? All those years wasted on hating myself, I —"

"Stop!" Trammel could see his friend spiraling down into a black hole and knew he needed to stop it. "You can't do much about what's already been done, Adam. All you can do is face today, then maybe tomorrow, if you're lucky. Who you were yesterday doesn't matter much. Who you are today means everything. You're a full-grown man, no matter what your last name really is. You get to decide what happens from here on out. From this moment. Right now. Are you a Hagen, a cripple, or a saloon owner? A friend or an enemy? You can't choose your blood, Adam. You can only choose the man you decide to be."

He stood up and checked on Bookman. The ramrod was still unconscious in the hall and hadn't shown signs of moving.

Hagen wiped away the tears with his sleeve. "What brought you back here so quickly? Had anyone searched my office?"

"You were right," Trammel said, hoping it would make him feel better. "I found out Bookman was working with Springfield to break into your office and look for the ledger. All they got was a bottle of whiskey. Springfield got it anyway. He went in first on account of him not wanting Bookman to get it."

Hagen laughed as he continued to wipe his face with his sleeve. "Springfield always was a weasel. I knew he had a second key made for the new lock, which was why I never kept anything important there. I hope he liked the whiskey, though."

"Springfield said it was the best he ever tasted."

"As long as someone enjoyed it. If he's smart, he'll be out of town before my feet hit the floor. It'll save me the trouble of shooting him for treachery." Adam looked at Trammel with reddened eyes. "And I don't expect any trouble from you when I do. None of this murder or manslaughter nonsense. If anyone has a bullet coming, it's that weasel Springfield."

Trammel ignored Hagen's threats against the bartender's life. "You didn't ask me if Bookman found the ledger."

"That's because I know he didn't," Hagen said. "And I didn't tell you they would. I said they'd most likely look for it in my office because I believed that's what I told Father in my stupor. In reality, I keep the ledger much closer to home. And don't bother asking where because I won't tell you."

"I don't need to know where it is," Trammel said, "but I'd like to know how you were able to send them on a wild-goose chase while you were half out of your mind with fever."

"I was full out of my mind with fever," Hagen corrected, "and I have no answers on that score. I just as easily could have told them where it actually was instead of in my office. But, at least one thing is certain. We know Father's true intentions toward me and how much he despises me."

He caught himself. "I suppose I should stop calling him that. He's not really my father. More like my uncle, if anything." His eyes got soft and drifted up toward the ceiling. "Yes. My *uncle.* That explains quite a bit, doesn't it?"

Realizing there wasn't much he could say to make his friend feel better, Trammel decided it was best if he left. "I'm going to run Bookman over to the jail and begin the paperwork on his arrest. He'll be away for at least five years for what he did here today. I don't think Mr. Hagen will do much to help him this time."

"Don't be so sure," Hagen said from his fog. "Bookman's been doing the ranch's dirty work for more than thirty years. You've already had one standoff with 'Mr. Hagen' over Bookman, and that was with three of us standing against him. With me laid up and Hawkeye unable to even stand, you're in no position to hold off another siege from . . . the ranch. Get Bookman down to Laramie immediately. My *uncle* will not be able to lay siege to that jail. Sheriff Moran is nobody's boy, least of all a loyal subject of King Charles the First." Hagen closed his eyes. "And, if I have anything to do with it, the Last."

Trammel knew Hagen's plan made sense, but he still did not like it. It was true the new sheriff of Laramie, Rob Moran, was an honest and tough man with his own crew of new deputies, but Charles Hagen was still one of the most powerful men in the territory, certainly in that part of it, anyway. He could easily influence a judge to set Bookman free, which Moran would be powerless to prevent.

Bookman's groans snapped Trammel out of his own thoughts and he had to make a decision quickly. "I don't like the idea of leaving you unprotected."

"They've no reason to kill me now that I know the truth. Bookman was acting to protect my father, not on his orders, or he would have brought more men with him. Don't waste time worrying about me. You must get Bookman to Laramie without delay. And after you drop him off with Sheriff Moran, be sure you swing by Judge Bishop's place. Let him know the nature of the charges against Bookman. Particularly his assault against me."

Trammel knew there were three judges in Laramie. "Why Bishop?"

"Because he has several lines in my ledger and knows it is in his best interest to deny bail to anyone who has attacked me. You're not to say that to him, of course. The implication of the threat should suffice."

That made sense to Trammel, except for one concern. "I've never really had the knack for being subtle."

"Fortunately for both of us, I do." Hagen nodded toward the door. "Quickly, before news of Bookman's arrest reaches the ranch and they send men to stop you. You can be there and back within a matter of hours."

Trammel headed out into the hall and took hold of Bookman as the prisoner got to his feet. The sheriff turned back to Hagen. "I'll send someone over here to keep an eye on you."

"Let me worry about me. You just get him behind bars as soon as possible. And don't forget about the Pinkerton men. They may already be in Laramie when you get there."

Trammel grumbled as he steered Book-
nan toward the front door of the hotel.
'The Pinkertons. How could I ever forget
:he damned Pinkertons?"

CHAPTER 23

Trammel and Hawkeye had tied Bookman's feet in the stirrups and his hands to the pommel of his saddle before leading his horse behind Trammel's on the trail south to Laramie. The ramrod was still dizzy from the blow he had received that had rendered him unconscious. Having a hard time staying upright in the saddle, his bindings kept him from falling over several times.

"You can untie these ropes now," Bookman said when he had regained his senses. "I don't need any help staying mounted anymore."

Trammel ignored him and kept the mounts moving at the same pace.

Bookman was not as cordial a second time. "Damn you, Trammel, I said untie me. I was riding a horse a long time before you ever saw one, you damned city boy."

"You might give the orders on the Blackstone Ranch, Bookman, but we're not on the Blackstone Ranch right now. You're under arrest, and we're headed to Laramie, where you're going to spend the next three to five years doing hard labor. Best save your wind for the courtroom. You're going to need every puff you can muster."

Bookman didn't seem to have any intention of quieting down. "What did I ever do to you, anyway? The only problem between us has been over Adam Hagen. Hell, I gave you that star on your chest."

"Sheriff Bonner gave it to me before he skipped town," Trammel said. "And you and I didn't have a problem until you stuck a gun against my head in your boss's office."

"I did that on Mr. Hagen's orders. I had no choice. I warned him against the notion before you even got there, but he wouldn't listen. You've got the old man spooked, Sheriff. Really spooked. I've worked for King Charles for upwards of thirty years and I've never seen anyone get to him like you have. You've got him talking to himself and losing sleep. Hell, he ordered me to draw on you, boy. It wasn't even my choice."

"I don't care who gave you the order," Trammel said over his shoulder. "You decided to do it and that's what makes it personal."

"But I had no choice," Bookman said.

"That was business."

"So is this. Now shut your mouth for the rest of the way, or I swear I'll gag you."

They rode together in silence along the well-worn Laramie Road. The sky was just beginning to think about changing over to darkness, but Trammel figured they would be in town before it finally did.

Bookman didn't appear to be in the mood to appreciate the coming sunset. "You want an apology? Is that it?"

"I don't want anything from you, Bookman. So shut your mouth."

"Well, whether or not you want one, you're getting one," Bookman sneered. "I'm sorry. Sorry I didn't pull the trigger on you when I had the chance."

"No you're not." Trammel glanced back at him. "But you will be."

Sheriff Rob Moran was a big man, though not as big as Trammel. Few men were. But few men made Trammel feel as inadequate as Moran did. Even from his time on the Metropolitan Police back in Manhattan, Trammel always felt like he was a goon playing a lawman. He enforced the law, if you could call beating people up police work, more through his strength and size than any intelligence or style.

Rob Moran was a lawman through and through. At just over six feet and a few years over thirty, Moran was one of those lawmen who had not hit his prime yet, and would be a formidable presence in town for decades. He had been brought to town from Abilene by the Laramie Businessmen's Association several months before and had handily won election over the previous sheriff who had openly been in Lucien Clay's pocket.

Moran was no one's man, however, and had a reputation for being as fair with the law as he was in handling a gun. He was the kind of lawman every town in this part of the country wanted, but few had. He was the kind of lawman Trammel wished he could be, but knew he never would.

The sheriff of Laramie did not look happy as he read over the hastily written report Trammel had given him. Moran's hat sat crown down on the corner of his desk. His jet-black hair was just beginning to show specks of gray at the temples.

Trammel imagined he still had a few years before he started showing gray, but did not care if his hair turned orange as long as he had the chance to keep it. His father had been as bald as a bean, and he hoped the same fate did not await him. He flattened down that hair as he watched Moran finish reading his report.

"I must tell you this is a highly irregular request, Trammel," the sheriff said as he set the report aside. "Usually we make arrangements in advance for the arrival of prisoners. You're lucky we had enough space for this Bookman character or else I'd have had no choice but to ask you to take him back with you to Blackstone."

"Then I count myself lucky."

Moran sat back in his chair. "I've heard about your run-in with Mr. Hagen last week and those damnable bounty hunters who shot up Adam and your deputy. Is that why you were in such a hurry to bring Bookman down here?"

"It's part of it," Trammel admitted. "They're the best shots I've got and, with the two of them laid up, I'm the only able-bodied gun in town. The shopkeepers mean well, but I can't give them too free of a hand or they'll kick the hell out of the saloon patrons. Since the drunks and the ramblers like to spend money, too, I'm trying to strike a delicate balance."

Moran set his elbows on the arms of his chair and folded his hands across his flat belly. "You sure this was a good time to go picking a fight with a man like Mr. Hagen,

Buck? King Charles has a lot of friends in this part of the world."

"He's got a lot of people he owns," Trammel said. "There's a difference when loyalty comes at a price."

"Loyalty always does." Moran smiled. "You know, you're building quite a reputation for yourself as a gunfighter."

"Don't remind me." Trammel didn't smile. "It's not by choice, believe me."

"I know, but you're getting that reputation nonetheless. I heard about some of that bounty hunter talk here in town and did my best to clamp down on it. I think I may have saved you some grief by running some of the braggarts out of town, but it's the professionals you have to worry about. You can see the amateurs coming from a mile away, but the professionals know enough to stay quiet until the shooting starts."

"It was amateurs that put Adam Hagen down," Trammel pointed out. "We're still not sure if he'll be able to keep the arm, much less use it again."

"I heard that from his doctors when they came back to town." He pointed at Trammel's report. "It doesn't match up with what you write here. If you think Mr. Hagen sent Bookman to kill his own son, then why did he go through all the trouble of trying to save him when he got shot? It just doesn't make any sense to me."

It would make plenty of sense if you knew they were only keeping him alive to question him about the ledger, Trammel thought, but dared not say. He imagined Moran had probably heard rumors about the ledger since becoming sheriff of Laramie, but Trammel had no intention of confirming them. The fewer people who knew the damned thing actually existed, the fewer who would come looking for it, which would make Blackstone a safer place.

"Mr. Hagen's a strange man," Trammel said. "I don't know if Bookman tried to kill Adam on his own or on orders from his boss. All I know is that I caught him trying to smother Adam with a pillow after he busted up his office looking for something. I suppose the rest of the facts will come out at trial."

"That's what trials are for," Moran agreed. "But you're the biggest mystery in this whole thing as far as I'm concerned."

"Me?" Trammel was genuinely surprised. "Why?"

"Because you spent half a day running Bookman down here when you know Mr. Hagen's going to send one of his men to talk to a judge and get him sprung before dinnertime. Hell, I expect a Hagen man to come walking through that door any moment and demand we take Bookman before a judge to release him right now. I'm surprised one of them didn't beat you here."

Trammel decided to test one of Adam's theories. "Is Judge Bishop in charge this week?"

"This entire month," Moran corrected him. "And he's been known to be partial to ruling in Mr. Hagen's favor in the past. I see no reason why he wouldn't do so in this case."

"You leave that to me." Trammel stood and Moran stood with him. "The judge in his office upstairs?"

"Didn't see him leave, so I suppose he is. Why?"

"Just want to have a word with him is all." He held out his hand to Moran, who eagerly took it. "Thanks for taking Bookman for me, Rob. I know he's in good hands with you and your men."

"He is until a judge cuts loose of him," Moran said. "After that, it won't matter how good my hands are."

Trammel already knew that. "I appreciate it just the same."

As he turned to leave, Moran stopped him by saying, "There's something else, Buck. It

301

goes to what we were talking about earlier . . . about bounty hunters. There are some Pinkerton men in town."

Trammel stopped, but didn't turn around. "What?"

"Been here a little less than a week," Moran explained. "They set up shop over at Lucien Clay's new place. The Molly Malone."

"How many of them?"

"An even dozen near as I've been able to figure. Thirteen if you count the man running them. He's a man who goes by the name of Jesse Alcott. Ever heard of him?"

Trammel closed his eyes. He remembered the man and the name from the train ride out to Laramie from Ogallala last spring. The same man he had humiliated on the train was in town, leading a posse of trained killers come to finish him off. "Yeah, I know him."

"Was a riverboat gunman on the Mississippi back when I first heard of him. As nasty with a gun as he was with a knife, near as I can remember."

Trammel only remembered the man being on his hands and knees on the floor of a train car six months before. He was certain Alcott remembered it, too.

"They say what they're in town for?"

"That's why I'm mentioning it," Moran said. "They haven't said why they're here, but I'd imagine it's got something to do with you. I heard Mr. Hagen had Mr. Montague buy them off, but I don't know if the word reached them before they got here. What I do know is that they've been spending a lot of time at Lucien's places. Throwing out rowdies and the like. Have to admit they've been a good bunch to have around. I've only got four deputies, and with the Pinkerton men minding the town, we're able to cater to the problems in the areas outside of town we can't always get to. Rustlers, things like that."

"Yeah." Trammel tried to fight down the bile rising in his throat. "Rustlers."

Trammel's worst fears were coming true. Clay and the Pinkerton men were working together. He had no idea what it might be, but whatever it was, would probably involve Blackstone before long. "Thanks for telling me, Rob."

"I'd advise you to head back to Blackstone as soon as you can," Moran said, "and be sure to watch your back trail when you do. I don't know what kind of arrangement Clay is cooking up with Alcott and those Pinkerton men. I'm not saying you can't go near any of Clay's places. I'm just saying it might

303

not be a good idea is all."

"I appreciate you looking out for me, Rob. I sincerely do."

Moran sat back down. "Hell, Buck. I'm not asking you to stay away for your sake. I'm asking you to stay away for their sake. You're liable to kill those boys, and I could do without the dead bodies."

Trammel smiled as he left the office and walked upstairs to Judge Bishop's chambers.

"How dare you, sir!" Judge James K. Bishop thundered at Trammel after he had delivered Adam Hagen's message. "Do you have any idea who you're speaking to? You are not speaking to a man right now, sir. You are speaking to a *judge.* One who has taken an oath to interpret the law. The very embodiment of justice in all of its forms. One who —"

"Whose name appears in a ledger listing numerous illegal activities." Tired of getting yelled at, Trammel continued. "A ledger that shows how much he charges for an acquittal or a bail hearing or a guilty verdict, depending on who is paying the fee. A ledger that shows you ruling favorably for every wealthy rancher and landowner in this territory when they met your price and against them when they didn't."

Trammel didn't know if any of what he was saying was true, but from the look on Bishop's face, at least some of what he had just said made the judge worry, so he kept going. "A ledger that shows you've got a real cozy relationship with Charles Hagen. It would be a real shame if someone from the press got hold of the information in that ledger. Some could say it would end your career, maybe land you behind bars in your own jail with some of the men you stuck there."

Bishop, a small round grayish man with a perpetual sneer, laughed. "If Madam Pinochet has not been able to pull me off this bench, sonny, I doubt a one-armed gambler from Blackstone will be able to do it. And yes, I know all about Adam Hagen's injuries. I'm only sorry one of those pellets didn't hit his heart."

"It's a mighty small target," Trammel admitted. "And there is a big difference between Madam Pinochet and Hagen. He's free. She's not. And unless you want your wife to read about every dirty secret you have in the morning paper, I would advise you to do what Adam says and deny bail to John Bookman under any circumstances. You would be justified, based on the types of charges I have leveled at him. And the charges will hold up in court." Trammel pointed at him. "Your court, Your Honor."

"I refuse to be blackmailed by you or anyone else." Bishop pounded his desk and pointed at the door. "Get out of here before I have the bailiff take you into custody."

Trammel stood slowly so the judge could fully appreciate the difference in their sizes. The corrupt jurist took a few steps back and fell into his chair.

"You do what you want, Your Honor. But if you grant Bookman bail, you'd better resign and leave the county right after or you'll find yourself in the same cell Bookman just vacated."

The judge continued to yell at him as he left his office and began walking downstairs.

Trammel was not happy to find Sheriff Moran and one of his deputies waiting for him at the base of the stairs. Did Judge Bishop have some kind of bell he rang under his desk to signal the deputies he needed help? He didn't know what they wanted, but was glad his coat was open and his Peacemaker within easy reach under his left arm. He hoped it did not come to that. "What's wrong, Rob? Miss me already?"

"It's not me who misses you," Moran said. "Our famous prisoner has requested an audience with you, Buck. Madam Pinochet would like to have a word."

"You're kidding," Trammel said.

"I wish he was," the deputy said. "I don't know how she found out you were in town, much less in the building, but she did, and she's been demanding I bring you down there to see her since I locked up Bookman. She's been asking nonstop for the past hour."

"I can't make you go down and see her," Moran added, "but I'd consider it a personal favor if you did. She seems insistent as hell on seeing you, and she won't let up until she gets what she wants, which are good qualities in a woman at the right time," Moran teased.

"But not when she's in a cell waiting for the hangman," the deputy said. "Would you talk to her, Sheriff Trammel? I don't think there'll be any end to her griping unless you do."

Trammel did not know why Madam Pinochet would want to talk to him, but he intended to find out. He walked down the stairs toward them. "Lead the way, Deputy."

"That's where I come in," Moran said. "We don't allow firearms in with the prisoners. Sets up a dangerous situation." He nodded at the Peacemaker under Trammel's left arm. "I'll need that Colt before you go downstairs."

For a moment, Trammel wondered if this might be some kind of trap on Clay or Alcott's part. A way to get him to give up his gun and leave him an easier target for a bullet.

But he quickly discarded the notion. Sheriff Rob Moran had never been anything but fair with him and he did not peg him for a Lucien Clay stooge. Trammel was not in the habit of trusting people, but his instinct told him he could trust Moran. He slowly reached for his Colt, eased it from the holster and handed it to Moran, butt forward.

Moran took it. "You'll get it back as soon as you come upstairs, I promise. If I'm not here, the man at the desk will have it waiting for you."

Trammel followed the deputy down to the basement where the county jail was housed. He was expecting a dank cellar with bars cut into the bedrock that lie beneath the busy streets of Laramie. Instead, he found a structure that was no different from the offices upstairs. It was well lit by oil torches, and a neat row of iron bars constituted the cells where the prisoners were kept.

The area was three times the size of the cells in his jail, but being that far underground gave Trammel an uneasy feeling. "What's your name, Deputy?"

"Beau Stiles," the man said quickly. He was older than Moran and Trammel. Maybe about forty or so, but only looked it if you stared at him long enough. "Can I ask you a question, Sheriff? Why do you wear you gun like that? Under your arm, I mean. I've always preferred it on my hip where I can get at it easy enough."

"You learned to shoot different from the way I learned," Trammel said. "I worked in New York and other cities were men couldn't wear their guns out in public. I got used to a shoulder holster, and I suppose I still like the feel of it."

"Seems to be that way, if what I hear about you is true." Stiles stopped as he opened the door to the cells. "Did you just say you've been to New York?"

"I did," Trammel told him. "In fact, I was born there."

"Is it as fancy as I've heard?"

"No." Trammel nodded at the door. "Now how about you open that up so we can find out what Madam Pinochet has to say?"

Deputy Stiles opened the door and allowed Trammel to walk by himself down the aisle between the cells. He ignored the glares and curses and other things the prisoners hurled his way until he found Madam Pinochet's cell on the right. The cell across from her was empty, and blankets had been hung on both sides of her cell in an attempt, Trammel thought, to give the female prisoner some measure of privacy. They did not have a jail exclusively for women in Laramie, and he imagined Madam Pinochet deserved some measure of consideration, even while she awaited the noose.

Madam Pinochet looked up when Trammel's shadow fell across the floor of her cell. She no longer had a thin veil to hide the burn marks on her face. Six months of prison food and a lack of sunlight had served to shrink her from a grand dame to a skeletal remnant of the woman she had once been. Her gray prison smock was a far cry from the lavish black gowns she had been known to wear back when she ran her criminal empire from her lair in Blackstone.

The only thing Trammel could still recognize about her was the look in her eyes. They still bore the same hate that had blazed there the day he had dropped her off at this same jail in the spring.

"So you really are here, aren't you?" She sneered up at him, showing a row of jagged yellow teeth. "You —"

"Say no more." He had already been insulted enough for one day. "You asked to see me. Say what you want me to hear and make it quick. I've got a long ride ahead of me."

"And I've got a long drop at the end of a short rope waiting for me because of you." Her voice still bore a trace of her native France. "The event of my death will be your doing, Trammel."

"Your death is no one's fault but your own." Despite his size, reputation, and chosen profession, it was against his nature to be coldhearted, especially where a woman was involved. But Madam Pinochet, or Madam Peachtree as the locals had taken to calling her, deserved no such consideration. She had lorded the contents of the ledger over the territory for years, using it to solidify her hold over most of the leading officials as she consolidated control over the opium and gambling markets.

She had somehow lost the ledger to Sheriff Bonner of Blackstone just before Trammel had arrived in town and taken Bonner's place. When Trammel accidentally discovered the ledger, he thought it was in code since he couldn't understand it. He asked Adam Hagen to look at it to see if he could understand its contents.

Unfortunately, Trammel learned later that it had not been written in code but only in French, Madam Pinochet's native language. A language Adam Hagen spoke well. Now he was in possession of the ledger and had taken her place atop the criminal element in the Wyoming Territory. She had ordered her men to kill Trammel, which was what had led to her arrest and soon her execution in Laramie.

Madam Pinochet continued to glower at him as she said, "A lot has passed between us, Sheriff. A surprising amount, given that we've barely spoken to each other two or three times."

"If you hadn't tried to have me killed, maybe we would've been better friends."

"I tried to buy your friendship, but failed."

"Having your men try to kill me is a hard way to buy friendship," Trammel said. "Besides, my friendship isn't for sale. Neither is my loyalty. Never has been. Never will be. Now, if you've got something to say, better get on with it before I leave. This is likely the last time you'll ever see me."

She drew herself to the bars and whispered. "You need to be very careful, Sheriff Trammel."

"I've been alive long enough to understand that."

"I mean careful with everyone. Danger surrounds you at every turn. You have few friends and a great many enemies. More than you know, back in Blackstone and here in Laramie."

"You're not telling me anything I don't already know. And you're beginning to waste my time. I'll find a preacher and ask him to say a prayer for your soul."

"I don't need your prayers, you damned fool," Madam Pinochet spat out. "I need you to listen. I need you to understand that no one is your friend, save for that pretty doctor widow at the edge of town. Adam Hagen is a man bent on revenge against a father who never loved him. He has my ledger and has added a great deal to it in an effort to topple his father and his allies. No good can come of this, and you must be careful to avoid being caught in the middle of their fight. There will be only one winner, and it will not be you."

"I've been looking out for myself for a long time."

"Yes, in cities where men have rules of conduct they must follow and laws that can be enforced. Laramie and Blackstone are unlike any place you have been, Sheriff. Even Wichita. Life is more brutal here. More personal. Men out here do not forgive slights so easily. And they do not give up when prudence dictates otherwise."

Trammel did not like the direction this conversation was headed. "Speak plain or don't speak at all."

"I still have a few friends who like to visit me, even here in this dingy place," Madam Pinochet said. "They tell me Lucien Clay has formed an alliance with Jesse Alcott and the Pinkerton men who came here from Chicago. Clay has learned of Adam's shooting and has spent the last week solidifying power among the county leaders. A steady stream of them has supposedly paraded through town like some kind of pageant."

So Clay was making the most of Hagen's disability. Since Clay was a criminal, Trammel had not expected him to keep a vigil by his partner's bedside. He expected him to do what criminals do — exploit a weakness for their benefit. "So what?"

"So this," Madam Pinochet went on. "Lucien Clay is not the oafish brute Adam or others would have you believe. He is a cunning man who plans to use the Pinkerton men to not only help him take down Adam Hagen, but retrieve my old ledger. He is reportedly willing to stop at nothing, including burning down all of Blackstone, to accomplish this if necessary."

Trammel did not believe a word of it. 'That's impossible. Mr. Hagen paid off the Pinkerton Agency a while ago."

"He may have paid off *Mister* Pinkerton," Madam Pinochet clarified, "but Mr. Alcott and his men have been offered positions in Lucien Clay's new organization if they are successful in their efforts to retrieve the ledger. They have promised to become Clay's personal army, which will give him complete control over a sizeable portion of the territory, if not all of it."

Trammel still wasn't buying it. "Rob Moran and his men would never let that happen."

"They won't be foolish enough to take on Sheriff Moran at first," Madam Pinochet said. "They will have no qualms about coming after Blackstone first. Your celebrity makes you an inviting target, Sheriff Trammel. Once they make an example out of you, who else could dare to believe they could stand up to them and win?" She smiled that crooked yellow smile again. "So you see, Sheriff? Your greatest strength has been made your greatest liability. Such is the way when dealing with men like Lucien Clay. And Adam Hagen."

Trammel grabbed the bars before he lost his balance. He was not sure how much stock he could put in the ravings of an insane woman staring death in the face on the gallows, but every single thing she had just said made complete sense to him.

It explained why Alcott and his men had not already ridden to Blackstone since arriving in Laramie, much less catching the next train back to Chicago.

He did not know much about Lucien Clay except that the man had once worked with Madam Pinochet to kill him, only to call off his men when Adam Hagen made him a better deal, and eventually, his literal partner in crime.

The old woman had struck close enough at the truth to give Buck Trammel pause. Close enough for him to finally believe she just might be telling the truth.

"You're telling me a lot of things," Trammel told her, "but you're not telling me what I can do about them. Any of them."

The prisoner's laugh echoed through the cell block, causing the other prisoners to yell for her to be quiet.

Madam Pinochet spoke over the clamor. "That's what I'm telling you, Trammel. There's absolutely nothing you can do about any of it, except maybe run. This is my parting gift to you from the gallows. Pure terror."

Trammel had to appreciate the depth of the woman's hatred. He imagined she didn't care enough about people to actually hate them, but Buck Trammel was obviously an exception. In an odd way, he was proud of himself. "Thanks for the thought, but if I worried about everyone who threatened to kill me, I'd never go outside."

"You might make it out of the territory before Clay and his hounds find you," she went on. "Though I doubt you'll get very far in a wagon with that pretty doctor and her dead husband's mother in tow."

Trammel banged his fist against the bars.

Madam Pinochet didn't flinch. "The truth hurts, Trammel, and inside a place like this, the truth is all I've got left. The truth is all there is to keep me warm at night."

"Good thing for you all of this will be over soon," Trammel wouldn't give her the satisfaction of seeing him rub his sore hand. "I've got a town to run. But don't worry. I'll see you at your hanging. Won't believe you're dead unless I see it with my own two eyes."

She rushed to the bars and howled after him. "I wanted you to know about Alcott. I wanted you to know he's coming, Trammel. Him and his riders are coming for you and Hagen, and there's nothing either of you can do to stop them. You might've gotten lucky against Clay's men the last time, but these aren't Clay's men. They are Pinkerton men. They hit what they aim at and they're aiming at you. Embrace the terror, Trammel. There's nothing you can do to stop it!"

Her screams echoed out from the cells and carried throughout the building.

Trammel exited the cell block, and Deputy Stiles quickly locked the door behind him. "I'm sorry you had to go through that, Sheriff. I sincerely am, but I'm grateful. At least now, maybe she'll shut up. If not, I can't dump a bucket on her and not get yelled at by the sheriff for being mean. It'll put me in a better state of mind."

Trammel kept walking up the stairs, anxious to retrieve his gun from Sheriff Moran. "That makes one of us."

CHAPTER 24

Trammel tugged his coat closed against the harsh Laramie wind as he stepped out of the telegraph office. The Colt felt good under his left arm again as he looked up and down the town's main street. Sheriff Moran had told him the Pinkerton men had not only come to Laramie, but had prospered under Lucien Clay's protection. They played a key role in his plans to grow past Laramie and throughout the territory, maybe even the entire part of the country. Adam Hagen's goals were at least simpler and easier to appreciate.

Trammel had no doubt that Alcott and the other Pinkerton men would go along with the plan. He couldn't blame them. Having spent a significant amount of time with the agency himself, Trammel knew it was a life of interminably long train rides and in carriages and on horses riding to follow orders from a man you didn't know to protect people you often did not like. The pay was decent enough for the labor required, but it was nothing compared to the untold riches Lucien Clay was undoubtedly promising them. The worst part of it all, at least from Trammel's perspective, was that Clay wasn't lying to them. If his plan worked, they would all be very wealthy, powerful men.

Hell, had Trammel still been with the agency, he probably would have taken Clay's deal, too. Offer a man a place in this world and some money in his pocket? Only a fool would turn that down. Trammel had been given a similar chance when Adam Hagen had taken him to Blackstone, and he had grabbed the opportunity with both hands. He saw no reason why the Pinkerton men would not do the same thing, even if it meant killing Buck Trammel in the process. The life of one man did not mean much when compared to the futures of twelve or the future in general.

Thirteen men, Trammel reminded himself. He had to count the ramrod of the Pinkerton outfit, Jesse Alcott.

Trammel tried to remember what the man from the train had looked like as he looked at the faces of the people passing by him on Laramie's Main Street. He remembered the name and he remembered their run-in on the train, but for the life of him, he could not remember what the man looked like. And he knew that ignorance may very well cost him his life. Alcott could walk right up to him and Trammel probably wouldn't see it coming until it was too late.

He kept a sharp eye as he went to the livery to pick up his horse and Bookman's horse that he had ridden down from Blackstone. He paid the liveryman for feeding and grooming the horses, then mounted up and began riding out of Laramie. It may have been well past dusk, but the sky was still bright with the promise of a coming moonrise to follow. He imagined there would be enough light to help him make his way back home easy enough. After what Sheriff Moran had told him, he didn't dare spend the night in Laramie. He had tempted fate by being there as long as he had been. Besides, Blackstone needed a lawman who didn't get sick every time he tried to stand up.

As he followed the dark trail back home, Buck Trammel admitted to himself that he was worried that Hawkeye's head might be permanently ruined. He cared less about it affecting his role of deputy than altering the rest of his life. The boy was barely twenty and didn't deserve to spend the rest of his days as a cripple.

Adam Hagen was a different story. He'd lived enough life for ten men and likely deserved whatever he had coming to him. Whether he kept the arm, lost it, or could not use it again, Trammel had a hard time working up a lot of sympathy for his friend. He hoped Hagen fully recovered, but if he didn't, the man could hardly lay claim to missing out on a full life. Hawkeye deserved that same chance, and Trammel hoped he got it.

Riding along the path, as the moon rose and cast a gray light on everything around him, the sheriff wondered what Lucien Clay's strategy for taking control might be. Would he keep bringing the important men from the territory to meet him, slowly consolidating power while Hagen was laid up? That might give Trammel enough time to get Emily and her mother-in-law out of town before Alcott and his men ultimately came for him.

He knew he probably would not survive the encounter and he did not want Emily around to witness that. He didn't want her last memory of him to be his death. She had already lost one man. Like he wanted for Hawkeye, Trammel wanted more for her, too. More than being shackled to an addled old widow. More than mourning the loss of a dead lawman. She had plenty of life left to live, too, and he did not want her wasting it on him. He and Hagen had been given numerous chances to live life. Hawkeye and Emily deserved the same. They deserved better.

He felt Bookman's mare twitch and rear back as they came around a bend in the trail. He pulled back his own mount to compensate. He did not know much about horses — a fact Hagen and Hawkeye were all too ready to point out — but he knew they could see better at night than humans. They sensed things before a man could see them and, given how dark it was, he would be a fool to discount its reaction. Could be a wolf or a mountain lion. Could be the animal caught wind of something dead somewhere in the dense forest on either side of the trail.

Or it could be something a hell of a lot more dangerous than that.

He brought the horse under control and slid the tow horse's reins over his pommel as he pulled his Winchester from its scabbard. He levered a round into the chamber and listened.

"Look who's becoming quite the Westerner," said a voice from the darkness.

Trammel aimed the Winchester in the general direction of the voice. "Show yourself or I start shooting."

"I don't think even you are that naïve, Trammel," the voice said. "One shot will send at least one of your horses to bucking, maybe both of them. You'd be on foot and all alone in the middle of the trail with no one but me. I don't think you want that, now do you?"

Trammel did, indeed, feel the horses growing restless and struggled to keep them steady without daring to lower his rifle.

"And I don't believe you want to get shot," Trammel yelled back. "So how about you step out here where I can see you and we can have a conversation like two grown men. Unless you prefer to play kids' games like hiding in the darkness."

Trammel saw the glint of moonlight off the steel revolver in a gloved hand that emerged from the darkness. The horse and rider appeared on the trail about thirty yards ahead of him. The man wore a gray bowler hat and matching duster. He recognized both and did not need a formal introduction to know who this man was.

"Jesse Alcott," Trammel said

"Good memory, Sheriff Trammel. I didn't

think you'd remember."

"I didn't until Moran told me you were in town." Trammel looked over the man's rig. It was just like Somerset's horse and saddle up in Blackstone. A typical Pinkerton outfitting. He decided to not insult the man straight off. He could have shot Trammel from the darkness had he wanted to. He obviously had something else in mind.

"You're a long way from the Mississippi, Alcott. Not a riverboat in sight. What are you doing here?"

"Not all that far from the train from Ogallala," Alcott responded. "No, not that far at all. In fact, our last meeting is an incident burned into my memory. Haven't been able to shake it yet."

"Is that what this is about? Me knocking you senseless on a train six months ago? Don't tell me you're that fragile."

"I'll admit it may have started off that way," Alcott said. "It may have been the reason why I asked Mr. Pinkerton for the assignment when Mr. Bowman sent word he wanted to hire us to avenge his dead kin. But it has become about more than that now." His pistol didn't move. "Much more."

"Clay's not paying you enough to get killed." Trammel kept the Winchester leveled at Alcott's belly. "His money's no good if you're dead, Alcott. Best for you and your men to remember that before you come after me."

"Then I'll have to see to it that I don't get killed," Alcott said. "And fortunately for me, I've got twelve men around me to make that eventuality most unlikely. You, on the other hand, are alone in a town with only old men to help you. A one-armed invalid and a green gun hand who can't even walk a straight line anymore." Alcott sucked his teeth. "If I was you, Sheriff, I'd be thinking about picking up stakes and leaving the territory while I could."

"Seems to me you've got more practice at running than I do, Alcott. Never was graced with speed." He gripped his rifle tighter. "Guess that's why I've had to learn to hold my ground and fight."

"It seems to have worked for you so far, but as I and your friend Hagen will tell you, everyone's luck runs out eventually. It's running out for you now. Run, Trammel. Run now."

Trammel struggled to nudge his horses around as Alcott ever so slightly kept his mount moving to his right. He knew the gunman was doing it on purpose, but Trammel would be damned before he would allow himself to be flanked. He kept his

Winchester aimed at the belly of the Pinkerton man, even though he did not look very graceful doing it.

"My luck's been holding up just fine, thanks. What do you say we quit all this talking and do something about it instead? How about we throw down these guns and climb down from these horses and settle this like we started it on that train all those months ago? With our fists. Hell, I'll even give you the first shot."

But Alcott was shaking his head before the sheriff even finished his sentence. "I never claimed to be a particularly intelligent man, Trammel, but I'm not that much of a fool. Your skills with your fists are legendary in the agency. You killed at least five men with your bare hands while in service to Mr. Pinkerton. Two of them in one fight, from what I was told."

Trammel was disappointed but not surprised that his ploy didn't work. "The real number is actually closer to eight. There were a couple of specialty jobs Allan asked me to handle for him personally." He looked at Alcott closely. "He never asked you for any special favors, did he, Alcott?"

Alcott's frowning silence told Trammel all he needed to know.

Now that he'd found a sore spot, Trammel kept hitting it. "Guess that's why the old man took my leaving the agency kind of hard. He was awful sore at me for leaving. Said I was one of his best men and offered me all sorts of incentives to stay. Too bad none of them were a good enough reason for me to change my mind."

Trammel cocked his head as he looked at Alcott more closely. "I wonder how Allan will react when he hears you've decided to leave him and take a dozen of his men with you in the process. I wonder if he'll be mad. I wonder if he'll even care."

"He won't know for a while," Alcott said. "As far as he's concerned, I'm still here, trying to drum up some new business while waiting for a train back to Chicago. Saw no reason to let him think any different, either."

Trammel frowned. "Damn. Wish you'd told me that earlier."

Alcott's horse shifted as it felt its rider's nervousness. "Why? What did you do?"

"Sorry to disappoint you," Trammel said. "But when I heard you boys were overstaying your welcome in Laramie, I took the liberty of sending Allan a telegram before I left town. Thought it was the least I could do for him, even though we didn't leave things on the best of terms." Even in the weak light of the moon, Trammel could see

Alcott squint.

"You're lying."

"Sent it right before I left town. Got the receipt and everything if you'd like to look at it."

Alcott tightened the reins on his horse, bringing it to a halt. "Why would you do something like that?"

In truth, Trammel had done it to put a couple of kinks in Alcott's rail. Questions from Mr. Pinkerton were the best way he knew to throw Alcott and Clay's plan off balance a bit. When a man like Allan Pinkerton asked questions, they demanded answers and action, even all the way out in Wyoming Territory.

Sheriff Moran had been right. Trammel was outgunned and outmanned. He had to find some kind of advantage any way he could.

"I figured a man has a right to know when his men aren't doing what he's paying them to do. I also figured he wouldn't appreciate you two-timing him with a snake like Lucian Clay. But I wouldn't get too upset just yet, Alcott. Like I said, Allan and me didn't part on the best of terms. Maybe he'll just ignore it. But I'll bet one of his office boys will read it and make inquiries."

Alcott's mount, again feeling the tension

from its rider, began to stomp and grow restless. "You'd better be lying to me, Trammel, or I'll plug you right here and now."

Trammel smiled at the .32 caliber pistol. "With that little thing? It sure as hell won' kill me on the first shot and if you shoot you'd better kill me, Alcott, because I'll sure as hell kill you."

Alcott swore and his horse fussed some more. He tucked away his pistol and rode back to town, yelling over his shoulder. "You've done a lot of damage, Trammel! won't forget this, and next time, I won't be alone."

Maybe not, Trammel thought as he tucked his Winchester back into the saddle scabbard, *but I will be.*

CHAPTER 25

Trammel found Emily and Hawkeye in Adam's room at the Clifford Hotel when he got back to town later that night. He would have chastised his deputy for not taking better care of himself, but the kid already looked in horrible shape. His skin was pale, and he had huge bags under his eyes. Poor Hawkeye looked like he was getting worse instead of better, and he should have been in bed already.

"Who's guarding the prisoner while you're here?" Trammel asked his deputy.

"There's not much to guard, Buck," Emily answered for him. "Somerset has been fed and is locked up behind bars. He's not going anywhere with a broken shoulder and two injured legs." She looked at Hawkeye then back at Trammel. "Your deputy here was quite a different matter entirely. He wasn't looking so good and was beginning to run a fever, so I thought it best to bring him over here with me while I checked on Adam. If you're going to be angry about it, might as well be angry at me and not him."

"I've been protectin' them while you've been gone, Sheriff," Hawkeye said, half asleep in a chair in the corner. "Been keepin' an eye out the whole time."

"And I've never felt safer, I'm sure," Adam Hagen said from his bed. His tone struck Trammel as sarcastic and he couldn't blame him. Hawkeye was beginning to look as bad as Hagen, and that was not good considering the nature of their respective injuries.

"How did you do in Laramie?" Hagen asked him. "I hope you gave Lucien my best. Told him I'm in fine fighting form?"

"Didn't have the chance," Trammel admitted. "I saw Sheriff Moran when I dropped off Bookman at the county jail. He told me the Pinkerton men have been in town for about a week. Alcott and the rest of them seem to have thrown in with Lucien Clay. And, according to Moran, your partner has had a steady stream of territory elders visiting him in Laramie since Alcott got there. Seems like Alcott and his men have become an integral part of Clay's operation."

Suddenly, Hagen was the one who didn't look so good. "Have they, now? That's a most interesting development. I'm not even dead yet and they're already dancing on my grave."

"No one's dead yet," Trammel said, "least of all us. I'm betting Mr. Pinkerton won't be too happy about any of this."

"Mr. Pinkerton?" Hagen asked. "Is he in Laramie, too?"

"No, I sent him a telegram about it before I left Laramie. It was getting on dark, so I didn't wait around for a response. But I'm pretty sure he'll send one, and he won't be happy. I have a feeling Alcott will get a less cordial response, and most likely an order to return to Chicago on the next train or face immediate termination."

Hagen looked impressed. "I didn't take you for a such a cunning man, Buck. Do you think Mr. Pinkerton will tolerate Alcott's insubordination?"

"Depends on if Clay is willing to buy him out of trouble with Allan. If your so-called partner has that kind of cash lying around to make Pinkerton forget about Alcott's treachery, then I might've just wasted a perfectly good telegram. But if he doesn't, I've just caused a hell of a lot of trouble for Alcott and his men. Clay's promises of future glory are all well and good, but the guaranteed wrath of a man like Mr. Pinkerton is never good for anyone."

"Do you think it will work, Buck?" Emily asked hopefully. "Do you think he'll send men here directly to stop Alcott before he can attack Laramie?"

"Even if he does," Trammel said, "it'll be a week before they get here. I don't think Clay will wait that long to move against us, especially now that most of the territory elders have seen that he has a small army of Pinkerton men behind him. Alcott claims to have twelve men who stayed loyal to him. I bet a couple of them will fall off once word of Allan's rage reaches them. Alcott's a boss and he has a name. A couple of gun hands without standing can be plowed under by the agency pretty easily. Allan's a prideful man, so there's an excellent chance he'll want to put down this kind of thing before others in the field get the same notion. But there are no guarantees in this kind of thing."

"So your telegram to this Pinkerton fella didn't do much," Hawkeye said.

"It caused Alcott to go on the defensive for the first time since this damnable business began," Hagen said. "That just might change things in our favor. Make those boys rethink things they thought of as certainties. With Clay appearing to galvanize his political and military forces, we need every single advantage we can muster." Hagen looked at Trammel. "Sending off that telegram was inspired thinking, Buck. I don't think I would've considered doing that, even if I had been up and about."

"Maybe you're starting to have an influence on me. And not in a good way." Trammel decided to change the subject. "How were things here? Any word from the ranch about Bookman's arrest?"

Emily said, "I saw Mr. Hagen ride into town to speak to Mr. Montague this afternoon after you left, but didn't see him ride out again. His horse is gone, so I assume he went back to the ranch. Hawkeye said he didn't go to the jail looking for you, and no one else in town remembers him going to their place to ask questions. It would appear his ordered attack on Adam has been the talk of the town. If he's planning to retaliate for Bookman's arrest, he's done a good job of keeping it to himself."

"Father has never been one to hold his cards close to the vest," Hagen said. "I'm sure the good people of town are preparing to take to the streets, torches in hand, to march toward the jailhouse to demand Sheriff Trammel hand over the man who dared raise a hand against their favorite native son." He laughed at his own bad joke and winced from the pain. "They couldn't care less as long as their liquor and beer and dope keep flowing, which I'm sure it is, to my great loss. Probably picking me clean as I speak."

Emily checked Hagen's bandage. "As a matter of fact, a surprising number of people were very concerned about your well-being, Adam. You should be honored."

"There were?" Hagen asked. "How many?"

"Why, there must have been two or three at least," she answered. "And they weren't even in this room!"

For the first time in days, the four of them enjoyed a good laugh. Even Hagen laughed, despite the pain.

At that same moment, in his office down in Laramie, Lucien Clay was not laughing.

Jesse Alcott slammed a telegram on Clay's desk. "Thanks to Trammel, me and my men have been recalled to Chicago."

Clay glanced at the telegram. "So, ignore it. Claim you never received it. Happens all the time."

"I can't do that, Lucien," Alcott said. "It's a personal telegram from Mr. Allan Pinkerton himself. To me. Personally. One doesn't just cast that aside."

"Is Mr. Allan Pinkerton himself some kind of a formal title, like royalty, or just something everyone has taken to calling him? An awful lot of people around here seem eager to pay deference to a round little Scot in Chicago."

Alcott was in no joking mood. "Damn it, Lucien. This is no laughing matter."

Clay poured himself another bourbon and shoved the telegram back toward Alcott. "I don't know why you're so upset, Jesse. You and your men have been overdue for a week. You knew something like this was bound to happen eventually. You didn't think the home office would just forget you were out here, did you?"

"No," Alcott admitted, "but I thought it would take a hell of a lot longer than a week. And it would have, too, if Trammel hadn't gone and sped things along by contacting Allan personally."

Clay took a drink. "I had heard that Trammel and Pinkerton hadn't parted company on the best of terms."

"They didn't," Alcott said, "but Pinkerton seems to still have a warm place in his heart for the thug, because he read and responded to his telegram damned fast."

Clay did not like Alcott's reaction to the telegram. He did not like it at all. Well aware that he had been taking a risk in attempting to corrupt the Pinkerton man, Clay knew there was always a chance a corruptible man could double-cross him somewhere down the road. Or, Alcott could remain loyal to the agency and serve as a double agent, placing the shackles on Clay while offering him up to his employer for a nice pat on the head and a modest bonus in pay.

Or a scenario Clay thought more likely — the cunning agent could have his men turn against Clay after learning enough about his plans to control the territory.

Fortunately, Alcott did not know Clay's men had already corrupted more than half of the former Pinkerton men. Alcott did not need to know it, either. For now, Alcott's reputation with the agency had served Clay well in his attempts to win the support of the territory elders. Alcott's presence gave Clay a sense of legitimacy that he did not have on his own, especially where Adam Hagen was involved.

Madam Pinochet had been able to win them over because she was a foreign-born woman and knew how to charm men through flattering their vanity. Adam Hagen had been able to win them over because he was the great man's well-traveled son and must have known what he was doing. And ny, did he make them laugh!

Lucien Clay did not possess a name or a history or charm. He was of the gutter born and had never been able to convince people otherwise. He insisted on wearing fancy clothes and adorning his office in ornate fabrics and furniture and had even hired a drunken actor from the London stage to help him lose his Arkansas drawl, but none of it had served to make him more than he was — a common street thug.

But with a man like Jesse Alcott at his side, Lucien Clay was finally in a position to impress upon the leaders of the territory that he was worthy of holding the reins of power. He had the discipline and the men to keep the political and criminal machines running as smoothly as they had always done and keep their pockets lined with as much gold as Hagen had, and Madam Pinochet before him.

After all, a man like Alcott would not just throw away his lucrative career with the Pinkerton Agency for just anyone, now would he? If Lucien Clay was good enough for a man of Alcott's caliber to take a risk on, then perhaps Clay was worth a try after all?

Now that he had the territory elders in his pocket, Lucien Clay wondered if Alcott was good enough to work for him. Clay was not so sure anymore. Why should the opinion of a fat old man over a thousand miles away in Chicago matter to a man who was on the verge of making so much money? The prospect of power and advancement of his own position should be enough to put Alcott at ease. Instead, he seemed to be hedging his bets, helping Clay as long as it did not damage his reputation back home.

Lucien Clay did not like that kind of thinking. What's more, he did not trust it.

Never a man to hold on to his thoughts for very long, especially when they were troublesome, he said, "I don't like that look on your face, Jesse."

"And I don't like Mr. Pinkerton's summons," Alcott answered. "He's expecting me and all of my men back in Chicago within a week at most. If we don't arrive or at least send news that we have boarded a train back within that time, it's entirely possible he will send another group to get us." Alcott looked at Clay. "That is the reason for my apprehension, Lucien. Mr. Pinkerton is a most stubborn man."

Clay still didn't see the cause for concern. "What makes you think this bunch will be any less corruptible than your bunch was? I'll just hire them on, too. God knows there's more than enough work to go around for everyone. Hell, three times that many."

"And what about after that?" Alcott asked. "He won't send a third group out. Mr. Pinkerton is a powerful man. His alliance with the railroads has given him many friends in governments throughout the country, especially in Washington. If he finds out about your plans to take over an entire territory, he could voice his concerns to the territorial governor. Maybe even the United States Army. Either could put a serious crimp in your plans, Lucien. And jail would be the least of our concerns."

"The governor," Clay laughed. "I already own the governor."

"But not the army," Alcott countered. "And you don't want to cross paths with those bluebellies. They're slow to rouse, but when they do, they ruin everything in their path. If Mr. Pinkerton uses his considerable influence to have them put their full weight against you, there's no stopping them."

Clay finally saw Alcott's reason for concern. He knew he did not have as much influence over the governor as he claimed. Hagen probably did, as he had that damnable ledger of his, but Clay's reach extended only by proxy. And when going up against Mr. Pinkerton's considerable influence, proxy would not be enough. Influence would need to be direct and final.

Those were terms Lucien Clay understood all too well. "Nothing is ruined, Jesse. Not yet, anyway."

Alcott staggered as he quickly got to his feet. "I don't think you fully grasp the extent of Mr. Pinkerton's influence in this matter. This isn't just some man who fires off telegrams at will, Lucien. Every word he puts to paper has considerable weight behind it. And influence as well. He likely understands the governor has been corrupted and may send his next telegram to President Grant himself."

"There you go with that *himself* business. Must be some kind of Louisiana thing." Clay selected a cigar from his box, bit off the end, and tucked it into the corner of his mouth. "I'm sorry to disappoint you, Jesse, but I simply don't share your fears." He struck a lucifer off the side of the desk and spoke out of the side of his mouth as he brought the flame to the cigar. "All Mr. Pinkerton's telegraph means is that we are going to have to speed up our plans a little. Everything proceeds as planned. Nothing stops. Nothing changes."

"But the order in which they happen changes drastically. We were going to pull down the rest of the ranches around Blackstone first. Now we don't have that kind of time."

"We always knew we would have to attack Blackstone and pull down King Charles Hagen from his throne eventually." Clay puffed on the cigar until the flame caught. He waved the match dead and tossed the matchstick into the ashtray. "Yes, we had hoped to squeeze the areas around him to the point where either he or Trammel got smart enough to run, but we no longer have that luxury. Instead, you and your men must take the town and the ranch of Blackstone first. But you must find that ledger so we can get the power we need to secure our hold over the governor and every other official in this territory. Their pledges of loyalty will be more secure with evidence to hold over their heads." Clay looked at Alcott through the thin veil of smoke. "Nothing stops, Jesse. It just happens faster." He watched Alcott as he chewed that over.

He did not seem to like the taste of it. "And what if we fail, Lucien?"

"Given the quality of our numbers, who could stand against us?" Clay eased the head of ash from his cigar into the ashtray. "But in the unlikely event that we fail, at

343

least we'll have the good fortune to know we won't live long enough to regret it."

CHAPTER 26

Trammel was having a tough time concentrating on his paperwork. The reports on the Somerset and the Blackstone Ranch arrests, followed by Bookman's times in jail, all *should* be finished and soon, but Trammel wondered if they *needed* to be done. If the whole town burned anyway, a few lousy arrest reports wouldn't matter worth a damn.

He knew that with Alcott and the Pinkerton men in Laramie, hell could break loose at any moment. An attack could come at any time, even at night. The men could ride straight for Blackstone and lay waste to the town. A few torches through a few busted windows would be enough to render the wooden town a wasteland in minutes. Only the bank, the Clifford Hotel, and the jailhouse would likely be all that remained. The town of Blackstone would be wiped off the map without a single shot being fired.

Or Alcott and Clay could continue to bide their time as they had for the past week or so. The sheriff did not know what was worse — the waiting or the unknown.

He went back to his reports, deciding it was best to focus on matters at hand. He needed to record an official account of what had happened so far, to get it all down on paper for Mayor Welch or Richard Rhoades from the *Blackstone Bugle* to read. Someone needed to know what had happened and why, especially if Trammel did not make it out alive. Someone needed to understand. By the time anyone outside Blackstone got around to reading it, he would most likely be dead.

He no longer had illusions about his survival. He was outgunned thirteen to one, at the very least, and it was only a matter of time before Alcott and his men finally came to town to clear him out. He had been asking for it long enough, and he imagined his telegram to Mr. Pinkerton hadn't endeared himself to Clay or Alcott. They were coming for him because he stood in their way. They would most likely hunt him, even if he had decided to run.

Trammel knew there was no one in town to help him, at least not in a meaningful way. The jailhouse was sturdy, but could not protect him forever. Alcott would find a way to breach its stone walls eventually. Trammel would do his best to take as many of them with him as he could when the time came, but his death was a foregone conclusion he had come to accept. It was time to pay for his sins. There were less noble reasons to die.

He looked up with a start when he heard Hawkeye shuffle into the jailhouse. The boy looked better than he had since the shooting, but was still so uneasy on his feet that Trammel imagined he should probably be in bed. He dropped into a chair by the door before the sheriff could rise to help him.

"What are you doing out alone? I thought I told you I'd bring you over to the jail this afternoon."

Hawkeye was breathing heavy. "On account of me having to tell you something important, Sheriff. Something that might not be my place to say, but I'm gonna say it anyway."

Trammel set his pencil aside. "I think we're beyond formalities here, Hawkeye. You might as well forget about what is and isn't your place and just tell me what's on your mind."

"I've been doin' a lot of thinkin' these past couple of days. I suppose I haven't been fit to do much except think as it's the only thing that hasn't made me dizzy or turn my stomach. I'd like to think I've put the time to some good use."

Trammel wasn't sure where this was going. "I'm sure you have. You're not stupid. Tell me what's on your mind."

The boy swallowed hard before saying, "Those Pinkerton men are coming and there's nothing we can do to stop them, is there?"

They had already discussed that the previous evening in Hagen's room. He wondered if the boy was beginning to suffer memory loss from his head wound. If so, it was a bad sign that the damage might be permanent. "That's true. We tried, but we don't know if it'll work. It probably won't work in time to stop them. Why?"

"That's what I thought," Hawkeye said. "So since we can't stop them, we're gonna have to find a way to control them somehow or a lot of people are gonna get killed. You know I respect you, Sheriff, and I owe you everything, but it's true. These men aren't reckless or desperate like them bounty hunters we went up against last week. Pinkertons are not stupid, and they've probably read every article about every run-in you've had since coming to Blackstone.

348

They know how well you handle yourself when the lead starts flying. They won't make the same mistakes others have done by coming at you head-on."

Trammel had though the same thing countless times along the ride from Laramie the night before. Hearing it said in the open did not make it any easier. "You're not wrong, Hawkeye. But there's nothing any of us can do about it except be as ready as we can when it happens."

"Now, that's where you and me happen to disagree, Sheriff. I think there's plenty we can do about it."

Trammel was obviously interested. "How?"

"On account of you being a lawman, so you're looking at it a certain way." Hawkeye aimed a thumb at his skinny chest. "But me? I grew up on a ranch. When I see a herd stampeding toward me, I don't think about how I can stop it. I think about how I can turn it, how I can drive it to where I want it to go."

Trammel could tell the kid just might be on to something. "Go on."

Hawkeye pointed in the direction of the Blackstone Ranch. "There's that rocky outcropping on the main road to the Hagen ranch, remember? The one we call Stone

Gate. I was able to watch Mr. Hagen and his men come down from there while I spied on him before they rode into town."

Trammel remembered it well. "It's like a natural gate to the Hagen spread."

"Nothing natural about it. Mr. Hagen blew a great big hole in the boulder on account of him wanting a straight rode into town to drive his cattle." Hawkeye waved off his digression. "But that doesn't matter now. Hagen and some other cattle outfits like to use the bottleneck as a way to get a better count on their cattle heads before they take them all the way down to the railhead at Laramie. I say we use that bottleneck not for cattle, but for slowing up Pinkerton men."

Trammel knew he did not have Hagen's mind for tactics or even Hawkeye's experience with cattle drives, but even a city boy like him could see the advantage of rocky outcroppings. It would force Alcott and his men into a bottleneck where Trammel could be hiding among the rocks, picking off at least a few of them before they returned fire. And when they did, he would be lost among a forest of rock. At least for a little while.

"I see where you're going with this," Trammel said, "but the ranch is on the other end of town. There's no reason for

Alcott and his men to head that way first before lighting a match to the town."

"Which means we're going to have to give them a reason, boss," Hawkeye pointed out. "And that reason is you and Adam."

Trammel tamped down the excitement he was beginning to feel. "Go on, Hawkeye. You're doing fine."

"The one thing we know is that, when these Pinkerton fellas come to town, they're going to be gunning for you and Adam first, right? It stands to reason on account of them hating you and figuring that the fall will be quicker if the both of you are out of the way."

Again, none of this made Trammel feel any better. "You've got a bleak way of putting things, my friend."

"That's when someone tells them that Mr. Hagen has taken Mr. Bookman's arrest mighty poorly and that he's holding you and Adam hostage up there at his ranch. I've got a feeling that would be enough reason to make Alcott ride up through the Stone Gate and finish both of you off once and for all."

Trammel took the thought all the way through to its conclusion. "And lead them into a fight against Hagen's ranch hands? Why, even though the Pinks would be outgunned, they would still be more than enough to put down a couple of cowpunchers, especially if they didn't know the attack was coming."

"That's why we won't tell them," Hawkeye said. "And they're not going to attack the ranch, either. You'll keep them bottled up at Stone Gate while I ride out to the ranch and let them know an attack is coming their way."

The idea was beginning to make sense to Trammel. "It just might work. Especially if they thought Mr. Hagen had the ledger."

Hawkeye grinned. "And I know a way we could make them think precisely that. Won't be all that hard to get them to think that way, especially coming from a dummy like me."

"You're no dummy, my friend," Trammel said. "The only problem is keeping them off me once I pick them off from the rocks." Some of the terms Hagen had used while they were on the trail from Wichita to Blackstone came back to him as he thought it over. "I'll have cover and the high ground, but even if I had all the ammunition in the world, I'd still be outgunned thirteen to one."

"Probably less than that if my plan goes accordingly," Hawkeye said. "Maybe nine or ten at most."

"That's still a lot of guns against me and a lot of lead coming my way. All it takes is one shot to put me down. Even at ten to one, I won't be able to hold them off forever."

"You won't have to hold them off that long," Hawkeye said. "Just long enough for the cavalry to arrive."

"Cavalry?" Trammel began to think his deputy may have been ranting this entire time after all. "There's no way the army will ride from Fort Laramie to get involved in a local dustup like this."

"We've already got an army in Blackstone, Sheriff." Hawkeye smiled. "One that's a hell of a lot closer than Fort Laramie, too. In fact, it's just right up the road from Stone Gate. Guess you might say it's an army fit for a king."

Trammel knew he was talking about the cowhands at the Blackstone spread. He had gone up against those boys a few times in the past and doubted they would be any match for Pinkerton men, but on horseback in a close-quarters fight like Stone Gate they would be. Their numbers might be enough to carry the day.

Hawkeye's plan just might work after all, but it was missing one key element. "We know how we're going to get them to the bottleneck when they come to town. Now we just need to find a way to get them to come to town on our own terms when we're ready." The more Trammel thought about it, the more it made sense. "And I think I've got just the man for the job."

CHAPTER 27

"I ain't goin'," Elmer protested.

"Can you give me one good reason why not?" Smith, the liveryman, yelled at him. "Hell, I'm giving you the best horse I've got, plus free care for your own animal for a whole month."

Trammel decided to sweeten the deal. "Not to mention twenty dollars for entertainment purposes once you get to Laramie. Twenty dollars can go a long way in a town like that."

"Can go a long way to gettin' me killed," Elmer protested. He looked at Smith. "If it's so easy, why don't you go?"

"I'll be glad to," the black man said. "Just run the livery for me while I'm gone." He stuck a crooked finger in Elmer's face. "Which means no drinking and mucking out the stalls every day. And tending to the —"

Elmer waved him down. "You made your

point, damn it. I've never been one for work, and I'm not gonna start now at this age." He looked up at Trammel. "Was that forty dollars you said in entertainment money?"

"I said twenty dollars." Trammel looked at the darkening sky. "But it can be forty if you get to Laramie immediately and start telling your story now."

Elmer rubbed his filthy hands on ragged pants. "And all I've gotta do is walk into the Molly Malone and tell 'em that I left here on account of bein' scared. How Mr. Hagen's men swooped into town and took the sheriff and Adam up to his ranch."

"And how you lit out of town the second you saw us bound and dumped into a wagon," Trammel repeated for his benefit. He had created a simple story Elmer would have no problem repeating when drunk. A story that should reach Lucien Clay and Jesse Alcott fairly quickly. A story both men could find believable enough to ride to town to see for themselves. "You don't know how many we killed, just that both of us are wounded. You saw blood, that's all you know."

"And then I'm out of it, right?" Elmer said. "No gunplay for me?"

Trammel placed a hand on his shoulder.

"You're free and clear, Elmer, with forty dollars in your pocket. A man could have himself a good time in Laramie on forty dollars."

The allure of whiskey and women was too great for the old man to resist. He slapped his legs as he stood and yelled to Smith. "My horse, good man! I have an appointment in Laramie!"

The next morning, Trammel slid his Winchester into the saddle scabbard and tied the three remaining rifles into a bundle on the back of his saddle. It wasn't the sturdiest set up, but it should hold until he got to Stone Gate outside the Hagen ranch. He had cleaned and loaded the rifles before he had gone to sleep the night before. His saddlebags were already filled with as many boxes of ammunition as he could carry. He doubted he would get close to using even one box, but just having them gave him hope. The plan he and Hawkeye had cooked up depended on how convincing Elmer could be. Relying on him to be a mouthy drunk in a bar was hardly a stretch for the old codger. But being believable was. Trammel hoped his tale would prove too rich for Alcott and Clay to resist. At this point, it was the only plan they had.

So deep in his own thoughts, Trammel had not heard Emily Downs enter the barn. She had a heavy wool blanket draped around her shoulders and her eyes were still puffy from sleep. When she got closer, he could tell they were not puffy from sleep, but from tears.

He had never seen her cry before. "What's wrong?"

"I know what you're doing, Buck, and I'm begging you not to do it."

Upsetting her was the last thing he wanted to do, which was why he was trying to get into position so early in the morning. He had hoped to leave before she woke. The image of her crying was not the last memory he wanted to have of her. "I'm not doing anything. I'm just staking out some positions in case the Pinkerton men come. Hawkeye's feeling better and —"

"He'd already told me about his plan before he went to see you last night," Emily said. "He was worried you might think it was a silly idea, and he didn't want you laughing at him. That poor boy idolizes you so much, he doesn't know his stupid plan is liable to get you killed."

He hadn't known Hawkeye had talked to Emily, but in a way, he was glad he had. It saved him from bearing the burden of lying o her. "His plan isn't stupid, Emily. It's the best chance I have of stopping Alcott and his gunmen without putting the town in any more danger than it already is. We've been damned lucky that no one has been hurt or killed in any of these dustups yet, and I want to keep it that way."

"By getting yourself killed in the rocks by the Hagen ranch?" she cried. "Like some damned goat? If Alcott's men don't shoot you from one side, Hagen's men will shoot you from the other."

"Hagen's got no quarrel with me anymore," Trammel said, trying to ease her mind. "If he was going to come after me, he would have done it yesterday after I arrested Bookman."

"He's had a grudge against you for months. For siding with Adam over him. For not genuflecting every time he walked into a room. You'll be in an impossible position up there, Buck, and I don't want you killed in some kind of cross fire. You're too important to the town for that." She threw her arms around him and pulled herself tight to him. "You're too important to me." Her embrace warmed him against the cold Wyoming morning air.

"I'm not going out there to get killed. I'm going out there because it's the best chance

I've got to live. And Hawkeye's plan is sound, Emily. I wouldn't be doing it if I thought otherwise."

Her voice was muffled as she spoke into his coat. "If it works."

"If it works," he agreed. "And it will work, I promise you."

"And if it doesn't?"

He tried to make her smile. He needed that last memory of her before he rode off to whatever fate awaited him at Stone Gate. "If it doesn't, then you'll just have to patch me up after it's all over. You've been giving Adam a lot of attention lately. I could be forgiven for being jealous."

She pulled away from him, laughing through the tears. "I'll never forgive you if you go and get shot on me, Buck Trammel. I don't want to be a widow before I've even had the chance to get married again."

He gently raised her head and kissed her as softly and tenderly as he knew how. He kissed her as if it was for the last time, because they both knew it may very well be.

He reluctantly broke off the kiss. "You know how many people have been trying to kill me since I got to town. That doesn't even count all the times before. What makes you think someone's going to be able to do it now?"

"I hope I never have to find out. I know no amount of begging from me will make you stay, so if you're still of a mind to go, you might as well go."

Knowing his gear was all packed, Trammel slid his foot into the stirrup and swung himself up into the saddle. He had not planned on saying a formal good-bye, so he was not prepared to say anything special. He wanted to tell her he loved her. He wanted to thank her for giving him a home and for being the closest thing to a family he had known in years. He wanted to say a lot of things to her, but everything sounded like a good-bye and he could not bear to say good-bye to her. Not now. Not ever. He dare not even think it, because thinking about it could make it real, almost as real as saying it.

"Check in on Adam for me," he asked her as the mount moved toward the open barn doors. "I'll be back before supper."

He touched the brim of his hat the same way he had seen Hagen do it dozens of times before, and rode toward Main Street and the road up to the Hagen Ranch.

He did not look back. He did not dare.

It was already well past sunrise by the time Jesse Alcott and his men had made it to

Blackstone.

Alcott had made a point of riding ahead of the column of mercenaries. He imagined the men thought him a martinet for doing so, but he did not care what they thought. He only cared that they obeyed his orders when the time came. And he had a feeling that time was at hand.

Even if everything that old drunk Elmer had spouted off about in the Molly Malone the previous evening had been an exaggeration, there was enough truth in his story to show it was the time to strike Blackstone and strike it hard. They may not get the chance at taking down Trammel, both Hagen men, and the Hagen ranch all at the same time. If they were successful, then Lucien Clay's dreams of controlling the territory would be that much stronger upon their return to Laramie.

Alcott held up his hand, bringing his column to a halt as they approached Main Street.

He brought his horse around to address the men behind him. "Looks like we are finally here, gentlemen. As I told you before we left Laramie, I have no idea what we will be riding into, either here in town or up at the ranch, so you must keep your eyes open and your hands close to your guns at all times. I don't think we will face much resistance, but you never know what kind of courage a man like Trammel can inspire in some of the more gullible men. I have absolutely no intention of getting shot by a storekeeper from Blackstone, and I hope all of you have the same ambition."

The men surprised him by laughing at his rare attempt at humor. "Follow me and keep your eyes open. If you can, call out before you shoot. I don't want to start a fight yet if we can avoid it."

Alcott dug his heels into his horse's flanks and rode down Main Street at a trot. His men followed in two columns of six. He enjoyed the looks on the faces of the townspeople as the Pinkerton men rode by. He knew they were a sight to behold. All of them were large, sturdy men clad in gray dusters and bowlers. They clearly were not from these parts. They had not come to be reasonable or friendly. They had the look of danger about them, a look Alcott was all too happy to cultivate.

His eyes swept back and forth across both sides of the thoroughfare as they rode, watchful for any pistols or rifles aimed in their direction. But mostly, it was just shopkeepers looking up from wagon beds and old biddies interrupting their gossip session to watch the thirteen armed men ride into their town.

Alcott brought his mount to a halt in front of the jailhouse. The front door was closed, as were the shutters. He wondered if Trammel had been taken prisoner like the old drunk had said or if he had decided to barricade himself in the jail with Somerset — if the man was even still alive — in the hopes of brokering some kind of peace. But as the spy had failed to meet them at the predetermined time in Laramie, the man had already outlived his usefulness and his life was forfeit. Trammel could do with him as he wished, as long as Trammel died in the process.

Alcott motioned for his men to spread out as he dismounted and tied his horse to the hitching rail. He had just stepped up onto the boardwalk when the jailhouse door opened inward.

Alcott's pistol was in his hand before a sleepy, gangly young man of about twenty stood in the doorway. A bandage had been wrapped around his head and a deputy's star pinned on his shirt.

The boy looked at the pistol in Alcott's hand as he stifled a yawn. "What can I do for you, mister? And be quick about it, because I'd like to go back to bed."

Alcott pushed the door all the way inside and the young man along with it. "Where's Trammel?"

"You mean the sheriff?"

Alcott was beginning to lose patience. "How many other Trammels live in town, boy?"

The young man appeared to give it some thought. "None that I know of. As for Sheriff Trammel, he ain't here and he ain't been here since Mr. Hagen and his men took him and Mr. Hagen up to his ranch. And by Mr. Hagen, I mean the other Mr. Hagen. Adam, that is."

Alcott lowered his pistol. *So the scared old rummy had been telling the truth after all.* "Why the hell would Mr. Hagen do that?"

"On account of the sheriff arresting Mr. Bookman, I suppose," Hawkeye told him. "And for letting Mr. Hagen get shot on account of that bounty put out on both of them. And by Mr. Hagen, I still mean the other Mr. Hagen. Adam. Got shot in his shoulder. The left one I believe." He scratched his head. "Or was it his right? I can't remember for certain. I got hit on the head a while back, see, so my memory ain't what it oughta be."

Alcott walked to the back where the cells were and found a prisoner lying on a cot.

His right arm was bandaged and his two legs looked like they were in splints. He called out to the prisoner. "You Somerset?"

"Damned right I am," the prisoner said. "Allan send you?"

"He most certainly did." Alcott looked over the man's injuries. "Well, at least I know why you didn't meet us when we arrived in Laramie."

"I'd have been there if I could've been," Somerset said. "You can ask Mr. Pinkerton himself if you want to. He knows I live up to what I'm paid to do, if I can." He looked himself over. "And obviously, I wasn't in a position to be able to do that."

Alcott didn't care about the man's competencies, only about what he had learned while he was in Trammel's custody. "You have any idea where Trammel is?"

"Heard a scuffle out there yesterday," Somerset said. "Lots of screaming and hollering. Then I didn't hear a thing until that idiot out there came in to take away my chamber pot in the night. I usually see Trammel at least once a day, or hear him, but there's been nothing since that scuffle."

Alcott found this news most encouraging. "And what about Adam Hagen's condition?"

"Haven't heard from that loudmouth in

over a week, by my counting," Somerset said. "Lost his right arm, from what I've been able to gather back here."

Alcott had heard the same thing in the week since the shootings, then from Elmer and the deputy. He imagined Somerset was the most believable, as he was the only one on-site and the most sober. Alcott was heartened to hear the rumor had some validation.

Realizing Trammel probably wasn't hiding in the building, Alcott tucked away his pistol. "Rest easy, Somerset. I'll see to it you're taken back to Laramie to receive proper attention for your wounds." He walked back out to the jailhouse boardwalk, ignoring Hawkeye on the way. "I need two of you to fetch a wagon. Buy it if you have to, then take Mr. Somerset in there back to Laramie. Set him up with a doctor."

"Ain't he a Pinkerton man?" one of the men asked. "Like we used to be?"

"Why not just shoot him?" asked another. "He didn't warn us about Blackstone like he was supposed to. Made us ride in here blind."

Alcott saw the insubordination he had feared beginning to raise its ugly head. "This man is one of Mr. Pinkerton's favorite operatives. If we send him back to Chicago in one piece, it may foster good feelings toward us from our former employer. Good feelings that may work in our favor in the near future." He felt his temper rise within him and got hold of it before it got completely away from him. "But for now, you're doing it because I told you to do it, so get cracking." He pointed at two random men. "Both of you! Now!"

The two men traded glances before riding off in search of a wagon to borrow or steal.

Alcott knew that left him with only ten men, which should be more than enough to undertake a visit to the Hagen Ranch. Even twenty farmhands were no match for his men. "As for the rest of you," he said to the ten men remaining, "we will ride north to the Blackstone Ranch, where we believe Buck Trammel and Adam Hagen are being held by none other than King Charles himself."

"You got a plan about what we'll do once we get there, Mr. Alcott?" one man asked. "We came ready to hit a town. A ranch is another thing entirely."

"Lots of land," said another. "Lots of ranch hands, too."

Alcott looked directly at the man, a former Kansas City thug he recalled being called Ty, though the rest of his name eluded the ormer Pinkerton man at the moment.

"Are you saying you're cowed by a bunch of cowpunchers, Ty?" Alcott had to admit he enjoyed the irony.

"No," Ty answered. "I just like to make sure I know what I'm riding into. We had a plan for killing a one-armed gambler and a sheriff in a sleepy town in the middle of nowhere. Going up against a ranch full of armed, able-bodied men is a different sort of fight and requires a different sort of plan besides riding up there and hoping for the best."

"It's not as easy as just riding up there," said a man he remembered being called George. He remembered it because it was his last name. "We need to ride in slow on account of there being no element of surprise. And you need to know who's going where so we don't have any gaps in our line. Cowpunchers or no, they're men with guns who know how to use them."

"You think about any of that before you decided to have us just ride up there, Mr. Alcott?" Ty asked.

Alcott knew this was not simply a matter of insubordination. This was the men's way of testing him to see if he knew what he was doing. To see if he could be trusted. These men had never ridden with him before and their only experience with him was a betrayal of their employer. True, they had decided to follow him, but if they were going to continue to follow him, they would need a reason.

They were all on equal footing, equally hunted in the eyes of Mr. Pinkerton, so if Alcott wanted to remain the top dog in the pack, he was going to have to fight for it. Or at least prove he knew how to do more than sniff out an opportunity and betray a confidence.

"Of course I planned for this contingency," he lied. "We always knew we would have to go up against Charles Hagen eventually, so this comes as no surprise. The house is usually lightly guarded, if at all. I will ride ahead and enter the ranch under the guise of a visitor. As Trammel and Adam Hagen have no allies on the property, I doubt the house will be under guard. Once I'm there, I'll gauge the situation and act accordingly. Once I am inside the house, I'll expect you men to ride soon after in a loose circle whereupon you will form a loose arc facing the fields. Any cowboys coming to their master's aid will naturally give pause once they see ten uniformed men around their employer's home. If anyone gives you cause, feel free to shoot them."

He decided to put a finer point on it. "We go in loose, then tighten up if we need to. Beats riding in there, guns blazing, doesn't it?"

The men exchanged looks and seemed to come to some kind of silent agreement that the plan was a good one.

Alcott untied his horse and swung into the saddle. He saw the simple-minded deputy still standing by the jailhouse door, as bewildered as ever. "Will you release your prisoner to my men or should I just shoot you now and be done with it?"

"Got no reason to shoot me, 'cause I've got no reason to stop you," the boy said. "I 'spect the sheriff keeps the keys around here somewhere. I'll open the cell as soon as I find them. Your men won't get any trouble from me, mister."

Alcott was glad at least one person wasn't looking to challenge him that day. "Smart man. Now tell me the quickest way to the Hagen ranch. And if you lie to me, I'll come back and shoot you."

"Got no reason to lie, either, mister." The young man pointed at a well-worn path just off Main Street. "You ride up that road and keep going until you see the house. Can't hardly miss it. You're going to have to pass through an outcropping known as Stone

Gate a ways up the road, but when you see it, you'll know you're in the right place."

Alcott wondered if he shouldn't simply shoot the lad just to be on the safe side. He decided against it, as he doubted his men would care one way or the other. If the day went as well as he hoped, he would have plenty of chances to show them his mettle before the day was out.

He wheeled his horse around and steered her toward the road the boy had pointed out. The ten men followed him, and they rode together up the trail toward the Hagen ranch.

CHAPTER 28

As soon as the last of the Pinkerton men rounded the corner and rode out of sight, Hawkeye tossed off his head bandage, ran back to Somerset's cell, and opened it.

"What the hell is this?" the prisoner asked. "After all of this, you're just going to let me go without a fight?"

"You're free," Hawkeye said as be unlocked the back door. "Congratulations."

He ignored the prisoner's other questions as he untied Daisy from where he had hitched her behind the jail and rode away. As he passed Bainbridge Avenue, he saw Doc Emily try to flag him down with her blanket, but he acted as if he had not seen her. He did not dare stop to speak with her. If he did, the timing of their plan would fall apart and Sheriff Trammel would be a dead man.

He heeled Daisy and let the horse run full out. He figured the animal would be completely spent by the time they got to the ranch, but as much as he loved the horse, that did not matter to Hawkeye. The mare could rest for a week if she had to. Trammel, on the other hand, did not have that kind of time.

In fact, he did not have any time at all.

Emily watched young Hawkeye duck his head and speed up when he saw her try to wave him down. She knew he had seen her, but had sped up on purpose. She did not know if that was a bad sign or part of whatever plan he had cooked up with Buck.

She had hoped Hawkeye could tell her what had happened with the thirteen men she had seen riding into town. She imagined they were the dreaded Pinkerton men that Buck had been concerned about for so long. She wanted to know if anyone had been hurt or killed. Was the prisoner Somerset still alive? She wanted to know if Buck was still okay. She had no idea what he was planning, but knew that whatever it was had risked his life.

She stopped waving at Hawkeye when she realized she was doing so for selfish reasons, and this was not the time to be selfish. She did not know enough about Buck and Hawkeye's plans to interfere in them. Hawkeye was likely the best chance Buck had to live. Best let him get on with whatever business had to be done.

But there was still the matter of the crippled Somerset being left alone in the jail. A man she hadn't been allowed to tend to for a day or so. A prisoner, yes, who also happened to be her patient. A defenseless one at that.

Doubting Somerset could play much of a role in whatever Buck's plan might be, Emily decided to head to the jail to see what had happened for herself. She went back inside to grab her medical bag, then walked over to the jailhouse to see Somerset. Buck and Hawkeye may have their duties, but she had a patient to tend to. Besides, she hoped addressing his wounds might help keep her mind off thinking about what was happening to Buck at that very moment.

Her mind was still busy with worry as she walked to the jailhouse. Was Buck still alive? Shot? Wounded in some other way? The man could be so damned stubborn at times that she wondered if there could be a future between them. She had never thought she could ever love a lawman. Her husband had been such a quiet, unassuming type. Gentle and sympathetic. He was always willing to listen to reason and, more often than not, common sense prevailed with him.

Sheriff Buck Trammel was a different sort of man. He was a kind man in his own way, but given to violence in a way her husband had not. He was a stubborn man who followed his own sense of right and wrong, which she judged was correct more often than not.

His violent nature worried her and drew her to him. She did not fear him, but found herself fearing *for him.* Fearing what would become of him if he continued to live that way and take up the kind of fights he was taking up now. She feared allowing herself to fall in love with him so deeply that she would lose herself in him and find herself a widow once again. She did not know if she could live through another death. She was not sure she deserved that and began to wonder if solitude, though lonely, might be the safest and best option.

She only prayed that Buck lived through today so the decision was not made for her.

Glad to find the jailhouse door open and the door to the cells unlocked, she was alarmed to see Somerset's cell was open and the prisoner awake and laughing to himself.

"You seem to be in good spirits this morning." Emily pulled the heavy door open wider. "Feeling better, I take it?"

"Feeling better than I have since landing

here," he told her. "Yes, ma'am. I'm getting out of here today, one way or the other."

Once inside the cell, she set her bag on the chair and began examining his bandages. "I've been treating you for broken bones and strains, Mr. Somerset. I'm afraid your captivity has made you delusional. You're not going anywhere except straight to the county jail in Laramie as soon as you're fit to travel."

Somerset laughed. "Oh, I'm going to Laramie, missy, but I ain't going to any county jail. Not when I'll be a guest of Mr. Allan Pinkerton himself." He laughed again, then regarded her. "You know, you've been real good to me, Doc. Better than I thought a lady doctor could be."

"Considering the source, I'll take that as compliment." She checked his shoulder and found the splint was still in place. The splint on his left hand had become loose and required to be tightened. She moved to check his ankles as she rebandaged his left hand. "Your feet appear to almost be back to normal. I think you might be able to stand, maybe even walk if you're willing to give it a try after I'm finished with your left hand."

"No thanks, missy," Somerset said. "I'll just wait for my friends to help me out when they come back."

Emily was beginning to lose patience. "I'm afraid I'm the only friend you have in Blackstone, Mr. Somerset."

She looked up when she heard what sounded like a wagon in front of the jailhouse.

The prisoner seemed to enjoy her surprise. "If you could see the look on your face right now, missy. Makes me wish I had a mirror for the first time in my whole life."

Forgetting about Somerset's hand for the moment, Emily stepped outside the cell and saw a wagon had, in fact, pulled up in front of the jailhouse. Two men in gray dusters and matching bowlers were tying their horses to the hitching rail. She had never seen the men before, but knew who they were based on Buck's description.

Pinkerton men. The friends Somerset had just talked about.

Somerset laughed as she shut the cell door and hurried to fit the heavy key ring through the bars. Fumbling, she managed to lock the door, then clutched the keys to her chest and backed away into the corner of the cell — far from the door and the giggling prisoner.

"You've got spirit, missy," Somerset laughed. "I've got to hand it to you. It'll most likely get you killed before all this is over, something I'll greatly regret, but I sure do admire a spirited woman. I most certainly do."

Emily was too busy trying to mask her fear to bother answering him.

The two Pinkerton men entered the cell area with their pistols at their sides. She judged both of them to be in their late twenties and taller than most, but not as tall as Buck.

One of them looked in the cell and said to Somerset, "You the one Mr. Alcott sent us to fetch?"

"I'm Somerset out of the Chicago office, boys. Glad to finally meet the acquaintance of some colleagues. Now, if you'll be so kind as to get me out of here, I'll be happy to put in a good word for you with Mr. Allan Pinkerton himself as soon as I get back home to Chicago."

The other man asked, "Where do they keep the keys?"

Somerset inclined his head toward Emily. "Looks like the good doctor here has taken it upon herself to act the heroine. I'm afraid she's locked us in, boys, and she has the only key."

A chill went through her as both men looked at her.

379

The first one, Beau, stuck his hand through the bars. "Let's go, miss. Hand me them keys afore you get yourself hurt."

Emily held them closer to herself. "If you so much as touch me, Sheriff Trammel will kill you both."

The two Pinkerton men shared a laugh. Somerset joined in.

"Sheriff Trammel's got troubles of his own right about now," the second one said. "He's on his way to dyin' if he ain't already there. Now, come ahead with those keys before we lose patience."

The first one stuck his pistol through the bars, cocked the hammer, and aimed it straight at her head. "We're not here for you and what's goin' on here don't concern you, lady, unless you make it that way. Now, hand them keys over, or I'll shoot you and have Somerset here kick 'em over to us."

"No sense in getting yourself shot over a lost cause," added the second man.

Emily had never had anyone point a gun at her before. She felt her grip on the key ring loosen before it dropped to the floor. She could barely muster the strength to kick the ring over to the man at the door.

The three men laughed as one of the Pinkerton men unlocked the door and pulled it open. The two Pinkerton men crowded the cell, pulling Somerset off his cot.

"Take it easy," he protested. "My limbs are just about healed up. Don't need you two mules pulling on me."

Eyes clenched shut, Emily sat in the corner as they went about the slow work of easing the broken man to his feet. There wasn't much space between them and the open door, but there was some. She thought she might be able to make a break for it while they were busy with Somerset, but knew she would never make it in time.

She even hoped their labors with the prisoner would make them forget about her. She wished she could have pulled the shadows around her to make herself disappear entirely.

But there was nowhere for her to go until they were done.

She took cold comfort in the accuracy of her diagnosis as she saw Somerset was able to stand on his own two feet.

"You did it, missy," the prisoner proclaimed as he took one uneasy step followed by another with the support of the Pinkerton men on either side of him. "Looks like you did a good job patching me up. I'll send you something for your trouble as soon as I get back to Chicago."

"Her work's not done yet," said the first Pinkerton man. "Not by a long shot. She's coming with us."

Her eyes sprang open. *No!* she thought, though she couldn't bring herself to form the word . . . or any other word.

The first gunman slipped his hand under her arm and pulled her to her feet with such force that she almost fell over. She managed to catch her footing, refusing to grant him the indignity of seeing her stumble.

He pulled her along with him as both Pinkerton men followed Somerset shuffling out of the jail. "You behave yourself, miss, and you'll come out of this just fine. The way we figure it, there's plenty of shop clerk heroes in this town who might get it into their head to try to stop us taking Mr. Somerset out of here. With you along, they're liable to think differently about trying that. They couldn't live with themselves if they got a lady hurt."

The second one said, "Don't worry. We're not in the business of harming women. We'll let you go as soon as we clear town and let you walk back on your own, as long as you keep on doing what we say. Understand?"

"Yes!" she gasped. "Just don't hurt me."

"If you get hurt, it won't be from us," the first one said.

The second Pinkerton man stepped out of the jail and onto the boardwalk first, pistol drawn. He pulled down the gate of the wagon. "You can climb in this way and lay down if it's easier on you, Somerset." He nodded at Emily. "The lady here can drive the team for us while me and Beau ride our own horses. You know how to drive a team, don't you?"

Emily nodded that she did.

As the man helped Somerset angle himself into the wagon, Beau steered Emily toward the front. "I hope you're not lying about being able to handle a wagon. If you can't, you're going to have to learn in a hurry."

She climbed up into the seat and took the reins. "I can drive one as well as you can ride a horse, damn you." She quickly reached for the brake, hoping to catch the two men off guard and attempt some kind of getaway.

But Beau's hand fell over her own. "Easy on the brake, Doc. You thinking of making a run for it with a big old wagon and a wounded man in tow? That would be stupid. You're not a stupid woman, are you? Being a doctor and all?"

She couldn't find the words to answer him, so she simply shook her head.

"Good." Beau took his hand away. "That's

what I thought. Let's leave the brake on until me and my partner here are on our horses. We wouldn't want you getting any notions about taking off and leaving us behind. Safer for everyone that way, isn't it?"

She wiped her hand on her skirts. "That's the last time you touch me, understand?"

Beau backed away, smirking. "Feisty. I like that. Maybe before this is over, you'll like me, too."

A voice from behind them called out, "I doubt that very much."

Emily didn't have to turn around to see who was speaking, but she did so anyway.

Adam Hagen was not up at the Blackstone Ranch. He was standing in front of the Clifford Hotel in nothing but his britches and the black hat with the silver band that he favored so. His right arm was in a makeshift sling of black silk and he was not wearing a gun belt. His skin was pale and, though he masked it well given the angle, he was leaning with his back against the porch post in an effort to keep himself upright.

It was clear to her that he had no business being out of bed, much less facing down two gunmen. Unarmed, no less! In fact, he looked like a good wind might blow him over at any moment.

The Pinkerton man called Beau stepped away from the wagon and back up onto the boardwalk. "That you, Hagen?"

The gambler managed something of a grin. "None other."

"Hell, the two of us were told you were up at your daddy's ranch with your buddy Trammel."

"I'm sure the two of you have been told a lot of things," Hagen said. "Like you're tough men and good with a gun. You look like you're gullible enough to believe them, too."

The other Pinkerton man left the buckboard open and walked into the muddy thoroughfare, away from Beau. "You sure are a tricky son for a man who's supposed to be dying."

"And I intend to go on being tricky well after both of you are in the ground and forgotten," Hagen told them. "Now, let Doctor Downs go or face the consequences."

"Give me a gun!" yelled Somerset to his rescuers. "I have a right to defend myself."

"Shut up and lay down," Beau said without taking his eyes off the pale man with his arm in a sling. "This'll all be over in a minute and we'll be on our way."

Somerset said, "You haven't seen what

this devil can do with a gun. I have. He's armed somehow, damn it, so throw me some iron, now!"

"They've no iron to spare at the moment, Somerset," Hagen called out. "Just what's on their belts and the rifles still in their scabbards under their legs. You're in no condition to be handling a rifle, and these men are not about to give up one of their pistols for the likes of you."

Emily saw Hagen's eyes narrow a bit as he looked at Beau. "I know you, don't I?"

"Good memory, Lieutenant Hagen. Beauregard Hanson, formerly of the Seventh."

"That's right."

Emily thought she heard some of the old swagger return to Hagen's voice, but did not know if she had only wished it.

"A man of the Seventh," Hagen repeated. "Always a blustery bunch if there ever was one. I can't recall ever having much use for a man from the Seventh." He grinned. "But the Lakota sure had. Used them as target practice, near as I recall."

She could sense Beau tighten. "Only because I wasn't there. Custer always had a habit of overestimating his abilities."

"A failing that I hope hasn't filtered down to his former lieutenants," Hagen said.

"Was a captain by the time I left," Beau

answered.

Hagen feigned being impressed. "Why, bully for you. I'm sure your mama must be proud. Well, if she was good enough to raise you to be a captain in Uncle Sam's army, then let us hope she raised you to have enough common sense to recognize a fair offer when one is presented to you."

The second Pinkerton man said, "Like you're in a position to be making any offers." To Beau he said, "You want to shoot him or do you want me to do it?"

Emily could tell Beau was still stinging from Hagen's remark about the Seventh.

"Let him keep talking. It'll make me feel better when I ultimately plug him. I want to hear how he thinks he's getting out of this."

"My proposition is simple," Hagen explained. "You brave men let Doctor Downs go and I allow the three of you to ride off with Mr. Somerset and the wagon. As Sheriff Trammel and Deputy Hauk are occupied elsewhere and I am obviously in no condition to ride, you have my word that no one will pursue you."

"Don't listen to him," Somerset said from the back of the wagon. "That snake is fixin' to do something, I just know it. Just shoot him and be done with it."

Hagen remained leaning against the post.

"No one needs to get shot. Not me, not you, not even old Somerset there, if you two gentlemen just let her go and ride on."

The second Pinkerton man said, "We came here to do just that. After you're dead."

Emily saw Hagen's left hand flick to the sling cradling his right arm and draw a pistol he aimed at the second Pinkerton. Hagen fired before the man touched his pistol, much less drew. The slug struck the man in the throat, causing him to gag horribly as he staggered backward before falling to the ground, clutching his bleeding wound.

Hagen's aim switched to Beauregard Hanson, who had just drawn his gun, but hadn't raised it yet. Hagen had been that fast.

Beau froze as he stood.

"Offer still stands," Hagen called out to him. "Drop the iron, tie your horse to the wagon, and ride on back to Laramie with Mr. Somerset in hand. Could buy you some goodwill with Mr. Pinkerton if you do."

Emily watched Beau's gun hand twitch as he said, "I didn't much like working for Pinkerton."

Emily thought Hagen looked as though he may pass out at any moment, but his pistol had not budged.

"I'm sure you didn't," Hagen said, "but you'll like dying even less. Drop the iron. Let Doctor Downs go and ride away."

Beau twitched as he dove back toward the jailhouse.

Hagen fired. His shot caught Beau in the right side of the chest and came out the left. He was dead before he skidded into the open jailhouse doorway.

Emily jumped off the wagon and skipped over Beau's body as she ran toward Adam.

"Take your time," he managed to call out to her as he slowly slid down the porch post. "You are quite safe now."

She knelt before him and gently placed her hand against his forehead. His fever had spiked and his skin was damp. "Damn it, Adam. You should be in bed."

"And allow you to be taken captive by a bunch of scoundrels? I'd never be able to live with myself if that happened."

She tried to take the pistol from him, but he resisted. "I may need that yet, Doctor."

She let him keep it and checked on the bandages around his shoulder. Ideally, his arm shouldn't have been in a sling for weeks yet, but the bandages were dry and there was no evidence of fresh bleeding.

"By some miracle of God, your dressing isn't damaged."

Hagen coughed as he laughed. "I'm afraid God has ended his association with me some time ago, but thank you for thinking otherwise."

She flinched when he raised his pistol and aimed it back at the wagon. "Mr. Somerset! You damned well better be angling your way down from that wagon so you can return to jail."

Emily saw the wounded man had somehow managed to work his way up from the wagon bed and into the jockey box. Despite his right arm being heavily bandaged and his left hand broken, he had grabbed hold of the reins and was struggling to release the brake handle when Hagen had called out to him.

Somerset winced as he turned to look back at Hagen, his escape thwarted. "What the hell else would I be doing?"

"Might be thinking about snapping those reins and taking that team to Laramie. A hard task for a one-armed man, and I'd hate to send you to hell on account of a stupid mistake."

Somerset inched himself to the right until he was at the end of the seat. "I'm going to need some help getting down, though."

"You just stay there and rest a while." He looked up at Emily and winked. "I think we've all earned a rest, don't you?"

But Emily didn't smile. "Buck is out there alone, Adam. He's out there alone against Alcott and the rest of those Pinkerton men."

"Where?"

"He wouldn't tell me, but I know it's either at your father's ranch or somewhere on the trail before there."

"Stone Gate." Adam looked away. "I saw Hawkeye riding off in that direction before. I didn't know where he was headed, but I suppose that makes sense. If they're planning to hit Alcott anywhere along the trail, it's at Stone Gate. It's the only bottleneck between here and the ranch where a couple of men could hold off an army. At least for a while."

"Hawkeye's head wound is so bad, he can barely see straight, much less shoot," Emily said. "And that leaves Buck all alone between your father and Alcott's men."

"Not for long." He tucked his pistol back into his sling and wrapped his good arm around Emily's neck. "Here, help me up."

She did her best, but Hagen was remarkably heavier than she'd remembered him being when she helped move him. "Let's get you back to your room."

"Nonsense," he said as he struggled to his feet. "You're going to stick me in that flatbed along with all the pistols and rifles and bullets those dead men were carrying. You'll drive that team toward Stone Gate. When I give you the word, you'll throw the brake and get out of there. I'll draw fire and hopefully give Buck a chance."

Smith from the livery ran over to help Hagen along. "Those two came over to the livery and stole that wagon from me at gunpoint. Made me hitch up the team and everything. So if anyone's driving it anywhere, it's going to be me. This ain't no business for a doctor, much less for the only one we got in town."

Hagen swayed when Smith got him walking and struggled to compensate for the shifting weight.

Emily trailed behind the two men. "I don't think this is such a good idea, Adam. I know Buck needs help, but you'll be passed out by the time we get there and no good to anyone."

"Nonsense," Hagen said as he got a few steps under him. "I'll be fine once I can —"

Emily watched his grip around Smith's neck began to weaken as he lost consciousness. Fortunately, Smith grabbed hold of him in time and was able to push him toward a bench in front of the Clifford Hotel before he collapsed to the boardwalk and damaged his shoulder even more.

"You don't look so good, Adam," the liveryman said. "Maybe this isn't such a good idea after all."

Emily pushed Hagen's head upright and felt his forehead. His fever had returned with a vengeance, and his skin was clammy. The only place he was going was back to bed. His war was done.

She wondered what that could mean for Buck.

CHAPTER 29

Trammel's stomach sank when he heard a rider approaching through the dense woods that surrounded Stone Gate. Had Alcott sent a scout in advance of the main group to find a better route? Or had Alcott decided to risk leading his men to Blackstone Ranch through the forest?

He triple-checked the location of his rifles before he poked his head up from behind the rocky outcropping. He had his Winchester Centennial in his hand and three other fully loaded rifles staged at other points around the outcropping. Two on the left side and one on the right where he was currently positioned. He knew he'd have to move plenty once Alcott's men started firing at him, and he didn't want to be killed for lack of weaponry. He hoped to save the Colt under his arm for any close-in work that might be necessary, should he live that long.

When Trammel looked up, he was glad to see it was only Hawkeye racing toward him through the woods. For someone suffering from a bad head injury, the boy was riding faster and better than Trammel ever could.

His deputy brought his horse up short about thirty yards away, still maintaining the cover the woods afforded him. His horse had worked up a good sweat and was breathing heavily.

"Alcott and his men are coming this way," Hawkeye told him. "They're makin' a beeline straight for you, so be sharp. They'll be here in a couple of minutes or so."

Trammel was grateful for the advance notice. "Just remember to be careful while approaching Hagen's ranch. I don't want you getting shot for no reason after all we've been through."

"Don't worry," Hawkeye assured him. "The only one who didn't like me up there was Mr. Bookman, and he's in jail. I'll be back in a few minutes with some help. And if not, it'll just be me."

The boy took off again before Trammel could thank him. And for the first time since he had arrived at Stone Gate, the sheriff began to wonder if this crazy plan they had cooked up together just might work.

■ ■ ■ ■

Alcott brought his men to a stop as he saw the trail to Blackstone Ranch dip down and pass between an outcropping of stone that had clearly been dynamited at some point to allow the road to pass through.

The edges of the opening had been chipped down and smoothed by man and weather over the years, but the rest of the rocky mound remained. He judged the opening to be wide enough to fit four head of cattle through at the same time. It was probably a great way for Mr. Hagen and his ranch hands to count cattle before they were taken to market down in Laramie, but less than ideal for Alcott's current purpose.

"A bottleneck," Alcott said. "I don't like it."

"Makes sense it's there," Ty said. "The ranch probably uses it as a way to get a more accurate count on the number of cattle they take to market."

"I know why it's there." Alcott could barely hide his annoyance. "I just don't like going through a bottleneck with so many men."

"That idiot down at the jail said it's a straight shot to the ranch from here," Ty reminded him. "I say we barrel right through and get there as quick as possible. Besides, if anyone was up there waiting for us, they'd be shooting at us right now."

Alcott looked at the high rock walls on either side of the trail and the dense trees that spread out as far into the distance as he could see. There really was no better way to reach the Hagen ranch except through this narrow opening before him. And he did not like his options one bit.

"There's got to be another way. Ty, ride out and find another way around."

"Hell, Jesse," called out one of the men from the back. "There ain't nobody up there waitin' to shoot us. There ain't nobody looking to stop us because nobody knows we're comin'. Let's quit wastin' time and head on up to the ranch and get that Hagen fella to give up them men. The only danger we face is waiting like sittin' ducks on this damned road like we're doin'."

"The quicker we get this done," another man said, "the quicker we can get back to Laramie and Clay's girls and his whiskey. With the weather being as cold as it is, I aim to get my fill of both tonight."

"The sooner we kill those two we're after," still another said, "the sooner we can get back to the comforts of home."

The other men grumbled their agreement to keep moving straight ahead.

Alcott did not like caving to the opinion of the mob, but he also knew these men were more familiar with life in the wilderness than he was. If they were ready to accept the risk, perhaps he was making more of it than he should. He had been looking for a way to prove himself in front of his men. This minor test seemed to be as good a place to start as any.

He raised his hand and beckoned the column to follow him down the dip in the road and on through the opening the locals called Stone Gate.

Lying as flat as he could among the rocks atop the outcropping, Trammel watched the last Pinkerton man ride down the dip in the road. He had heard Alcott and the others deliberating before riding into the bottleneck. He had heard the men agree it was time to kill him and Adam.

It absolved him of any guilt he may have felt about the ambush. Everything he did from now on was in self-defense.

As he brought his Winchester to his shoulder, he dared not think of it as murder. He was giving these men more of a chance than they were planning to give him. He carefully drew a bead on the last man in the group and fired. The .45-75 round plowed through the Pinkerton man's chest and threw him down from the saddle.

The ten remaining riders struggled to keep their mounts under control as the shot echoed and the horses bucked amid the cramped confines of the narrow pass.

Trammel quickly levered another round into the chamber, aimed into the mass of man and horseflesh, and fired once again, hitting a rider in the upper chest. The round passed through him and slammed into the man behind him. Both men fell to the ground as the booming rifle shots and screaming men served to whip up the horses into a full-blown panic.

The man Trammel recognized as Alcott was caught between the main group and the entrance to Stone Gate, frantically waving at the others to head back the way they had come while he fought his own horse for control.

Trammel racked in another round as one of the riders managed to get off a shot that bounced off a rock somewhere nearby, but not close enough to his position to make him move just yet. In all of the chaos and confusion, they hadn't pegged his exact location, so moving might be more dangerous than staying put.

He aimed down at Alcott and waited until the leader turned his way before firing again. The shot was a bit rushed and caught his target lower than he'd aimed. The man doubled over, but somehow managed to remain in the saddle.

The Pinkerton leader yelled at his men over the sounds of screaming horses that echoed all around them and the men fired in Trammel's direction.

Time to move.

Trammel scrambled off the top of the outcropping and slid over to the Stone Gate entrance. He stole a quick glance through the opening to choose his next target, but had to pull back when bullets began pelting the stonework. The shots were all rushed and fired blind, but even a lucky shot could end his life. He knew it was only a matter of time before they rallied themselves and charged through the opening. That would turn his only advantage into a death trap. There was only one way to hold them off before help got there, if it was coming at all.

Trammel brought his rifle to his shoulder, levering and firing four rounds into the broiling mass of humanity and horseflesh in front of him as he moved from one side of the opening to the other. Gunfire and screams sounded from the riders and he lost count of how many men and animals he had hit as he reached the safety of the other side of the outcropping.

The gun smoke from his rifle and the weapons of the Pinkerton men grew heavy as more gunfire began to pepper the left side of the wall. He could hear more men and horses screaming than before, but their return gunfire was also heavier than before. He had no idea how many he had hit in that last outburst, but knew it had to be at least four, if not more. His upper back burned, and he realized a stray bullet must have grazed him when he had broken cover.

He had just levered another round into the chamber when one of the riders burst through the gun smoke and the stone opening. He was still on horseback, firing his pistol wildly. Trammel fell backward, ignoring the pain arching across his shoulders, and fired as soon as he hit the ground. The first round went wide, but he quickly levered a second round into the Winchester and fired. That round struck the man under the chin. The rider was still clutching the reins as he pitched back in the saddle, causing his mount to also topple backward and on top of him. The rider certainly would have broken many of the bones in his body had

he still been alive. Fortunately for him —
and for Trammel — he was already dead
before he hit the ground.

The panicked horse scrambled to get up
as bullet after bullet now peppered the
outcropping. The wild horse ran toward
Trammel, before veering away and darting
through the opening in the rock. As the
doomed animal absorbed round after round
intended for Trammel, the sheriff used the
confusion provided by the panicked horse
to run back to the other side of the wall. He
had no idea how many men he had killed,
and he had lost track of how many times he
had fired. He began feeding rounds from
his pocket into his trusted Winchester when
he realized the gunfire from the other side
of the wall had stopped.

Trammel's hands trembled as he fed more
rounds into the rifle. Alcott and the remaining survivors must be planning something.

The sheriff ignored the pain arching
through his back and scrambled up to the
top of the outcropping to get a better look
at what was happening. A shot rang out and
a bullet ricocheted off a large rock just in
front of him.

He laid flat as more rounds began slamming into the rocks all around him. He
pulled his legs to within the safety of the

rocks, but knew the game was up. His position had been discovered, and it wouldn't take long for the men to take him down.

It would be only a matter of time before one of the shooters got an angle on him and finished him off, or another one rode through the stone gate and finished him off from horseback.

Buck Trammel had done exactly what he could not afford to do.

He had allowed himself to be trapped by Alcott and his men.

As soon as he reached the ranch house, Hawkeye spilled out of the saddle and ran up to the porch steps to the front door. He didn't bother tying off Daisy, because the poor animal was too spent to move.

Ignoring his own dizziness, he began pounding on the front door, hoping Mr. Hagen or someone else was inside. The gunfire from Stone Gate had just increased from a couple of shots here and there to a thunderous barrage of gunfire echoing throughout the valley. He had never been in a war but imagined it must sound something like that.

Hawkeye hoped he would be able to convince Mr. Hagen to help Trammel, if the sheriff was not dead already.

The front door of the great house swung

inward, and Mr. Hagen stood by the door with a shotgun by his side.

"Who the hell is damn fool enough to go banging on my door?" He squinted as he looked at Hawkeye. "You that idiot that works for Trammel? What the hell are you doing here, boy? Your place is in town."

Hawkeye was still trying to catch his breath, so Mr. Hagen gestured toward the trail. "You two responsible for all that noise down there?"

"Raiders," Hawkeye managed to say when he had caught his breath. "Raiders from Laramie come to burn down your ranch. The sheriff and me found out about it and headed them off in time at the Stone Gate, but you need to come fast. The sheriff is holding them off all by himself, but he won't be able to hold out much longer. Please! You and your men have to get down there, quick!"

King Charles Hagen pushed past the deputy as twenty of his men began to ride in from their respective fields and fill the area in front of the main house. One of them was trailing Mr. Hagen's horse, a black mare Hawkeye recognized as a Morgan with a thick mane.

Hawkeye had never known so many men could move so quietly on horseback.

"Don't look so surprised, stupid," Hagen said as he climbed into the saddle. "Did you think I was just going to let anyone ride up here and shoot up my property?" He motioned for his men to move out down the road toward the gunfire.

All of them did, except for Mr. Hagen, who hung back. "You'd better get another mount if you plan on joining the fight. That one looks about played out and will die on you if you push her any harder. Take your pick if there's anything left in the barn."

Hawkeye watched Mr. Hagen ride away at a hard gallop. *My, that's a fast horse. Maybe the fastest horse I've ever seen.*

Then the world tilted as Hawkeye grew dizzy and collapsed.

CHAPTER 30

Trammel slid down the outcropping as bullet after bullet began to pelt the near side of the rocks he had been using for cover. It was only a matter of time before he got flanked or one of the shooters got lucky and took him down. He liked his chances on the ground better, especially since he could maneuver much better.

But he hit the ground crooked, lost his balance, and fell back against the outcropping. The fire in his back blew up and he cried out in pain. The echo of his scream had just died away when a white gelding burst through the opening of Stone Gate and charged straight for him. Instinct made Trammel push himself off the wall and swing his Winchester like a club up at the rider just as a pistol shot went off.

The butt of the rifle slammed into the rider's chest, sending him tumbling from the saddle. The gelding, without the burden of a rider, reared and broke away as it ran farther up the trail in the direction of the Hagen ranch.

Only then did Trammel get a good look at the man he had just knocked to the ground. Jesse Alcott.

And despite the fall, he still gripped his pistol.

Without thinking, Trammel stomped on his outstretched hand with his right boot and kicked the pistol away with his left. The weapon sailed harmlessly into the high grass on either side of the trail.

For the first time since the shooting had started, Trammel thought he had a chance to win. "Call off your men, Alcott. It's over."

Trammel saw the knife too late. Alcott buried it in his right leg and withdrew it before the sheriff could even react.

The sheriff bellowed in pain as another man tackled him from behind and slammed him to the ground.

He tried to use his rage to block out the pain shooting across his back and from his leg. His tackler broke his grip and tried to put all of his weight on Trammel's head in an attempt to push his face into the dirt. Trammel drove his right elbow back into the stomach of his attacker, but the grip held. He did it a second time, then a third time before the man's grip finally faltered and he stumbled backward.

Trammel pushed off his good left leg and rolled onto his back, drew his Peacemaker and fired up at the man. The bullet struck him on the left side just below the shoulder. He tumbled backward and was dead before he hit the ground.

From the right side, Alcott kicked at the pistol, knocking Trammel's arm away, but his grip on the Colt held.

Alcott stomped on Trammel's bleeding right leg, causing the sheriff to cry out in pain once more. He knew the Peacemaker still in his grasp was his only hope for survival, but he was too blinded by pain to aim at anything and wildly swung the big pistol with all of his might, driving the butt of the big pistol into Alcott's groin.

The Pinkerton man collapsed to his knees in silent agony.

Encouraged by knowing he had hurt Alcott badly, Trammel brought the pistol back again and clubbed the man in the temple. He fell across Trammel's legs like a rag doll.

The impact caused even more pain to shoot through Trammel's body. The knife wound in his right leg was still pumping blood, and he could feel the life slowly leaking from his body. The bullet graze along his shoulders still burned and grew even worse now that he tried to find a way out from under Alcott's deadweight. He had no idea if the Pinkerton man was still alive or dead and did not care. All he knew was that he was lying in the open with hostiles all around him and he could not move.

When Trammel reminded himself that he had to deal with one threat at a time, he ignored the fire in his back, forced himself to sit forward, and pushed Alcott off his legs. The unconscious man rolled off onto the ground flat onto his back.

Another Pinkerton man stepped through the Stone Gate and took in the scene. He had just enough time to glance down at Trammel — to see the man he had been sent to kill sitting flat on the ground like a kid who had just been bucked off his horse — when the sheriff shot him in the head.

The assassin fell back through the opening.

Trammel rolled away from where he had been as quickly as he could manage until he reached the relative safety of the Stone Gate.

Another man burst through the opening, trailing gun smoke behind him. Trammel steadied his aim on his good left leg and fired, cutting the man down where he stood and before he saw where Trammel was hiding.

He had lost track of how many rounds he had left.

He knew he had other rifles on this side of the opening, but as he sat against the wall, could not remember where he'd set them.

He had also lost track of how many he had seen riding up the road just before all of this started. He took a deep breath. *Alcott plus twelve. That means thirteen, right? Yes, of course it does. What's the matter with me?*

He felt the Peacemaker begin to grow heavy in his hand and almost dropped it in his lap. That is when he saw the hole in his right leg and saw all the blood pooling out onto the ground. The wound caused by Alcott's knife. It was his blood, he realized, though it seemed like it should belong to someone else. He was Buck Trammel. He was not supposed to get wounded. But there it was. Blood spoke for itself.

Trammel flinched when a bullet slammed into the wall to the left of his head, sending up a small cloud of stone dust with it.

He looked up and saw one of the Pinkerton men had crawled through the opening in Stone Gate. The front of his shirt was a red mess and the heavy Walker Colt shook in his hand. The man struggled to have the strength to say, "Look at me. You killed me, you good-for-nothing —"

Without moving the Peacemaker from his lap, Trammel was able to aim and fire. The impact caused the man to flop onto his back, dead. It was not until the smoke cleared that Trammel could see the bullet had struck the man just below the throat.

Trammel smiled through his drowsiness. "Now you're dead."

His last bit of strength ebbed and he fell back against the rock despite the pain from the bullet wound across his shoulders.

He had lost track of how many men he had killed. He had also lost track of how many there were still left to kill. He had watched enough men in his life bleed out to know the same was happening to him. Not in an alleyway or a boardinghouse or in the back room of a bar like his old mother had warned him. But out in the wilderness against a rocky outcropping in Blackstone, Wyoming. He was about to meet his end, no better than the mad dog his mother had always told him he was.

Trammel fought off the sleep that was pulling at him as he felt the ground begin to rumble beneath him. In his drowsy stupor, he wondered if it might be some kind of earthquake. Or was it common for people who were about to die to feel before they took that last great step into the unknown? Was it the beat of angel wings? Were angels coming to carry him up to heaven? Or the hoof beats of the Grim Reaper's pale horse to drag him down to hell? He was ready for either.

Buck Trammel fought with all of his might to remain awake so he could see his destiny approach. Death, he knew, was a foregone conclusion. He would never see Emily again. Not in this life, anyway. He wanted to know if he would see her in the next one. He had survived too much in life to allow himself to be cheated an answer just before his death.

His last vision before passing out was the sight of King Charles Hagen leading twenty of his men toward the Stone Gate. And toward him.

Trammel thought of raising his Peacemaker to defend himself against this last assault from Mr. Hagen. But the effort proved to be too much and the pistol too heavy.

And firing back suddenly didn't seem to matter all that much to Buck Trammel.

Trammel heard someone calling his name before he felt someone smacking his face.

Before he was able to open his eyes, instinct caused him to grab the hand that had been striking him before the next blow landed. "Stop."

"He's alive!" a young voice cried out. "See, Mr. Hagen! I told you he wasn't dead."

Trammel recognized that voice. It belonged to Hawkeye.

He struggled to open his eyes and saw he was bending his deputy's wrist at an awkward angle. "Why were you hitting me?"

"To bring you back, boss," Hawkeye said. "Could you let go of my hand now? It kind of hurts."

Trammel released his deputy and tried to get a better grip on his surroundings. He looked around and realized he was still at Stone Gate, but he was flat on his back. His hat was gone, but someone had put something under his head to help prop it up. He felt someone tugging on his right pants leg until he realized they were cutting it away.

That someone was Mr. Hagen. "This looks like a knife wound, not a bullet wound. That sound about right to you, Sheriff?"

"It's what happened," Trammel said, before a deeper, more intense pain than he had ever known spread throughout his

413

entire body and a horrible stench filled his nostrils. A vaguely familiar, but still wretched odor.

"Sorry about that, Sheriff," Mr. Hagen said, "but cauterizing the wound is the best way to stop the bleeding, at least until the doc can take a better look at you in town. Just wish it had been on your hindquarters so we could've put the Blackhorse brand on you."

Trammel heard a smattering of laughter, which he took to be from Hagen men.

"I'm sorry I didn't do a better job of warning you he was gonna do that," Hawkeye added, "but Mr. Hagen here said it might be best if you didn't know ahead of time."

Trammel blinked hard to clear away the tears that had risen in his eyes. The pain was still there, but had died away some. He decided he would die first before he told him about the bullet that had grazed his back. "What happened to the rest of the Pinkerton men?"

"I don't know what you did here," Mr. Hagen said, "but every one of them who could ride was already on their way back to Laramie by the time we got here. The ones left behind were either dead or too close to dying to bother marking the difference.

"We caught them all. Killed them all in the bargain, too. Lost one of my men in the exchange, but it had to be done." The rancher looked down at Trammel. "Thought we were going to lose you, too, for a while, Sheriff."

"Don't look so disappointed," Trammel said through the pain of his wound. "I might die yet."

"I doubt that." The rancher laughed without humor. "You're not the type." He stood to his full height and looked down at the human carnage around Stone Gate. "If you had told me about this plan earlier, I wouldn't have given a nickel for your chances up here, Trammel. Not up against eleven or so men. Lucky enough for you, three of them broke off when the shooting started, leaving you only a few to face, but still."

Trammel found a way to do the math despite his mind being fuzzy. "It was still eleven-to-one odds when the shooting started, Hagen. Sorry it wasn't enough to impress you."

The rancher toed one of the corpses on the ground. "Your deputy tells me this one here is the ringleader of the whole group. Man named Alcott."

Trammel raised his head and saw Alcott's

bloody corpse looking far more grotesque in death than it had only a few moments before in life. His vacant eyes stared at nothing and everything all at the same time. The fight that had begun the previous spring on a train from Ogallala had come to an end. Jesse Alcott was finally dead.

"Yeah." Trammel lowered his head back onto his pillow. "That's him."

Hagen cut loose with a stream of tobacco juice that hit Alcott's corpse in the face. "Well, like you said, Trammel. It was still eleven to one." The rancher walked to the opening he had blasted in the stone outcropping decades ago and looked at the carnage on the other side. "They'll be talking about this for generations, you know? I can hear the campfire stories now. How big Buck Trammel fought off thirty men or more single-handedly from his Stone Gate fortress with only his trusty rifle and a few boxes of bullets by his side." The rancher smiled as he shook his head. "Washerwomen get a bad deal when compared to how a cowboy can blow up a story. Yes, sir, Sheriff, you're about to become a mighty famous man after Mr. Rhoades down at the *Bugle* gets hold of this."

Trammel struggled to raise himself up on his elbows. Hawkeye helped as best he could. "That's why it's not going to be told that way."

Mr. Hagen looked back at him, making no effort to help Hawkeye pull the big man to his feet. "What are you talking about?"

"I'm talking about fame," Trammel told him. "I'm talking about how I don't want any more than I've already got. How fame is dangerous, both for me and for the town."

"Fame doesn't ask for us, boy. It just happens, and it happens after something like this occurs. Hell, you just fended off eleven men single-handedly, Trammel. Now, I might not care much for you, and I'll deny ever saying this, but that's one hell of a trick to pull off. You've got plenty of praise and admiration coming your way, and as much as it galls me to say it, you deserve it."

"We did this," Trammel said. "Not just me and Hawkeye. You and your men from your ranch. We fended them off together."

Hagen's eyes narrowed as he took a closer look at the sheriff. "You take a knock to your head, too, Trammel? You're starting to sound like the Hauk boy here."

"If I am," Trammel said, "then I'm making plenty of sense. If word gets out about me fending off this crew by myself, it'll bring trouble to town. Trouble that neither of us need. I don't want to be the next Bill

Hickok, and you sure as hell don't want to live next to a town that's a tourist attraction."

The rancher placed his hands on his hips. "Keep talking, Trammel."

"I've already got more of a reputation than I want. I don't want more people coming here looking to test it, hoping to make a name for themselves. We already had enough trouble with the bounty hunters who came around looking for money. Imagine the trouble that will follow when men come looking for fame."

Mr. Hagen signaled some of his ranch hands to help the sheriff to his feet. It took four of them to do it, but they got the big man standing on his own. Hagen beckoned them to stay where they were afterward. "You're saying you want my boys to share in the glory of what happened here?"

"No glory," Trammel said, winded from the effort of standing again despite the help. His right leg still felt like it was on fire, but at least the bleeding had stopped. "Not for me and not for your men. I'm going to have to write an official report on what happened here today and, when I do, it'll say I helped fend off an attack on the Blackstone Ranch by a group of assassins led by renegade Pinkerton man Jesse Alcott."

Mr. Hagen looked just as puzzled as his men looked pleased. They had probably planned on bragging about their exploits in the matter anyway, but now that they had the official blessing of the sheriff to do so, it made everything better.

"You going to get into their reasons for attacking my ranch?" Mr. Hagen asked. "Because that's going to raise as much trouble as you getting famous."

"The report doesn't have to get into motive," Trammel explained. "And I'm sure Mr. Rhoades will get into that in the newspaper articles he writes on the subject. We'll keep that vague until we know what we want it to say. But for the purposes of the report, this fight wasn't just me against eleven or so of them. It was the brave men of the Blackstone fighting off bandits. Me and Hawkeye just happened to help. That's all."

The Blackstone ranch hands were still cheering their newfound heroism when King Charles shouted at them to be quiet before shooing them away like pesky flies.

The rancher looked at Hawkeye. "No need for you to be here either, boy. This conversation's just for adults."

Trammel limped between them. "He was enough of an adult to save my life and he's adult enough to hear whatever you've got to

say to me. He's my deputy and he's entitled."

Charles Hagen didn't like the challenge,
but he seemed willing to tolerate it. "Have
it your way, Trammel. I'd like to know what
kind of game you're playing here. You and I
haven't exactly been on the best terms of
late, and you sharing this bit of glory with
my boys makes me a little suspicious. It
sounds like you're giving away a lot of valuable things, and I know for a fact that nothing valuable is ever really free. It always
comes at a price."

Trammel did not have the strength to
stand in the same place where he had just
killed so many men and debate a man like
Charles Hagen. But he knew the rancher
would not let him go until he got an answer,
so he gave him one. "I never thought I was
going to live through this dustup, Hagen, so
I didn't really think it through. But I've had
plenty of time to do that while I was unconscious just now and it all just settled into
place. We'll keep it real simple. By making
this thirty on eleven, we take the notoriety
out of what happened here. No legends, no
campfire tales, no glory. Blackstone goes
back to being a peaceful place and the
Blackstone Ranch goes back to lording over
the town like it always has."

"It's not that simple anymore, Trammel. Things have gone too far."

"That's just the way it's going to be, Hagen. You let Bookman go to jail for the attempted murder of your son and of me. In exchange for your silence, your name gets kept out of this. We pin all of the unpleasantness between us on Bookman" — Trammel eyed the rancher carefully — "and it all ends with him. No further questions about why he did what he did it. No further questions about who told him to do it."

King Charles Hagen walked away from Trammel and stared up at his ranch high on the distant hill. "John Bookman and I have ridden a good piece together. We've been through a lot. He knows a lot, too. Maybe too much for what you're proposing."

"Every journey comes to an end one way or the other," Trammel told him. "And Bookman knows an awful lot about an awful lot of people. Stands to reason there are some folks who won't want him to testify in court. Too much of what he knows might come out. No one wants that. Not you, not the judges, and not the county. Or do you?"

For the first time since arriving in Blackstone, Trammel felt Hagen's discomfort. This decisive man was actually struggling with what to do next. "Damn it, Trammel. You're practically condemning this man to a death sentence."

"He condemned himself the second he put a gun to my head. Anything that happens to him now is all his doing."

Hagen slowly turned to face him. "As I recall, I pointed a gun at your head the same time John did. That mean I'm condemned, too, Buck?"

Trammel was still angry about what had happened in the rancher's home not so long ago. He was embarrassed by the memory and angry that any man could claim they had been able to cow him like that.

He also knew that he was on the edge of brokering some kind of peace with Hagen that he needed. Trammel had been fighting too many people for too long. Adam Hagen, Charles Hagen, Lucien Clay, Jesse Alcott, the Pinkerton men, the bounty hunters. Not to mention all of the usual drunks and dregs that needed jailing in town. The drunks and dregs came with the job. The rest of it could go away with a simple peace, and he needed that peace with Hagen.

Trammel had been willing to give up glory by sharing the events of Stone Gate with the Blackstone Ranch. He had to be willing to be humble for the sake of peace.

"No, you're not condemned. But you quit trying to fight Adam and me. Blackstone is a town, Mr. Hagen, not a battleground. I won't have anyone treat it like one. Not you. Not anyone." It took him a great effort to swallow every bit of pride he had as he held out his hand to the rancher. And he could see King Charles Hagen struggle just as much to take it.

Trammel looked through the opening in Stone Gate when he heard the ranch hands call out that someone was approaching. He saw they were still in the process of pulling the dead men and horses from the road when a team of horses pulling a wagon appeared. Smith, the liveryman, was driving the team, and Emily was sitting right beside him.

Hagen broke their grip and stepped aside. "Looks like you don't need my help anymore, Trammel. You've got your own doctor."

Hawkeye rushed to greet her and help her down from the wagon. But, ever an impatient woman, she had already jumped down on her own and was running to Trammel before Hawkeye got there.

At the sight of her, his leg didn't hurt so much anymore. "Looks like I do at that."

CHAPTER 31

A week later on a crisp October morning, Sheriff Buck Trammel rode alongside the wagon Doctor Emily Downs was driving. She had operated properly on the stab wound in his leg and he was well on his way to walking without a limp.

Adam Hagen sat beside her, dressed in a black suit and matching coat draped around his shoulders like a cape on account of his arm still being in a sling.

The prisoner Somerset, still recovering nicely from his wounds, sat in the wagon's flatbed. His newly healed feet were tied together by a rope and his good left arm was tied to his waist. The broken fingers on his left hand were healing nicely, according to the doctor.

Deputy Hauk, his balance and vision restored to almost normal, brought up the rear. "Ain't life funny?" he observed.

Trammel had come to the conclusion that

his deputy's recent brushes with death had served to make him more introspective than before. The sheriff had never considered himself a thoughtful man, but had decided to indulge Hawkeye's nature until he had fully regained his faculties. "What do you mean?"

"I mean a week ago today, at this very moment, we was all doin' somethin' different. I was ridin' out to Stone Gate to warn you about Alcott and his men comin' your way before I rode up to the Hagen place and set them a-runnin' to you. Mr. Hagen here was defending Mrs. Downs from them Pinkertons while Somerset was thinkin' about all that freedom he was going to enjoy in Laramie.

"Now, look at us. Ridin' together on a beautiful day to watch Mrs. Pinochet swing for her crimes, and Somerset gets to spend a year or so in jail." Hawkeye shook his head. "Guess that's what I meant when I said life sure is funny."

"None of us are laughing," Somerset grumbled from the flatbed.

Trammel did not blame the prisoner for being sour. He was looking at several years in prison once he went before a judge. Allan Pinkerton might pull some strings to get his spy free, but given the recent embarrassment he had received over what the news-papers had come to call the Alcott Affair, his influence was not as great in Wyoming as it may have once been.

Trammel looked over at Hagen, who had made remarkable progress in the weeks since his shooting. Emily told him his shoulder was healing surprisingly well, and he was beginning to look more like his normal self.

"You planning to confront Clay about sending Alcott our way?"

"And let him know what we know? Non-sense." He pulled the black coat tighter around his shoulders. "I never allow my enemies to know my mind, Buck. We know Alcott and his men were working for Clay when they attacked us. I'll allow him to stew in his own anxiety for a while until I'm ready to exact my revenge, should I decide to take revenge at all. Until then, I'll just string him along and make him wait. Seeing what he does may prove interesting. He's gone after us twice now and failed. That must be weighing heavy on his mind."

Trammel knew all about heavy minds. A heavy mood had descended over town in the days since the Alcott incident. Despite the watered-down story he had written into his report, newspapermen from all over came to cover the Raid on the Blackstone Ranch. Alcott's attachment to the Pinkerton Agency only whetted their appetite for scandal in the hopes of painting Allan Pinkerton the one who had plotted everything from the beginning. Some chose to emphasize the renegade mercenary angle, but most of the reporters opted for the eastern aggression angle, painting King Charles Hagen as a pioneer's pioneer and a symbol of the new American Westerner.

Trammel had sought to curb the rancher's power. But all he had done was help make him even more powerful.

Maybe Hawkeye was right. Life sure was funny.

Trammel realized he had slipped into one of his introspective moods again when he snapped out of it and saw Emily smiling at him. He found himself smiling, too.

Life may be funny, he decided, but with a woman like her by his side, it could also be very good indeed.

ABOUT THE AUTHORS

William W. Johnstone has written nearly three hundred novels of western adventure, military action, chilling suspense, and survival. His bestselling books include *The Family Jensen; The Mountain Man; Flintlock; MacCallister; Savage Texas; Luke Jensen, Bounty Hunter;* and the thrillers *Black Friday, The Doomsday Bunker,* and *Trigger Warning.*

J. A. Johnstone learned to write from the master himself, Uncle William W. Johnstone, with whom J. A. has co-written numerous bestselling series including The Mountain Man; Those Jensen Boys; and Preacher, The First Mountain Man.